Applause for L.L. Raand's Midnight Hunters Series

The Midnight Hunt
RWA 2012 VCRW Laurel Wreath winner *Blood Hunt*
Night Hunt
The Lone Hunt

"Raand has built a complex world inhabited by werewolves, vampires, and other paranormal beings…Raand has given her readers a complex plot filled with wonderful characters as well as insight into the hierarchy of Sylvan's pack and vampire clans. There are many plot twists and turns, as well as erotic sex scenes in this riveting novel that keep the pages flying until its satisfying conclusion."—*Just About Write*

"Once again, I am amazed at the storytelling ability of L.L. Raand aka Radclyffe. In *Blood Hunt*, she mixes high levels of sheer eroticism that will leave you squirming in your seat with an impeccable multi-character storyline all streaming together to form one great read." —*Queer Magazine Online*

"*The Midnight Hunt* has a gripping story to tell, and while there are also some truly erotic sex scenes, the story always takes precedence. This is a great read which is not easily put down nor easily forgotten."—*Just About Write*

"Are you sick of the same old hetero vampire / werewolf story plastered in every bookstore and at every movie theater? Well, I've got the cure to your werewolf fever. *The Midnight Hunt* is first in, what I hope is, a long-running series of fantasy erotica for L.L. Raand (aka Radclyffe)."—*Queer Magazine Online*

"Any reader familiar with Radclyffe's writing will recognize the author's style within *The Midnight Hunt*, yet at the same time it is most definitely a new direction. The author delivers an excellent story here, one that is engrossing from the very beginning. Raand has pieced together an intricate world, and provided just enough details for the reader to become enmeshed in the new world. The action moves quickly throughout the book and it's hard to put down."—*Three Dollar Bill Reviews*

By Radclyffe

Romances

Innocent Hearts	The Lonely Hearts Club
Promising Hearts	Night Call
Love's Melody Lost	Secrets in the Stone
Love's Tender Warriors	Desire by Starlight
Tomorrow's Promise	Crossroads
Love's Masquerade	Homestead
shadowland	Against Doctor's Orders
Passion's Bright Fury	Prescription for Love
Fated Love	The Color of Love
Turn Back Time	Love on Call
When Dreams Tremble	Secret Hearts

Honor Series

Above All, Honor
Honor Bound
Love & Honor
Honor Guards
Honor Reclaimed
Honor Under Siege
Word of Honor
Code of Honor
Price of Honor

Justice Series

A Matter of Trust (prequel)
Shield of Justice
In Pursuit of Justice
Justice in the Shadows
Justice Served
Justice for All

The Provincetown Tales

Safe Harbor	Winds of Fortune
Beyond the Breakwater	Returning Tides
Distant Shores, Silent Thunder	Sheltering Dunes
Storms of Change	

Acclaim for Radclyffe's Fiction

Secret Hearts "delivers exactly what it says on the tin: poignant story, sweet romance, great characters, chemistry and hot sex scenes. Radclyffe knows how to pen a good lesbian romance."
—*LezReviewBooks Blog*

Wild Shores "will hook you early. Radclyffe weaves a chance encounter into all-out steamy romance. These strong, dynamic women have great conversations, and fantastic chemistry."
—*The Romantic Reader Blog*

In **2016 RWA/OCC Book Buyers Best award winner for suspense and mystery with romantic elements** *Price of Honor* "Radclyffe is master of the action-thriller series...The old familiar characters are there, but enough new blood is introduced to give it a fresh feel and open new avenues for intrigue."—*Curve Magazine*

In *Prescription for Love* "Radclyffe populates her small town with colorful characters, among the most memorable being Flann's little sister, Margie, and Abby's 15-year-old trans son, Blake...This romantic drama has plenty of heart and soul."
—*Publishers Weekly*

2013 RWA/New England Bean Pot award winner for contemporary romance *Crossroads* "will draw the reader in and make her heart ache, willing the two main characters to find love and a life together. It's a story that lingers long after coming to 'the end.'"—*Lambda Literary*

In **2012 RWA/FTHRW Lories and RWA HODRW Aspen Gold award winner** *Firestorm* "Radclyffe brings another hot lesbian romance for her readers."—*The Lesbrary*

Foreword Review Book of the Year finalist and IPPY silver medalist *Trauma Alert* "is hard to put down and it will sizzle in the reader's hands. The characters are hot, the sex scenes explicit and explosive, and the book is moved along by an interesting plot with well drawn secondary characters. The real star of this show is the attraction between the two characters, both of whom resist and then fall head over heels."
—*Lambda Literary Reviews*

Lambda Literary Award Finalist *Best Lesbian Romance 2010* features "stories [that] are diverse in tone, style, and subject, making for more variety than in many, similar anthologies…well written, each containing a satisfying, surprising twist. Best Lesbian Romance series editor Radclyffe has assembled a respectable crop of 17 authors for this year's offering."—*Curve Magazine*

2010 Prism award winner and ForeWord Review Book of the Year Award finalist *Secrets in the Stone* is "so powerfully [written] that the worlds of these three women shimmer between reality and dreams…A strong, must read novel that will linger in the minds of readers long after the last page is turned."—*Just About Write*

In **Benjamin Franklin Award finalist** *Desire by Starlight* "Radclyffe writes romance with such heart and her down-to-earth characters not only come to life but leap off the page until you feel like you know them. What Jenna and Gard feel for each other is not only a spark but an inferno and, as a reader, you will be washed away in this tumultuous romance until you can do nothing but succumb to it."—*Queer Magazine Online*

Lambda Literary Award winner *Stolen Moments* "is a collection of steamy stories about women who just couldn't wait. It's sex when desire overrides reason, and it's incredibly hot!"—*On Our Backs*

Lambda Literary Award winner *Distant Shores, Silent Thunder* "weaves an intricate tapestry about passion and commitment between lovers. The story explores the fragile nature of trust and the sanctuary provided by loving relationships."—*Sapphic Reader*

Lambda Literary Award Finalist *Justice Served* delivers a "crisply written, fast-paced story with twists and turns and keeps us guessing until the final explosive ending." —*Independent Gay Writer*

Lambda Literary Award finalist *Turn Back Time* "is filled with wonderful love scenes, which are both tender and hot." —*MegaScene*

First Responders Novels

Trauma Alert	Taking Fire
Firestorm	Wild Shores
Oath of Honor	Heart Stop

Short Fiction

Collected Stories by Radclyffe
Erotic Interludes: *Change Of Pace*
Radical Encounters

Edited by Radclyffe:
Best Lesbian Romance 2009–2014

Stacia Seaman and Radclyffe, eds.:
Erotic Interludes 2: *Stolen Moments*
Erotic Interludes 3: *Lessons in Love*
Erotic Interludes 4: *Extreme Passions*
Erotic Interludes 5: *Road Games*
Romantic Interludes 1: *Discovery*
Romantic Interludes 2: *Secrets*
Breathless: *Tales of Celebration*
Women of the Dark Streets
Amor and More: Love Everafter
Myth & Magic: Queer Fairy Tales

By L.L. Raand
Midnight Hunters
The Midnight Hunt
Blood Hunt
Night Hunt
The Lone Hunt
The Magic Hunt
Shadow Hunt

Visit us at www.boldstrokesbooks.com

HEART STOP

by

RADCLYffE

2017

THIS TRADE PAPERBACK ORIGINAL IS PUBLISHED BY
BOLD STROKES BOOKS, INC.
P.O. BOX 249
VALLEY FALLS, NY 12185

FIRST EDITION: JULY 2017

CREDITS
EDITORS: RUTH STERNGLANTZ AND STACIA SEAMAN
PRODUCTION DESIGN: STACIA SEAMAN
COVER DESIGN BY SHERI (GRAPHICARTIST2020@HOTMAIL.COM)

Acknowledgments

One of the pleasures of writing a First Responders romance is the chance to investigate and incorporate interesting professions into the story. Even more satisfying, though, is the chance to bring back characters from previous books in supporting roles. First responders, be they military, law enforcement, medical, firefighters, environmental protectionists, search and rescue, or any of a host of others, never work alone. Teamwork is the foundation of care, and at the heart of all these books is the dedication to caring for the welfare of others and the world we live in. If not us, then who shall we look to for that?

I especially enjoyed writing this entry in the First Responders series as I had a chance to revisit Philadelphia and the worlds of the Justice series and *Trauma Alert* (a spin-off of that series, one of the first I started). While this work stands alone, I hope those who are familiar with the setting will enjoy revisiting a few favorite characters, and of course, that everyone enjoys the romance at the heart of the story.

Many thanks go to: senior editor Sandy Lowe for her continued expertise in support of BSB's authors and operations as well as her invaluable personal support, editor Ruth Sternglantz for knowing my work so well I can count on her to keep me on the right road, editor Stacia Seaman for never missing the errors large and small, and my first readers Paula and Eva for taking time out of their busy lives to send invaluable feedback.

And as always, thanks to Lee for a heart that knows no bounds. *Amo te.*

Radclyffe, 2017

To Lee, from the heart

CHAPTER ONE

Olivia Price walked into the Graveyard at six a.m. Every autopsy bay she'd ever worked in had a similar nickname, and this one was actually on the tamer side—not to be repeated to civilians, of course. True, this was where the bodies rested until they moved on to some other place, claimed by families or relegated to a nameless plot marked only by a number in a potter's field, or what passed for that in the modern era. Her job was to help them find their way to wherever their journeys ended. She laughed at herself and the whimsical thought. She was a scientist, a doctor, not a priest. She dealt with corpses, the remains of a human being, whose spirit or essence, or whatever it was that made them unique individuals, had long since deserted the flesh. All the same, every body that came under her care was unique and special. Each still carried the outward and inner signs of a lifetime of living, no matter how brief that lifetime might've been. She was trained to read those signs, to take note of the evidence of disease or injury or injustice. She was the observer, the chronicler, the last biographer of those who ended up in the medical examiner's office—victims of accident, illness, or merely the passage of time.

She had always known she'd be a doctor to the dead, and she was never happier than at this hour of the morning, when she was alone, before the inevitable interruptions from colleagues, students, and trainees disturbed the peace. Of course, she could still work through the inevitable chaos—the dead didn't keep to a schedule or any other form of social convention—but she needed, relished, the peaceful solitude. She did her best work then, all thoughts orderly, efficient, and logical.

In the antechamber, she hung her white lab coat, a fresh one pressed and laundered every day, on the first hook inside the door, donned disposable booties over her flats, placed the gold ring with central opal on the thin gold link chain around her neck, and scrubbed her hands with the hexachlorophene-impregnated sponge. After drying off with the industrial blue paper towels, she tied on an impermeable green apron that draped from chest to knees, covered her hair, and entered the space that was more home than her own brownstone. Surprisingly bright and spaciously airy for a room underground, the twenty-by-sixty-foot suite held four stainless steel autopsy tables lined up down the center, leaving an aisle on either side and in between, each large enough to easily maneuver the gurneys. The floor-to-ceiling thermoregulated steel cadaver storage cubicles, each four feet square with a slot for the index card bearing the identifiers in black Magic Marker, occupied the far rear wall. Each long wall held waist-high counters with shelves and cabinets for equipment, extra-deep sinks, and several hoods for venting noxious fumes from chemically or naturally induced decomposition. Overhead cables, pulleys, and mechanical arms allowed cameras, spray washers, and X-ray devices to swivel into place above the tables. Wireless voice-activated recorders hung down above the tables, and computer monitors sat on shelves suspended from the ceiling at eye level.

The tables themselves were eight feet long and four feet wide, slanted at twenty degrees from head to foot so bodily fluids could drain through thin horizontal slats into the stainless steel basin below and from there into the special drain system designed to collect biological effluent for disposal. At the head of each table, a large hanging scale swung above an adjustable shelf equipped with a power saw and large-bore suction lines. In most respects, the autopsy suite resembled any other operating room.

Olivia checked the printout on the intake board next to the door, noting that another body had been delivered during the night, case 17A290-1: UM, TOA 0321. Unidentified male, time of arrival 3:21 a.m. Jane and John Does were denizens of the past, each body now being assigned an identifier that took precedence over their name, if that was even known. In this case, it wasn't. No one had been assigned to the case yet. She would take care of that before morning review. Right now, she intended to begin the autopsy on a case delivered late the day before, a young male victim of a drive-by shooting. Undoubtedly the homicide detective assigned to the case would be calling for information once shift changed at the police station.

She checked the file number against the intake sheet, typed in her password and the file number on the computer adjacent to her table, and activated the voice recorder. As the assistant chief, she had her own work space that no one else used unless they were overwhelmed with casualties. Once the file came up and she'd double-checked that all the identifiers matched, she printed a series of labels that included the case number and her ID number. Done with the critical documentation to secure chain of evidence, she opened the corresponding storage cubicle, slid out the tray holding the body bag, engaged the hydraulics to lower it to stretcher level, and transferred it, after years of practice, without difficulty. If the diener had been present, he or she would have insisted on doing the transfer. They were the official Graveyard techs, after all, but she rarely actually needed an assistant and had to remind herself to let them do their jobs. She pushed the gurney to the side of her table, quickly unzipped the bag, and in several practiced moves, settled the body onto the stainless steel table.

For the first and only time, she surveyed Dejon Barnes. After this, he would be case 17A285-1.

Hello, Dejon. I'm Dr. Price. It's my job to find out why you're here.

Determining manner and cause of death was not only a legal necessity but a moral one, in her mind. If he had family, they would want to know how he died, even if she could never tell them why. So would the courts, if this turned out to be a homicide. She never made assumptions—she only dealt in facts. Facts never lied. She owed him the truth.

Before doing anything else, she photographed him as he lay there, even though he would've been photographed at the scene. This was her scene now.

His clothes had been removed, already bagged and tagged by the night diener, and according to the on-scene report she scanned on her monitor, the crime scene techs had collected physical evidence at the scene. After she completed the photographs, she pulled on gloves and combed through his medium-length jet-black hair with a wide-toothed stainless steel comb, searching for any foreign objects that might've been caught there. More than once she'd found bullets or other fragments that ended up being critical evidence. Not today.

Once finished, she pulled the overhead spray handle into place and methodically washed the remains. She drew no conclusions as she worked, despite noting the two-centimeter circular wound just medial to his left nipple in direct line with his heart. The cause of death might appear obvious to a novice, but she knew better than to make assumptions. An external wound that *appeared* to be from a projectile might prove to be the cause of death, but she would not know that until she had examined the entire body, dissected the major cavities, and reviewed the toxicology report. While it did not appear that the wound had been inflicted postmortem, she had to be sure some other agent hadn't been the cause of death before the wound was suffered. Once she'd completed the wash down, she was ready for the first part of the autopsy, and everything she did and thought would be part of the official report.

She removed her gloves, engaged the recorder, and re-gloved.

"This is Dr. Olivia Price performing the external examination on case 17A285-1."

After waiting until her awareness of her surroundings, thoughts of her workday to come, of her very sense of self, receded and her entire focus was on the body, she began her observations, noting the overall appearance of the body, his apparent state of health and nutrition, the presence or absence of tattoos, scars, deformities—congenital or accidental—and the wound. When finished with the visual inspection, she measured his height, limb length, and the dimensions of the entry and exit wounds, turning the body as needed to perform the same thorough examination of the back. Once he was lying faceup again, she drew intraocular fluid for DNA, injected the material into a sterile test tube, and affixed a preprinted label with his identifiers. She removed her gloves and diagrammed the wounds electronically on the tablet attached to her computer.

The external examination took her forty-five minutes, a routine she had performed hundreds of times before and that never varied. Ritual in science ensured that vital information was not overlooked or forgotten. Once that portion of the autopsy was completed, she opened her instrument tray and lined up what she would need in the precise order in which she would use it, comfortable and secure in the knowledge her findings would be complete when she finished.

Just as she reached for a new pair of gloves, the door behind her opened. She stiffened, a rush of annoyance breaking the clean white canvas of her concentration. She hadn't expected anyone to be in this early. The other MEs didn't start their workdays until after the eight a.m. review.

"I thought I saw your car out back," a gravelly male voice announced.

"Morning, Dr. Greenly," she said without turning. Her boss's voice was unmistakable, as was the faint aroma of cherry smoke, the pipe tobacco he routinely used.

"Getting an early start, I see." His tone held the slightest hint of censure that might just as easily be her imagination, but she didn't think so.

"We have a busy day ahead," Olivia replied neutrally, aware that her associates found her work habits curious, probably found *her* curious as well. She was used to it, had always been the odd one out, the too studious, too humorless, sometimes too weird one in any gathering. She couldn't remember if she'd ever minded the persistent sense of being slightly out of step with everyone else, but she was so used to it now she ignored the sidelong looks and semi-snide comments about setting a bad example for everyone else that were sometimes directed at her. "I don't want anyone to get overloaded."

"I expect your staff can handle things without you burdening yourself too much," he said, and she wondered if he was subtly trying to suggest that, like him, she needn't spend too much time in hands-on work. *Setting a bad example.*

But then, she wasn't like him, content to be only an administrator, to shuffle papers and study budgets and deal with the politics of running a city-funded department with close ties to one of the largest and most affluent medical centers in the nation. She would have to deal with that balancing act someday, when he retired and she took over his position. Which she would, she was certain. She had the training and the will. Running a big-city ME's office was her destiny. But not now, and even when, she would never give up the practice of her craft. She was a medical examiner, and that was what she would be for the rest of her life. This was the one place where she fit.

"The best way for me to train residents is to spend time with them," she said, although she knew that wasn't what he was talking about. Teaching was not a requirement for bureaucrats. What she didn't say was she needed to see the staff at work too, to be accountable for the department's results.

"Yes, well, I won't argue that point." Greenly tipped his chin toward her table. "You'll have to put this one on hold for a little while, I'm afraid. I've scheduled an interview for you at eight."

Olivia frowned. "An interview? I wasn't aware we had any positions open at the moment."

"This is for the fellowship program."

"We've already interviewed all the applicants. I was planning to call the candidates to offer positions this morning, in fact."

"Yes, well, that's why I want you to interview Dr. Reynolds before you do anything. That way, you can decide which of the others you'll move to a wait list."

"I'm sorry," Olivia said. "I'm confused. Who is Dr. Reynolds? We already have three excellent candidates, all of whom are highly qualified and could go anywhere. We're lucky to get such top choices."

"You'll want to take this one in place of one of those three," he said flatly.

Olivia's jaw tensed at the obvious order. "Oh? And why would that be, considering I don't even know who he is?"

"She. *She* is," he muttered, waving a hand. "It's a bit of a long story, but I've already spoken to the appropriate people and gotten clearance for this. A bit unusual, I agree, but I think you'll find it will all work out."

"Sir," Olivia said, trying hard to keep the irritation from her voice, "what is this all about? Who requested this?"

"Dr. Reynolds comes highly recommended from the chief of surgery and several other prominent university officials, and they would like to see her placed in our program right away."

"And what is the incentive?" Olivia couldn't miss the stench of politics, a lot like a decomp—impossible to wipe out or wash off. She'd never been able to hide her disdain for the power games, and some game was under way here. She resented being forced to play without even knowing the ground rules.

Greenly's chest expanded, his look supremely satisfied. "I've just gotten approval to budget in the new DNA analysis lab *and* the upgrades to the chemical and mass spec units."

Olivia tasted defeat, at least for this round. A state-of-the-art DNA sequencer would make a huge difference in many of their cases, where identifying the victim was often the first challenge. She understood how difficult it would be to turn that down for something that seemed on the surface as simple as accepting a new fellow on the recommendation of some obviously well-positioned physicians. All the same, she resented being told she didn't have a choice in choosing who her fellows would be for the next twelve months. She'd already spent dozens of hours reviewing applications, reading letters of reference, and interviewing potential candidates. Being forced to take someone, sight and credentials unseen, went against everything she considered important. This was not the way things should be done. In her experience, deviating from the tried and true always led to disaster.

"Is there some reason Dr. Reynolds can't enter the next applicant pool so that we have a chance to—"

"No, I'm afraid that won't work. She's ready for placement now, and her circumstances…Let's just say a number of people feel it's important that she get started."

"I'll speak with her, of course, but this is highly irregular, and I have to insist that I have the final say in this. The fellowship program, after all, does fall under my—"

"Of course, of course."

"I'd like to review her file before we meet."

"I'll have it sent round to you. I'm sure once you've had a chance to look at all the information, you'll be perfectly happy to take her." Greenly smiled. "I know you have only the best interests of the office at heart."

Olivia smiled rigidly. "Of course."

After he left, leaving a trail of smoked cherries behind, she carefully rebagged the body, noted the time on the tape, and stripped off her contaminated boots and gloves and garments by the door. She washed up and donned her lab coat before walking back to her office. Once there, she texted the diener scheduled to cover the Graveyard that morning and requested he return the body to storage until she could resume her autopsy. With her morning plans in shambles, she determined to reestablish her routine. She checked her mail, reviewed the lab reports that had come in after-hours the night before, and signed off on the completed charts awaiting her attention. Once she was done with that and somewhat back on schedule, she went outside to the last food truck in line, her favorite, for her morning coffee and returned to her desk at 7:55. Since there was still no sign of the file, she called Greenly's office to ask his secretary to bring it over. No one answered, and she left a voice mail.

When a knock sounded on her door, Olivia straightened and noted the time. Exactly eight a.m. Pleased with that, but in no way ready to accept Dr. Reynolds just because she'd been ordered to, she straightened the file folders into an orderly pile and folded her hands on her desk. "Come in, please."

CHAPTER TWO

Olivia's first thought was that Dr. Reynolds was older than she expected. Most applicants for a fellowship had had four years of college followed by medical school and almost as many years of residency, putting them in their late twenties. This woman looked to be a decade older. Maybe she was wrong about the age estimate, though, considering how haggard and not quite well she appeared. Used to avoiding assumptions, Olivia tried not to ascribe the gaunt frame that could use another twenty pounds and still be considered lean, or the hollow-eyed look in the dark-haired woman's gray eyes, to the scar that ran down her left temple almost to her cheekbone and the limp she tried to hide. However, the cane that assisted her in moving into the room toward the single metal folding chair in front of Olivia's desk was impossible to ignore. Logic concluded this woman had been through something seriously damaging in the not too distant past.

Olivia stood and held out her hand. "Dr. Reynolds, I am Dr. Olivia Price, the assistant chief medical examiner."

Jay shifted the cane from her right hand to her left and held out her hand, mentally ordering the tremor to diminish. It never worked, but she couldn't seem to stop trying. Gratefully, the woman across the desk appeared not to notice as she gripped Jay's hand firmly and held it for a second.

"Jay Reynolds," Jay said, embarrassed that she couldn't hide her weakness and wondering if she'd ever get used to it. Knowing that she wouldn't.

"Please," Price said with a cool, clipped voice, "have a seat."

Jay lowered herself onto the hard, narrow chair and extended her bad right leg. Her knee still throbbed like a son of a bitch if she kept it flexed for too long, but at least it held her up. She scanned the room and the woman watching her as she settled. She'd been in plenty of hospital offices in her life, and she couldn't remember a single one as ruthlessly organized as this one. Every book on the crammed floor-to-ceiling bookcase was vertical and appeared to be exactly the same distance from the edge of the shelf, as if lined up with a ruler. Not a leaning one among them. Price's desk was clear except for one absolutely square stack of folders in the corner, a phone, and a computer. There was an ornate patterned rug covering ninety percent of the institutional tile floor, thick and expensive looking, without a trace of lint or a stray hair. The only oddity aside from the unusual lack of chaos was the tri-level game board of some kind sitting on a carved, dark wood pedestal table in the far corner behind Price's desk. Small shiny stones lay scattered on each level. She tried to pull the name of the game from her memory and came up blank. That didn't happen nearly as often as it had six months ago, but the hot wave of frustration never lessened.

"What is that?" she muttered.

Price followed her gaze.

"Go."

Price's tone and expression never changed. Impersonal, cool, not exactly unfriendly, but no flicker of warmth either. Jay was used to making quick assessments and rapid judgments in the trauma bay, and her assessment of Olivia Price was that she was direct, reserved, maybe a little cautious, and despite that icy shell, a hell of a lot more attractive then Jay had anticipated. With her willowy build, honey-blond shoulder-length hair, deep green eyes, and near-porcelain skin over perfectly proportioned facial bones, she would probably be beautiful if any part of her face smiled, but not even her eyes held a hint of warmth. They were steely and appraising and remote. Jay straightened under the scrutiny.

"I'm afraid your interview was scheduled before I had a chance to review your file." Olivia Price sighed. "In fact, I don't *have* your file, and for that I apologize."

Jay waited. She hadn't known about the damn interview until the night before when Ali had called her, and if Ali and Vic hadn't ganged up on her she wouldn't be here now. Looked like Dr. Price hadn't been briefed either. Great. Maybe this would be short and sweet and she could get the hell out of this dungeon. Hell, there weren't even any windows down here. Not that there were any in most ORs either, but at least everyone there was alive. Mostly.

Price broke the silence. "Tell me how you come to be here, Dr. Reynolds."

"I'm here to interview for the forensic pathology fellowship," Jay said, treading carefully around what she felt was a whole battlefield full of land mines waiting to blow her out of the air.

"As I understand." Price's thin smile undoubtedly covered annoyance. "What's your background? Where did you do your pathology residency, for example."

Jay swallowed a laugh. Nothing about Olivia Price suggested humor would get through to her or impress her. All business. Super serious. And none too happy, if Jay still had any ability to read people.

"I didn't...take a pathology residency, that is."

Olivia's evenly arched brows flattened as she frowned. "Then why are you here applying for this fellowship?"

"Quite a few people think it's a good idea."

"And you don't." No challenge, more a statement.

She was quick, and Jay respected that. Her direct gaze never wavered. Not someone to fuck with. "All things considered, it's the best offer I've had in a while."

"What is your training, then?"

"Surgery," Jay said. "I'm board-certified in general surgery and... and that's it."

"No pathology training?"

"Actually, I *have* had more than most. My surgery training program required a year in the lab and I spent it doing gross pathology—surgical specimens, mostly."

"Gross and histologic?" Olivia asked.

"That's right."

"That hardly makes you qualified for this position."

"That's what I've been telling everyone, but the pathology chair is willing to credit my surgical training and the year I spent in the lab toward the path residency. Along with this fellowship, and a concurrent six months of histo-path, also done here, and they'll certify me to sit for the pathology boards."

"You're not presently qualified for a forensic fellowship here."

"Why not?" Jay said, even though an hour ago she'd had no interest in the position. Now being told she wasn't good enough, when she'd been telling herself for almost half a year she wasn't good for much, only made her want to prove this woman was wrong.

"Really, Dr. Reynolds, you don't strike me as naïve or inexperienced. You must know this is an advanced program for physicians with much more formal experience in pathology than you've had. We don't have time to provide remedial training. Our fellows are expected to work at a high level of competence from the moment they arrive."

"And what makes you think I can't do that? I've been performing at a high level all my life. I don't think your..." She searched for the word and didn't know what to call them. They weren't patients. They weren't clients or customers either. They were corpses.

"'Cases' is the word I think you're looking for," Olivia said smoothly, the ice growing thicker in the room by the moment.

"At least there's no urgency," Jay finished.

Olivia sat forward, glacial gaze narrowing. "That's just one of the many ways in which you are wrong, Doctor. Many things hinge on a speedy and accurate diagnosis of cause and manner of death. Death certificates are necessary before families can bury their dead, collect life insurance or other benefits, dissolve partnerships, execute wills, and of course, in the case of unlawful deaths, before the authorities can investigate properly. We must be as accurate and as efficient as any other emergency medical doctor."

Jay bit back a retort, noting the ME hadn't mentioned closure for the family in her list. Arguing over which specialty was more important was locker room banter, and besides, Price had a point. All those things mattered, maybe not quite as critically as a ruptured aorta, but medicine was about more than the moment. Maybe she'd fare better when she talked to the chief ME. She didn't know where Olivia Price fit in the chain of command, and as much as she'd been willing to walk away from the whole crazy idea of a pathology residency at breakfast, now she wasn't willing to burn her bridges.

"You're right," Jay said, "and I misspoke. In the trauma bay, the patient's life depends on split-second decisions. I only meant that there is a slightly larger window of time to do the job that needs to be done in your field."

Price tilted her head infinitesimally. "I will grant you that."

Score one for me.

"Still, that does not excuse incompetence."

Jay bristled. "I may be inexperienced in the specifics, but incompetence cannot be assumed, only observed, wouldn't you agree?"

Olivia Price smiled, a genuine smile, and the impact was as unexpected and shocking as a sucker punch. Jay's heart nearly stopped in her chest, and since she knew what that felt like, she was light-headed for a second. Where once there had been ice and stone, now there was heat and sunlight. For a heartbeat, less, Olivia was radiant. And if Jay hadn't been absolutely positive she'd seen it, she wouldn't have believed it.

The absence of that heat a second later sent a chill down her spine.

"You may not be aware," Price said slowly, "but the job itself is physically rigorous. Every staff pathologist performs at least one autopsy a day, if not several, sometimes half a dozen or more, which requires standing, lifting, transferring bodies. Physical stamina is essential."

As she talked, Jay's jaws clenched and now her teeth ached. She knew what Olivia saw—skinny as a stick, pale as the *patients* Price probably labored over every day, weak and damaged. She couldn't argue with what was evident to anyone who cared to look at her. "As I said before, that's something that remains to be seen."

"How long have you been out of the hospital?"

The gentleness of the question was worse than the previous distance. Jay would've liked to lie, but there was no point when the facts could be checked and probably would be before the day was ended. "A few months."

"Rehab?"

Jay blew out a breath. "Three mornings a week, the hours can be flexible. I'll work around it."

"That hardly seems advisable."

"My physical condition shouldn't concern you as long as I can do the job."

"And that's exactly what does concern me. You are eminently unqualified on every level."

"Is there anything else you need from me, then?" Jay asked. This was going nowhere, and she had better things to do than beat her head against the wall. Actually, she didn't, but she could beat herself up all on her own.

"I have a question," Price said. "It's the same one I asked you when you first arrived. Why do you want this position?"

"I don't, at least I didn't," Jay said, surprising herself with the words. But faking anything was never in her tool kit. "I'm a trauma surgeon—that's all I've ever wanted to be." She huffed and looked down at herself. "As you can see, that plan has gone off the rails. I'm well trained and I can do the job you're offering."

"I can't use anyone who isn't one hundred percent committed." Olivia Price rose. "I'm sorry."

Jay pushed herself up and steadied herself with the cane. "Thank you for your time."

"Of course," Olivia said, watching as Jay crossed the room and let herself out. Jay Reynolds carried herself with pride, despite her injuries, visible and otherwise. A tragedy, one of dozens Olivia witnessed every day, although usually those were the kind that ended in death. Then again, there were more kinds of death than just physical. She knew that all too well.

A knock at her door brought her back from the brink of memory, a mental lapse she rarely allowed. For a second she wondered if Jay Reynolds had returned to plead her case again. But no, Jay didn't look like the kind of woman who would do that—beneath the battered exterior and that hint of dark defeat in her eyes, her spirit still seethed.

"Yes?" Olivia called.

The door opened a few inches. "I've got that file you called about, Dr. Price."

"Morning, Pam. Bring it in."

Pam Hernandez, Greenly's secretary, crossed the room with the file extended and a look of chagrin she couldn't quite hide. "Sorry. Dr. Greenly couldn't put his hands on it right away."

"I imagine," Olivia said. "Thank you."

"Sure thing," Pam said, beating a hasty retreat.

Olivia squared the file in the center of her desk and studied it, much as she did a body before she began the actual physical examination. The manila folder looked just like that of all the other applicants, but this one was brand new and uncreased. Whatever was inside, no one else had ever looked at it, and she doubted there was much of anything to see. Certainly not the reams of material they generally collected on an applicant, sometimes going all the way back to college—transcripts, medical school records and recommendations, copies of licensure, test scores, and personal affidavits. This was hastily thrown together to satisfy protocol.

Protocol. She checked her watch. 8:42.

She was already late for morning review, and what did it matter now what the file said. The decision was already made. She knew it and so did Jay Reynolds. Morning review was the time when pending cases were assigned. Presumably Greenly was running the session in her stead, which only meant she would have to go over all the cases set for that day with their assigned pathologists to be sure everything was in order and on schedule. Well, she'd be there in a few minutes. Another minute wouldn't matter.

She opened the folder and drew out the three single pages, the first a half dozen lines of demographic material—name, DOB—she'd been wrong, Jay was only thirty years old—and a medical school dean's letter dated six years previously. The summary stated the applicant, Jay Emerson Reynolds, was an excellent candidate for surgical training, having earned an honors grade in all her core courses and junior internships. *Excellent* was a code word for top of the class, which most medical schools didn't actually stipulate in so many words, but everyone understood. The next page held a copy of her board certification in general surgery earned the year before, putting her on time, according to Olivia's mental math, in her training schedule. The final page was a personal letter of recommendation from Ali Torveau, MD, the chief of the surgical trauma division at University Hospital, their affiliate institution next door. Olivia had talked with Ali Torveau a few times in the eighteen months she'd been with the ME's office when she'd needed clarification about a case that had previously been Torveau's. Her impression had been Torveau was bright, scrupulous about details, and not afraid to admit a surgical outcome was less favorable than she desired. Olivia had never found any indication an individual's demise had been due to a surgical mishap in Torveau's department. She scanned Torveau's recommendation, focusing on the final paragraph.

"Dr. Jay Reynolds is a superb clinician, technically and intellectually, and will be a superior addition to any department lucky enough to secure her in the future. Her tenure as a trauma fellow at University Hospital proved her to be exemplary in judgment, skill, and dedication. I recommend her without reservation for a training position in pathology, for which her previous training affords her unique qualification."

Olivia closed the folder and sat back. Well, that told her not much more than she already knew—Jay Reynolds had a lot of people in her corner, including quite a number of important and influential ones. That might mean she was well liked or it could mean she was simply well positioned politically. Torveau obviously held Reynolds in high regard, and like most surgeons, thought surgical training equipped someone to do just about anything as well as the experts in the field. As Jay herself had stated, though, she didn't want to be a forensic pathologist. Her only interest was trauma surgery, and that road was clearly closed to her.

Olivia keyed her computer, entered her ID number and password, and scrolled into the statewide medical records database. Her department had access to online hospital records, since many of the cases they cleared originated as inpatients. Deducing Jay would have been treated at the hospital where she trained, Olivia searched the University Hospital records first. Jay's name came up on-screen with an intake date of nine months ago. She hovered the mouse over the link for an instant and then closed the database.

Whatever was in that record would give her the facts, but she'd already seen the results. She spent her life steeped in the tragedy of others, witnessing day in and day out the aftermath of accident, illness, and crime. She didn't search for reason, only for cause, and she couldn't do the work she did if she allowed the concept of fairness to cloud her judgment. Still, for an instant, she mourned Jay Reynolds's lost dreams.

CHAPTER THREE

Jay left the ME's building less than an hour after she'd entered. Still early morning. This time nine months ago, she would've been in the OR, scrubbed and just starting the first case of the day, or making rounds with the team in the trauma intensive care unit. Instead, she was standing on the street corner at loose ends. All she had to look forward to for the rest of the day was a rehab session, which at this point, she could do on her own. Her personal effects were still in the TICU locker room. No one had said anything to her about clearing it out, and she hadn't been back since she'd been discharged from the hospital. Like if she didn't empty out her things, she wouldn't have to face the hard fact that she was never going back. But she knew she was done, *everyone* knew she was done, and pretending things were going to be any different some magical time in the future was a loser's game. Sitting in Olivia Price's office, passing on a job she could do if she'd been willing to jettison her empty wishes, made her realize she was stuck in some self-appointed limbo, feeling sorry for herself. The admission made her wince.

Time to change the channel.

She got a coffee and a cinnamon roll from a food truck and ate standing out on the street corner, watching the traffic go by on University Boulevard. The light rain didn't bother her, not with the smell of spring in the air. Most of the snow had melted and green poked up from the ground and blossomed on the branches. She looked at her watch. April 1. She grinned, accepting the irony that appeared to be her life. She admitted having been fooled—the question was, where to next.

"Time to get on with it and find out." She tossed back the rest of the coffee, dumped the paper cup in a trash can, and made her way down the long delivery drive separating the ME building from the rear entrance to the medical complex. University Hospital had grown up over a couple hundred years, starting back when the medical school was established by Benjamin Franklin. Now it was a two-block-long labyrinth of mismatched buildings cobbled together and connected by hallways that started on one floor and ended on another. Only experienced residents were aware of the circuitous back routes, and part of the training tradition was losing the newbies the first time a code was called. Jay smiled to herself, thinking about the days of rushing headlong from the cafeteria on the ground floor through the hallways with her team, people parting to let them pass, some turning to watch, taking the stairs two at a time to the main level and shouldering through the trauma doors ready to take on any challenge. The Gods of War.

Yeah, right.

Not anymore. Her days of running anywhere apparently were over. The rehab doc assured her she'd be able to walk without a cane at some point, once she retrained the rest of the muscles on the right side of her body, once the ligaments in her knee got solid again and didn't fold up every time she tried to climb a set of stairs faster than a snail. He wasn't quite so optimistic about her arm, though. All the joints worked and the muscles were supposedly undamaged, although it felt weak to her, but the mainframe sending signals from her head to her hand wasn't working right. The tremor was probably permanent, although she was learning to work with it. Good thing she'd always been fairly ambidextrous, and her motor skills on the left were pretty damn good.

Not good enough to operate, but she could hold a scalpel. For what, she didn't know, but it mattered to her that she could. She flashed on Olivia Price studying her without a hint of pity, which she appreciated, even if she didn't care for her conclusions. *Unqualified.* Dismissing her without a second thought, cool and impenetrable, except for those few moments where a little bit of sympathy peeked through, which Jay didn't need, and that blazing instant when she'd smiled. Now, *that* Jay wouldn't mind witnessing again.

And bullshit to the unqualified. Hell, she could hold a scalpel to cut a cadaver. She knew more about anatomy—okay, as much about anatomy—as Price. She didn't need any training there. The rest she could get if she had a chance to get her hands dirty. Her chest tightened thinking how much she missed putting her hands to work.

She shoved the thought aside as she walked into the hospital feeling like a thief sneaking around. The halls were bustling, and no one paid her any attention in her civilian clothes. She was just another visitor to what had been her life. She keyed in her ID code on the pad next to the swinging doors at the trauma unit and, miracle of miracles, it still worked. She should have figured that, though. Ali wouldn't have shut her out.

Hoping she didn't run into anyone, she hurried as fast as her leg could manage the short distance to the locker room and pushed her way in. It was empty, and the relief made her a little dizzy for a second. She didn't want to see anyone, hated the look of sympathy in their eyes or, not quite as bad, the discomfort mixed with embarrassed gratitude it hadn't been them out on that highway. She parked her windbreaker along with her cane on the bench that ran the length of the room between the lockers and opened number 72. Her scrubs were stacked on the top shelf, her clogs on the bottom, and her lab coat with her name stitched on the front and *trauma surgery* on the arm hung from a hook. The pockets of her coat were filled with the usual equipment—a stethoscope, stainless steel bandage scissors, a couple of rolls of tape, a folded sheet of paper with patient names and work lists. She tossed the scrubs into the used clothing bin and stared at the coat, not sure what to do with it. After a minute, she retrieved the stethoscope and scissors and stored them on the empty top shelf of the locker. Somebody would use them or toss them, didn't matter to her. She rolled up the coat and shoved it into the trash bin along with her OR clogs.

"Cleaning house?" Ali asked from behind her.

"Thought it was time," Jay said, still staring into the empty space where her identity used to reside.

"How'd the interviews go?"

Jay closed the door, let the lock fall shut, and turned with her back against the bank of lockers. Ali leaned against the row opposite her, shadows under her deep brown eyes, her shaggy dark hair shaggier than usual.

"Long night?" Jay asked, avoiding the inevitable.

Ali Torveau nodded. "You know how it is with rainy nights and MVAs. Had a two-car head-on from the expressway about three."

"Just finishing up?"

Ali grimaced. "Yeah. So?"

"No go."

Ali's eyebrow rose. "What do you mean? How do you know that already?"

"Have you ever met Olivia Price, the assistant chief ME?"

"Not in person but I talked to her a couple of times, I think. Sounds young, smart, no bullshit?"

"Yeah, that's her. She informed me that I'm unacceptable on every level—I think that's how she phrased it."

"Does she know Andrews already approved you for the path residency?"

"I told her, but I got the idea she hadn't been briefed on anything. I don't think it would matter. I am an unorthodox candidate, and she's a very orthodox, by-the-book kind of person."

"Well, don't be too sure yet. It sounds like she just didn't get the whole picture."

"I'm pretty sure she did." Jay grinned. "And I probably didn't help when I told her I didn't really want to be a pathologist."

Ali pressed her lips together and shoved her hands into her pockets. "*Ookay.* Talk to me, Jay. What do you want to do, then?"

"I've been asking myself that since I left Price's office. A little late, I guess. I've been pretty much of an ass, haven't I?"

"No, you haven't. At least"—Ali smirked—"no more than ever."

Jay laughed. Ali was as much a big sister to her as Vic. Her older sister and Ali had been best friends since grade school, and Jay had been the younger kid sister, tagging along whenever she could. They were so tight, and she looked so much more like Ali than her blond-goddess sister, people always thought they were a trio of sibs. She'd grown up wanting to be just like both of them, following them to medical school and surgical training and, she thought, into trauma surgery. Ali could kick her ass like nobody else in her life except her big sister Vic, and the two of them hadn't been kicking her at all since the accident.

"Maybe you should've booted me in the ass a little sooner than this," Jay said.

"You weren't ready to be booted. Besides, it's better if you boot yourself, and it sounds like maybe you are. What brought the change of heart?"

Jay shrugged, not entirely sure herself. "Being told I wasn't good enough, maybe. Looking at a long day ahead of me and nothing to do that mattered."

"Sounds like a good place to start."

"Yeah, but I just blew my chances."

Ali looked unperturbed, just like she always did when a problem cropped up, never deterred or discouraged. "Did you see Greenly?"

"For about five minutes right after Price. He didn't have much to say except the standard line—he'd heard good things about me, glad I was interested, certain everything would work out. And then he was gone."

"Well, he's got the final word."

Jay sighed. "Not if Dr. Price has anything to say about it."

"Like I said—don't be so sure."

"I'll work on that."

"Good. Beau says hi, by the way, and to get your butt over for dinner."

"Tell her I'll be there next time."

Ali nodded and blew out a breath. "I have to get going, but I'll check with you later after I've made a few calls."

"Look, you don't have to—"

"Yeah, I do. You're one of mine, remember?" Ali stepped over the bench and cupped the back of Jay's neck, looking her in the eye. "You always will be. And you need to get your ass back to work."

"Thanks," Jay murmured as Ali disappeared around the corner. She leaned her head back against the lockers and closed her eyes. She needed to do something to feel worthwhile again. She wondered if she'd be able to convince Olivia Price of that.

❖

As soon as roll call ended, Sandy slid a dollar into the antiquated vending machine in the hall outside the muster room and grabbed another coffee. Trying to drink and walk upstairs to the Narcotics Enforcement Unit on the second floor of the precinct house without burning her mouth and other critical structures, she mumbled bleary *morning*s to the officers she passed on her way. She ought to be used to working days by now, but even after a year she still preferred nights. When she'd walked the streets instead of working them, she'd never crawl out of bed before ten at night, stroll until dawn, cadge breakfast one way or another from a friendly café owner, and crash by noon. Now she was up at six, showered, dressed, and at the precinct house by seven, pretending to be awake for roll call. At least she could work in a polo shirt and chinos instead of a patrol uniform, so she didn't have to polish shoes or brass. Small blessings and fifteen minutes saved. She'd cut her hair to collar length and styled it in loose layers so it didn't need anything except a finger comb. Lucky for her, Dell liked it short as much as she had long and tangled. According to Dell, as long as it was still blond, she was happy. Sandy smiled to herself—as long as Dell was getting laid regular, which she was, Dell was happy. Keeping her that way was no hardship, for sure.

The only reason she didn't mind days at the moment was Dell was working days too—so she got to curl up with her after they had night sex and wake up to morning sex. That made the misery of early wake-ups worth it. Sex with Dell anytime was *always* worth it. Except she usually fell asleep after having been properly tended to—thus round two of the coffee this a.m.

She'd barely made it through the dispatches on her desk from the night before when the phone balanced between her desk and her partner's rang. Since she was the only one sitting there, she grabbed it.

"NEU—Sullivan."

"This is Palmetti, Homicide. Where's Nunez?"

Sandy ground her teeth. Another dickhead who thought he was too important to talk to the rookie, even though she hadn't been a rookie for a year. She scanned the room for her partner. Oscar Nunez was leaning against the water cooler, flirting with one of the uniforms.

"Busy with his hand on Turner's ass."

Palmetti laughed, a husky cigarette bark. "Yeah—that sounds right."

"What can I do for you?"

"We got a DB we think has your name on it."

Figures, a personal call could only mean they were trying to turf one. Sandy slugged the coffee she wasn't going to get to finish, winced at the taste, and pulled over a pad and pen.

"*It* being male or female?"

"Female, youngish. Crack house down on Delaware."

"Who called it in?"

He scoffed. "Landlord—at least that's who he says he is. Came looking for rent."

"And we want this why?"

"Couple of glassines next to the vic look designer—got a marking we've never seen before."

Sandy perked up. "What kind of marking?"

"Weird waves with some kind of wings inside a circle."

"Like a canceled stamp?"

"Yeah—could be that, if you close one eye and squint. You coming, or do I have to buy your dinner first?"

"Maybe you could bite me instead."

Palmetti laughed. "I'll be waiting, sweetheart."

"Uh-huh. You do that."

Still laughing, the homicide dick gave her the address. "Body still there?"

"You're my first call. CSU's doing their thing. We'll get the MEs rolling next."

Sandy sighed. A DB likely drug overdose wasn't going to get priority attention if there was more on the docket. "Try to get them there before noon."

"I'll work on it," Palmetti said and disconnected.

Sandy stood, shoving the scrap of paper with the details in her pants pocket. Oscar was still romancing the pretty redhead from records. "Hey, Oz, we caught one."

Oz gave the redhead another grin, murmured something no doubt smooth and soulful in her ear, and lazed his way over to Sandy. His sharp gaze belied his bedroom manner. "What you got?"

"A turf from homicide."

"You let them talk you into that?"

They'd been partnered for three months since Sandy transferred into the drug division from a stint with vice, but they meshed like they'd been together a decade. Funny, since they couldn't be more different— Oz had six years' more street experience, two previous wives plus a sorta-serious girlfriend, four kids to support, and an eye for everything in skirts. Sandy was only a year out of the academy and had spent her life on the same streets Oscar had been walking, but she'd been trolling them for johns before working as a civilian CI for the High Profile Crimes Unit. That was how she'd met Dell and everyone else who mattered to her, and now she was on the job, settled down with her forever woman, who just happened to be the sexiest detective in the whole department.

"Remember the briefing about the new designer scag that showed up in NYC and Chicago—the super-deadly one?"

Oz's brows drew down over his dreamy chocolate eyes. "Wings or something, right?"

"Bird—but the brand is supposed to be a wing. Anyhow, this might be it. So if you're done romancing the next Mrs. Nunez, we should probably check it out."

He waggled his brows. "Always so serious, partner. You gotta loosen up."

She grinned. "I got plenty of excitement in my life, don't you worry about it."

"Do tell me about it sometime."

"Don't you wish." If she told him just how hot Dell was in bed, or what a rush it was when Dell went undercover and Mitch came home, pumped up and ready for action, Oz would think she was making it up. Besides, the fewer people who knew about Mitch, the better. "Your heart couldn't take it."

Sighing, he pulled his topcoat off the back of his chair. "Just what we don't need. Another goddamn epidemic of deadly shit on the streets."

"Might be just another routine OD." Sandy slouched into the bomber jacket she'd borrowed from Dell and never returned, and followed him into the hall. She liked wearing Dell's clothes, even though they were all a little too big for her. Felt like carrying a little piece of Dell around with her.

He gave her the eye as they tromped down the stairs. "Routine OD. Yeah, right. You feeling lucky?"

"Don't believe in it. Worse case, it'll be a short batch and the mess will run its course before the ODs start stacking up on us."

"We can only hope." He didn't sound convinced.

Chapter Four

Olivia reached the auditorium only forty-five minutes late for morning review. She slipped through the door at the rear so as not to interrupt the presentations, and stopped short. The lights were on, but the tiered rows leading down to the stage and podium were empty. The screen at the back of the stage where the case summaries, X-rays, and histo slides should be projected was blank. Where was everyone? By her account, another ME along with Dr. Greenly, the lab techs, and at least two path residents should have been occupying the first few rows. She checked her watch even though she didn't need to. She knew what time it was.

Of course, she should have known if Dr. Greenly was running the morning meeting, it would be brief. He'd probably called an end to the meeting as soon as the new cases were logged and distributed. Usually, each ME and resident presented their ongoing cases as well as those that had just been closed, giving everyone the opportunity to comment or sometimes provide very valuable feedback on those cases that were less than straightforward. She sighed. Well, at least she could get on with her day. Once she finished the autopsy she'd started earlier, she could check with everyone else on the status of their cases. Not the way she'd like to do things, but thus far the entire morning had been out of sync. Oddly, she felt out of sync too, as if she'd overlooked something important or failed to recognize the significance of some subtle but key finding. The sensation of things spinning outside her control was disquieting.

Luckily, she knew how to settle her unusual case of nerves.

Turning to leave the room, she texted the diener to prepare case 17A290-1 for her. By the time she got down to the Graveyard and prepared, he should have the body ready. When she entered the anteroom to don her protective wear, she glanced through the glass partition separating the prep area from the main autopsy room. Several other procedures were under way. At least everyone was working. Frowning, she checked her table. It was empty. Just as she hung her lab coat on its customary peg, the diener came through the outer door behind her.

"Morning, Doc."

The thin redhead was dressed in his usual maroon scrubs, the ID clipped to his chest pocket so faded with time, Olivia suspected it was close to her in age. "Morning, Elliot. I texted you, but I guess you didn't get it."

He frowned. "No, I got it. But then I ran into Dr. Greenly and he asked me to get his car ready, and when I told him I was on my way down here to prep your case, he told me I didn't need to."

"Sorry? Did he say why?"

"No, ma'am. He just said you wouldn't be doing the case until later."

Sending the morgue attendant to bring his car around was exactly something Dr. Greenly would do, and she couldn't say a thing about it. His use, or rather misuse, of department personnel and in all likelihood other things was simply not something she could change. Seeing how distressed Elliot was by the lapse he had no control over, she smiled. "That's fine, just miscommunication. You can get the body ready for me now."

"Absolutely." He pulled on a fresh pair of shoe covers from the blue plastic bin by the inner door. "Won't take me a minute."

The hall door opened again and Dr. Greenly filled the frame, holding the door ajar with one arm. "Ah, Dr. Price, there you are. I've been trying to reach you."

Olivia checked her phone and didn't see a message. "I'm sorry. I didn't get anything from you."

"Well, no matter. I've got you now. I'd like to see you in my office for a moment."

"I was just about to start a case. Could we—"

"No, no, that's fine. This won't take but a minute. Elliot can wait, can't you?"

"Yes, sir—no problem at all."

"You go ahead with the rest of your work, Elliot," Olivia said. "I'll text you when I'm ready."

"Sure thing, Doc," he said, looking from Olivia to Greenly with obvious confusion.

Olivia grabbed her coat and followed the chief down the hall to his office. He held open the door and allowed her to step through before him.

"I thought you might want to reorganize your schedule so you could introduce Dr. Reynolds to everyone and give her an idea of how things run around here." Greenly crossed to his desk and hiked a hip onto the front edge.

Olivia stopped short. "I'm afraid I don't understand. I spoke with Dr. Reynolds this morning as you requested. She's obviously a very accomplished physician, but she's not right for—"

"I understand your reservations," he said with surprising sincerity. "The circumstances are unusual, I agree, but Philip Andrews feels confident that with her previous clinical experience along with the advanced laboratory year in pathology she's already completed and some intensive direction from us, she'll meet the requirements to sit for the pathology boards with no trouble."

"Of course, Dr. Andrews is in charge of his training program, but that doesn't mean that our training program is flexible enough or that we should compro..." She struggled for words that wouldn't be completely insulting to her superior. "I simply want to be sure we don't alter our standards."

He held up a finger. "And neither do I. That's exactly why I'm assigning her to work with you exclusively for the time being. As things progress, we can reassess the supervisory details." He checked his watch. "She should be here anytime. I called her just a few moments ago and gave her the good news."

"I am sure she was quite surprised," Olivia said dryly.

"That's an understatement," Jay said from the open doorway.

Olivia turned. Jay wore the same plain dark trousers and blue pinstripe shirt she'd worn for the interview, although her thick dark hair and the shoulders of her light jacket looked sodden. "Still raining, I see."

"Spring showers." Jay flicked wet strands off her neck with a slim, long-fingered hand.

Surgeon's hands, Olivia couldn't help but think. "Do you have any business to wrap up with your previous department?"

"Nope. I'm free and clear." Jay's gaze was direct as she met Olivia's. "And I appreciate the opportunity to work."

"All right then." Olivia bowed to the inevitable. If Greenly had approved this special program, she would have to make the best of it, at least if—or until—it became apparent Dr. Reynolds could not meet the same standards as the other residents. Were that the case, then they would need to dismiss her without jeopardizing her eventual career path. She would be certain of that when she wrote a recommendation for whatever position Dr. Reynolds planned to pursue next.

"Well then," Olivia said, "let's start—" Her phone vibrated and she pulled it from her pocket. "It's intake—excuse me a moment…This is Dr. Price."

"It's Bobbi, Dr. Price. We've got an unattended DB, PPD just called it in."

"Address?" Olivia asked, switching to a text screen and typing in the address. "I've got it. On my way."

"We're rolling now," the investigator said. "Meet you on scene."

"I have a new fellow with me, so wait after photos if we're held up."

"Roger."

Olivia slid her phone away. Jay watched her expectantly, and she motioned her to follow. "Well, your training is about to begin. We've got a scene investigation to do."

"What is it?" Jay asked.

"Unattended death. It's up to us to determine if it's an automatic autopsy or a natural death."

Dr. Greenly said, "Dr. Reynolds probably wants to get settled before she—"

"Sounds good," Jay said, keeping her gaze on Olivia. "Just tell me what you need me to do."

"Come with me," Olivia said, "and I'll get you a field kit."

"Thanks."

"Well then, good luck," Dr. Greenly called as Olivia and Jay slipped into the hall and let the door close behind them.

"So how does this work?" Jay said as they walked. "Do you… attend every death the police investigate?"

"If the police are involved, probably ninety percent. Any violent death, accidental or otherwise, requires an autopsy by law. In the case of hospital deaths or when the circumstances are otherwise clear-cut, the medical investigators who do the initial phone intake may just arrange for transport or release the body to the family." Olivia turned a corner into the brightly lit equipment bay. "The ME and the MLIs—

the medicolegal investigators—will respond to any suspicious death, suspected suicide, potential homicide, MVA, mass casualty, and the like."

"And you're on call today?"

"This month. If I'm tied up at an active scene, the second call will take over."

"Sounds familiar," Jay muttered.

"Somewhat, I'm sure." Olivia pointed to a row of wide gray lockers. "You can claim one of those to store your personal effects. Some people prefer to work in scrubs, but you will be suiting up in the field if necessary, so street clothes are appropriate if you prefer. When doing an autopsy, you'll also be wearing an impermeable cover gown, but you'll probably be most comfortable in scrubs."

"I'm good for now."

"Fine. Let me show you where the field kits are, and we'll sign one out for you." Olivia led Jay into the adjoining room, really a big walk-in closet, with shelves on either side and red tackle boxes lined up on the bottom row.

"Do we use the same kit every day?" Jay asked.

"I prefer to keep my own field kit and restock as needed." Olivia handed one to Jay. "You can either pick up a new kit when you're on call or keep one and restock as needed. I advise you to check the contents before going out if you're not stocking yourself."

"And restocks?"

"Right here." She pointed to the shelves. All the bins had coded locks. "You punch in your code for each item when you restock so we can keep track of inventory and, obviously, what each individual is using." She handed Jay a clipboard. "You can sign right here for the kit. I'll go over its contents with you when we have a chance."

"All right, thanks."

"We'll take my car, it's out back."

"I haven't felt quite so green since my first few days of medical school," Jay muttered, keeping pace with Olivia despite the faint protest in her knee.

"I'm sure you'll feel more comfortable after a few days."

"I'm a pretty quick study," Jay said.

Olivia did not reply.

❖

"I'm over here," Olivia said, leading the way across the gated lot behind the empty building.

Jay scanned the vehicles, looking for some kind of coroner's wagon or van. When Olivia keyed the doors on a battered gray Chevy Tahoe that looked like it might have been new when Clinton was president, she said, "You drive your personal vehicle?"

"I like having all the gear I need accessible." Olivia slid behind the wheel. "I know I'll have what I need if I transport it myself."

Jay hastened to climb in as Olivia started the engine. Glancing over her shoulder, she took in neat stacks of equipment cases and wrapped packs of coveralls. "Is that a metal detector back there?"

"Mmm—similar. It's a sonar of sorts—detects uneven density in the ground."

"Like buried bodies."

"Yes."

Jay tried to picture Olivia marking off a grid, searching for buried bodies. Yeah, she could, absolutely. Olivia was no desk jockey—she looked capable of any kind of fieldwork, looked like she was the kind of chief to get her hands dirty. That suited Jay just fine—she wanted to learn from a hands-on expert. "So what do the MLIs do, exactly?"

"Much the same things that the police CSIs will do, but from a slightly different viewpoint." She pulled the big rig out into traffic, continuing as she adroitly maneuvered between the slower-moving vehicles headed into Center City. "Photograph the body, preserve evidence in the immediate vicinity of the body, note environmental temperatures, disturbances in the physical terrain, and any other data that may impact our investigation."

"And what do we do?"

Olivia cast her a quick glance. "*You're* going to be my scribe."

"Is that an ME term for scut monkey?"

Olivia smiled, almost laughed. Jay felt a thrill of accomplishment. If she worked at it, she might actually discover some way to provoke another one of those full-blown smiles. Right then, she decided that was going to become her real goal if she stuck with this crazy idea of training to be a pathologist.

"No," Olivia said, "it's a learning tool. And while in this situation not entirely critical, it will be when we're dealing with a mass casualty situation, for example. It's impossible for an examiner to stop and record everything, and it's essential to have every observation noted."

"Just how am I supposed to do this?"

"I have a tablet with the templates you need, and if we find something beyond routine…well then, you'll scribble."

Jay laughed. "I sort of like the term scribbler better than scribe. Sounds more contemporary."

"For today, we'll double-record and then go over everything when we get back." Olivia pulled onto the expressway to circle around downtown Philadelphia to the broad boulevard that ran along the river, separating the city from New Jersey across the way. "Compare notes and impressions."

"Sure," Jay said, not relishing being relegated to the position of student again. She'd climbed the Mount Everest of surgical hierarchy without much trouble, but somehow, this mountain range looked a lot more formidable. She might as well get rid of the elephant hulking on the console between them. "I guess my turning up again was unexpected."

"This entire morning has been unexpected," Olivia said dryly.

"How many other fellows are you taking this year?"

"Ordinarily, we take three. I'm not sure what we'll do now, but the conventional two-year fellowship starts in the summer."

"So I'm an add-on."

"That remains to be seen."

Jay began to see the problem with Greenly's abrupt edict to bring her into the program under less-than-ordinary terms. "So I might be taking someone else's place?"

"As I said—"

"No wonder you're not happy."

"I'm neither happy nor unhappy," Olivia said. "It wasn't my decision to make."

"But you're stuck with me."

"That's not how I think of it," Olivia said.

Jay shifted, stretching out her knee, subtly hoping to ease the cramp in her calf. "How do you look at it, then?"

Olivia shook her head. "Dr. Greenly has accepted you on somewhat unusual terms, but you're here now. As long as you are here to work and to learn, I'm going to do my damnedest to make sure you do both."

Jay grinned. "I can get behind that."

Olivia shot her another look, and this time there was a hint of fire in her eyes that rocketed a bolt straight to the center of Jay's chest. She'd been wrong in her initial assessment. There was nothing icy about Olivia Price. She was a banked fire, smoldering and ready to flare, but only on her own terms. A twist of interest coiled in Jay's belly, a feeling she hadn't experienced in a long, long time. "Why did you choose forensic pathology?"

"It suits me." Olivia looked back to the road and didn't answer.

So there was the barrier—the personal. Intrigued, Jay wanted to probe but decided to wait until she understood the ground a little better. If she made the wrong move one time, she'd never get anther chance with Olivia.

"This looks like it," Olivia said, pulling over to the curb behind a cluster of police cruisers with light bars flashing and a couple of unmarkeds with blue dashboard beacons. The empty vehicles blocked most of the street in front of a ramshackle row of deserted buildings. A red and white van pulled behind them as they were getting out of Olivia's SUV. A man and a woman, both wearing blue nylon windbreakers with *Medical Examiner* stenciled in yellow block letters on the back, jumped down and hurried over to them as Olivia opened the rear of her Tahoe.

"Hi, Doc," the curly-haired blond female said.

The African American man who had been driving nodded to Olivia and looked at Jay's cane quizzically.

"Darrell, Bobbi, this is Dr. Reynolds." Olivia passed Jay a plastic pack containing a white Tyvek coverall. "She's a new fellow who will be working with us."

The techs both said hello, and the group headed down the cracked and uneven sidewalk toward the building with the crime-scene tape blocking it off from the street. Jay dodged piles of trash, dog litter, and foul-smelling puddles, doing her damnedest to keep her pant legs from getting soaked in biohazardous swamp water.

A bored-looking uniformed police officer stood on the sidewalk in front of a brick building with broken-out windows, a doorless entryway above a crumbling set of concrete stairs, and the desperate look of a dying time written all over its façade. The officer seemed to perk up as they approached.

Olivia held out her ID. "Dr. Olivia Price, medical examiner's office."

"Hey, Doc. Maybe now we'll be able to wrap this up." He noted something on a clipboard as Olivia passed.

The blond MLI paused and took out a tablet. "You first on scene?"

"Yeah." He winced. "My lucky day, all right."

She stayed behind talking with him as the other MLI went on ahead. Olivia waited at the top of the crumbling steps for Jay to climb them.

Following Olivia, Jay stepped into a dark, dank hallway and uncharted territory. The only thing she knew with certainty was that Olivia Price held her future in her hands.

CHAPTER FIVE

S andy paced in the hallway beyond the yellow plastic tape the CSU guys had strung to keep lookie-loos from further trashing the scene. The landlord, the EMTs, and the first officer on scene had already tracked muddy water across the stained, torn linoleum that covered the floor of what was once the parlor of an elegant town house. A hundred freaking years and a different world ago. Now the big room with the blown-out windows was an empty shell, everything of value, like the lifestyle of those who'd inhabited the house so long ago, stripped away. The ornate woodwork framing ceilings, doors, and windows had been pulled down by the homeless to fuel a barrel fire in some alleyway, the cast-iron radiators carted away for the scrap, and the hammered tin torn from the ceilings. She'd seen a hundred rooms just like it, even slept in a few, but the one thing she'd never done was stick a needle in her arm for a few hours of forgetfulness like those who inhabited this place now.

Not that she'd been any smarter or better than the girl on the floor—from what she could see, the DB wasn't much older than late teens—she'd just refused to surrender. As long as she could think, she could fight. It had helped that Frye had taken an interest in her, even if the cop had been pumping her for information. Frye fed her, paid her, and kept an eye out for her long before Dell and the others had come along. Long before she'd traded in her miniskirts and halter tops for these ugly-ass cop clothes.

She had Frye to thank, and her own stubbornness, for ending up different than the girl on the floor in this cold, forgotten wasteland.

"You're gonna wear out the floor, partner," Oz said as he leaned against the wall scanning his phone.

"I hate waiting."

"Part of the job."

"Yeah, yeah, I know." She frowned. "Palmetti and Chu sure lit out like their pants were on fire."

Oz snorted. "That's 'cause we took the bait. We don't even know if we got a crime scene yet."

"What, you think she lay down in there for a nap and died in her sleep?"

"If she OD'd and the MEs call it accidental, we got nothing to investigate."

"Unless we got a new poison on the streets."

Oz's eyes darkened. "Yeah. But one case doesn't mean anything."

One case might just be the first case. Sandy went back to pacing.

❖

From what Jay could see of the first floor, the place was unoccupied. At least by conventional tenants. A dingy passageway ran straight to the back of the building. Doors hung askew or were entirely absent, and piles of trash billowed out from the rooms on either side of the hall. A bit of daylight filtered through a small grimy window at the top of the back entrance. What was left of the staircase hugged the wall, the banister missing sections and leaning dangerously out into the air. They were apparently going up, as voices and footsteps echoed above them. Olivia, already on the stairs, turned on a flashlight and passed it back to her.

"Watch where you're stepping," Olivia said. "Some of these treads are about to disintegrate, and the place is probably full of needles."

"Right," Jay muttered, alternating her light between the stairs beneath her feet and the landing above. She was careful not to brush her shoulder against the wall. Whatever was growing there, she didn't want it on her jacket or anywhere near any part of her. She started to itch just thinking about it. The OR was as sterile an environment as possible outside a research lab. She'd somehow ended up in the mirror image of that world, where the living were dead, order gave way to chaos, and she was no longer a king but a peasant. She swiped at a cobweb that laced her cheek and swore.

As if reading her thoughts, Olivia said, "When we get back, I'll show you where the showers are."

"Thanks." Jay was pretty sure she heard Olivia laugh again, and spared a moment to be sorry she hadn't witnessed it before concentrating on avoiding some level 4 biohazard. "Where do I get one of these flashlights?"

"There's one in your kit," Olivia said.

"Right." Of course, that was tucked under her arm, and since she hadn't had a chance to go through it, she had no idea what goodies might be secreted away there. What a way to start her new job. This reminded her of the first day of her internship, when she'd shown up at six thirty a.m., sparkling clean in her white coat, stethoscope in one pocket and a manual of emergency care in the other one, and her chief resident had said, "Welcome aboard, here's your list of patients, and remember, to call for help is a sign of weakness. See you tomorrow."

And she'd been left with an intensive care unit full of critically ill patients and another twenty-five post-ops on the floor, first call and green as spring grass. She'd survived that, so she'd damn well survive this too. If she didn't die of disgust.

Olivia waited for her on the landing.

"Darrell will photograph the scene before we do anything else. Unfortunately, any number of people have probably already trekked through it."

"I thought everyone was supposed to protect the integrity of the scene," Jay said, using the terminology that everyone seemed familiar with from watching television.

"Well, that's the theory, and the protocol is supposed to prevent disruption of the scene, but usually the way things happen, someone calls in to report the body to 9-1-1, who are then obligated to call emergency services to determine that, in fact, the individual in question is really dead. If they should be alive still, they'd need emergency treatment and transport to hospital. So once the EMTs assess the victim to assure the individual is indeed dead—which almost always involves them touching if not actually moving the body—they'll notify the police, who may or may not examine the scene before contacting us. They will also alert the Crime Scene Unit if a crime is suspected, and their control of the scene supersedes ours. Our calls go through communications to our investigators, who get as much information as they can to make a determination as to whether we need an on-scene investigation or can transport." Olivia shrugged. "Multiple levels in the chain of command."

"Lots of opportunity for people to tramp around, you mean."

Ever cautious, Olivia only smiled, but even in the dim light cast by a couple of bare bulbs dangling from the ceiling, her eyes sparkled.

Damn. She was beautiful. And Jay needed to stomp on that little bit of interest right now. Hospital romances were legion, and she'd indulged in a few herself. Hell. Everyone was adult, often well past thirty, and even those still in training were licensed professionals and hardly impressionable students. But she was in unfamiliar terrain with no idea what the hell she was doing, and the last thing she needed was to have a little fling and then, when it was over, have to maneuver the awkwardness or worse, by seeing the ex every damn day. Assuming, of course, Olivia had an interest. Big assumption there. "So, after the photographs?"

Olivia gave her a curious glance, almost as if she knew Jay had just taken a mental detour. "Then you put your gloves on—and don't touch anything before you do have them on."

"I'm good with that." Jay hefted the pack. "When can I put this on?"

Olivia laughed. Jay's resolution not to be affected by her flew out the window. She swallowed around the fist in the throat. Yeah, Olivia was a heart-stopper.

"Save it until we actually cross the perimeter to the scene," Olivia said. "Those suits are hot."

"To say nothing of ugly," Jay muttered. "So what's first?"

"Then we'll start at the outer perimeter of the room and work our way around, slowly circling in until we reach the body."

"What about...determining time of death and all that."

"That's important," Olivia said, "and much less precise than popular fiction would have people think. She's already dead, and another few minutes won't make any difference in our determination. Missing something else in there might make all the difference if this turns out to be homicide."

"Right."

A young blonde in a navy polo shirt, dark pants, a kick-ass leather jacket, and even more kick-ass three-inch, square-heeled boots came toward them with her gaze nailed to Olivia.

"Are you the ME?" the blonde asked.

"That's right, Olivia Price, assistant chief medical examiner." Olivia held out her hand and the blonde shook it.

"I'm Sandy Sullivan, Narcotics Enforcement Unit. CSU is just finishing up in there. Can we get a look at the body now?"

"It will be a while yet," Olivia said. "Darrell, get started on the photos as soon as CSU clears out."

"Got it," Darrell rumbled. He pulled on his Tyvek coveralls, shoe covers, and hat.

"What do we know about her?" Olivia asked Sandy.

"Not much," Sandy said. "We might be looking at a designer drug new to the area. CSU bagged a couple of envelopes that we'll be testing, but you know how long that takes. Tox on the vic will be key."

"Let's ascertain she's an overdose first," Olivia said. "Once we've finished here, I'll need you to fill me in on this drug."

"No problem. I was planning to hang around until you took her."

"Good."

Olivia moved off and Jay kept pace.

"The first thing you need to learn, and remind yourself of frequently," Olivia said quietly, "is not to let the expectations of the other professionals color your observations or your judgments. Your job is not to solve crimes. Your responsibility is determining the cause and manner of death."

They stopped in the doorway and Jay watched as Darrell moved around the outer edges of the room with the grace of a dancer, despite his heavy frame. He adroitly stepped over the piles of trash and remnants of old mattresses and other things Jay couldn't identify, photographing the body and the contents of the room from multiple angles.

"The difference between cause and manner being?" Jay asked as she watched.

"The cause of death is whatever disease or biological incident led to cessation of life—overwhelming sepsis, heart failure, massive stroke, blood loss. The manner of death, at least in this state, is one of six—homicide, suicide, accidental, therapeutic misadventure, natural causes, and undetermined."

Jay worked her way through the mental exercise. "So just assuming that our…subject…actually did die of an overdose, her cause of death would probably be respiratory failure, and the manner of death would be accidental, assuming she didn't intend to die."

"Very good. Just remember, the most obvious answer is not always the correct one."

"I've already learned to tell the difference between zebras and otherwise."

"You'll be dealing with an entirely different zoo now."

"No kidding," Jay said, hoping she wouldn't be bringing any of the local wildlife home on her.

"Ready for you, Doc," Darrell called.

"Let's get a look at the body while Darrell works the room," Olivia said. "Suit up, Doctor."

Jay checked her gloves just to be sure they were intact. In her years of surgical training, she'd punctured dozens of gloves during a particularly difficult dissection or when suturing, and she'd never particularly worried about it. Somehow, the specter of death felt far more dangerous than working with living patients, even those who were seriously infected and contagious. Just another way her world had flipped, and day was night and night was day.

Olivia stopped a foot from the body, and Jay paused beside her.

"The first step in every examination is to look," Olivia said.

"No different than in the trauma unit."

"Agreed," Olivia said.

The body of a young Caucasian female lay curled on her side, her hands pillowed beneath her head as if she had lain down to take a nap. Her shoulder-length brown hair was tangled but fairly clean looking, as were her black knit miniskirt and lacy off-white T-style top. Her legs were bare and, rather than being drawn up into a fetal position as was common when asleep or falling into a drugged coma, were splayed and fully extended. A sandal matching the one on the girl's right foot lay a few feet from the body. Kicked off when she seized, maybe? Jay frowned. "The position doesn't look at all natural. I've never seen anyone lie down exactly like that. If she seized from an overdose, I'd expect some sign of fluid on or under the body. Don't see any."

"No," Olivia said, "neither do I." She shone her light over the body from head to toe, slowing over the eyes, the lips, and what was visible of the hands and feet. "What else do you see?"

"What I *don't* see," Jay said, "is any blood around the nose or mouth or anywhere else on the body, for that matter. No obvious trauma of any kind. Her skirt is zipped in the back and"—she knelt, taking care not to touch anything, even the floor, and angled her head—"she's wearing panties." She straightened with difficulty, careful not to put her cane down and disturb anything near the body. "She's also wearing a tank top. Suggests she wasn't assaulted, but doesn't rule it out." Jay scanned around the room. "I don't see anything that looks like a coat, but maybe she didn't have one."

Darrell moved like a shadow behind them, and as he passed, he muttered, "Pretty good eye for a newbie."

"Go on," Olivia said.

"I'm not sure what else I should be seeing."

"Fair enough." Olivia handed Jay a tablet and pressed the on button. She tapped an icon. "This is the on-scene report. Bobbi will be taking care of most of the standard metadata, gathering it from the police and whatever witnesses she can find. Date, time of day, ambient temperature...here and here. Darrell will do the same for general contents of the room. You and I will focus on the body."

"Is this the part where I get to be the scribe?"

"Actually, I believe that would be *scribbler*."

Jay's head jerked up, looking for a sign of amusement, but Olivia had already turned her attention back to the body. But Olivia had remembered, had even teased her a little. An unexpected wave of heat flowed through her, as pleasant as it was confusing. Jay pushed it aside and pulled the stylus from the small loop on the side of the tablet. "Okay. Your scribbler awaits."

A stillness came over Olivia as she began to speak, her voice thoughtful, precise. Jay checked boxes, entered observations, said nothing, recognizing Olivia had moved into another space where all her senses were attuned to what she was observing. The entire process was intriguing.

"Look at the body again," Olivia said as she crouched by the girl's side. "Take your time. There are no right or wrong answers. Tell me what else you see. What you deduce from that."

Jay took a breath, forced herself not to jump to conclusions. Tried to open herself to what was there before her. "She doesn't look like a drug addict."

"Tell me why," Olivia said softly.

"She's not malnourished, her hair is clean, her fingernails still have remnants of polish here and there." Jay moved closer, bent her good knee, squatted awkwardly. "Can I borrow your light?"

Olivia handed it to her.

Jay did as Olivia had done, shining the light over the body, slowly, from head to toe. "There's some kind of bruise over her rib cage—you can see it where her top is pulled up. Discoloration extending down onto her flank. Looks like it might go all the way to her hip beneath her skirt."

"Lividity."

Jay paused, dredging up old information from medical school. "I thought...I thought that was due to blood settling in dependent tissues."

"It is."

"Then why is this on the side that's facing upward?"

"Darrell?" Olivia asked, quite certain Darrell had been listening to everything they'd been discussing.

He suddenly appeared right beside Jay. "Because somebody moved her."

"So she didn't die here?" Jay said.

"Not necessarily," Darrell went on. "Could've been one of the EMTs or any of the police. Hell, could've been someone going through her clothes earlier, just looking for whatever fun stuff she'd taken."

"Did you see anything that suggests she'd been dragged in?" Olivia asked him.

"No. I've got standard and infrareds of the floor and outside in the hall too. We might see something on them, but she could have been carried and we wouldn't pick that up."

"Any sign of a needle?" Olivia asked.

Darrell scoffed. "Only about a hundred. The CSIs are bagging everything. I don't envy them running the scene."

"Let's get a liver temperature before we move her."

"You got it." Darrell opened his kit.

Olivia touched the body for the first time, gently flexing an arm. "Lividity is well established. She's been dead for some time, but there's no animal activity. She hasn't been here very long."

"No needle marks on her forearms," Jay said.

"No needles in the immediate vicinity," Olivia noted.

Bobbi appeared in the doorway. "No name, nobody saw her come in. There are a couple of kids stoned in a room on the first floor. They can't remember when they got here, but she wasn't with them."

"Thanks, Bobbi." Olivia straightened. "So we have an unidentified female, death under unexplained circumstances, possible OD. She's one of ours."

"What do you think?" Jay said, feeling the excitement of solving a puzzle despite thinking the dead would never call to her.

"I don't think anything, Jay. I only have questions to be answered."

"Yes, Obi-Wan," Jay murmured.

Darrell barked a laugh. Olivia regarded her with one elegant brow arched. "Why don't you help me turn the body."

CHAPTER SIX

Detective Lieutenant Rebecca Frye's cell phone vibrated in her pocket as she walked down the steps from the courthouse at Sixth and Market. She stepped out of the way of a group of tweens and the harried-looking older guy trying to shepherd them all inside—must be a field trip of some kind—and checked the readout on her cell. She recognized the number and swiped to answer. "Frye. What's up?"

JT Sloan replied, "Maybe nothing—but we pulled a few snippets you might be interested in."

Rebecca started walking again, deciphering Sloan's message while headed around the corner to the parking lot. Her cyber chief never trusted a phone line, and she was used to Sloan's cryptic verbal shorthand. The gist of this message was clear—Sloan had gotten a hit on a wiretap. They had only one major tap running, the one they'd set up on Zamora, and that had been dry for weeks. They were nearing the point when the DA would pull the warrant for it. Since they'd broken up Zamora's prostitution ring and derailed his trafficking of young women from Eastern Europe, Zamora had scaled back on his high-profile activities. Rebecca had no doubt Zamora's operation was still running drugs and girls and probably producing porn, but he'd clamped down on chatter from his people, upped security around his home and offices, and the streets were quiet. No doubt his enforcers were discouraging anyone from passing on info to the police. Even the best CIs were reluctant to risk bodily harm for a few bucks. Times like this she missed Sandy Sullivan working the streets. Sandy was turning out to be a solid cop, and she'd been a solid CI too. She'd been able to cut through the tangle of rumors always hovering over the streets like a spider's web and tease out the bits of chatter that turned into a lead.

Frye grimaced. Sandy was safer now, and that was what mattered. "Something I should see?"

"You ought to drop around," Sloan said.

Rebecca keyed her department vehicle, a nondescript gray Ford sedan, and slid in. "Fifteen minutes."

"See you then."

Rebecca tossed the phone onto the passenger seat and pulled around a slow-moving horse-drawn carriage on Fifth occupied by a pair of intrepid early spring tourists hunched in their too-light jackets. The rain had stopped and skies were clearing, but the temperature wasn't going to top out much above fifty. Brisk weather in an open-air carriage.

The possibility of having a thread to pull that might unravel a weakness in Kratos Zamora's highly sophisticated network made all the weeks of scratching for leads and coming up empty fade into the background. She and her team had known they were playing the long game—Zamora ran a legitimate import business in addition to being the head of a shadow enterprise with ties to prostitution, pornography, human trafficking, drugs, and gambling. The team had come close to snaring him after breaking up an operation that brought girls in from Eastern Europe and funneled them into a high-class prostitution ring, but Kratos had slithered free and let his brother Gregor, the muscle not the brains of the operation, take the fall. Gregor had died in prison soon after his arrest, and Rebecca would have bet her last dime Kratos had ordered the hit. Even family didn't get between Kratos and the bottom line.

With Kratos upping security and muzzling all the small-time operators he employed, Rebecca and the rest of the High Profile Crimes Unit had been reduced to long-distance surveillance. And hoping for a lucky break. Maybe they finally had one.

Zamora's main offices occupied a top floor in an exclusive high-rise overlooking the harbor. Sloan had set up her tap location a block away in an apartment with a clear sight line to Zamora's glitzy office and an internal floating feed from the phone company switch to calls going in or out of his location. They had to filter through a lot of junk, but Sloan's cyber sleuths were used to it. Every job had its tedium, and in this case, the payoff would be worth it.

Rebecca parked two blocks north of Sloan's location and walked the rest of the way, just being cautious. Zamora almost certainly had eyes on his building, and his guys would recognize her if they saw her on the street, since she'd been the one to lock up Kratos's brother Gregor.

As a brisk breeze tossed bits of trash around the sidewalk, she was glad she'd listened to her wife and worn a topcoat. She almost never wore more than a blazer, even in the winter, but Catherine was slowly breaking her of that habit. Subtly civilizing her. Smiling to herself, she climbed the brick stairs of an unassuming brownstone, one just like half a dozen others on the inner-city residential blocks that surrounded the new waterfront developments, and once inside, took the stairs to the fourth-floor apartment where Sloan and her cyber cops had set up operations.

When she knocked on the door to the street-facing apartment, a woman with a cap of sleek dark curls, honey-gold skin, striking green eyes, and a hint of playfulness in her smile opened the door for Rebecca to enter. In her form-fitting jeans and a T-shirt with a rock band logo, she'd easily pass for a tenant to anyone she passed in the hall or leaving the building. As she shut the door, she said, "Hi, Loo."

"Sergeant," Rebecca replied to the newest member of Sloan's cyber division. Bianca Cormey had transferred in from Fraud after hearing Sloan give a presentation to the department about the rise in hacking, from both within and outside the country, and what Sloan's freshly minted civilian-police blended unit was designed to do. Bianca had ten years' experience working computers, tracking credit-card phishing schemes, and digging out hidden bank accounts. She'd told Sloan she was looking for a detail where she could go after high-profile criminals instead of low-level hacks, and Sloan had offered her a place in the HPCU.

Sloan, in her standard white T-shirt and dark jeans, sat in a wooden swivel desk chair working a keyboard in front of a bank of monitors as big as Rebecca's TV. Rebecca tossed her coat over the back of a leather sofa that had seen better days and dropped into a chair next to Sloan.

"What you got for me?" Rebecca asked.

"Minute." Sloan barely registered Rebecca's presence, typical for her when she was on the hunt. Her dark gaze scanned from monitor to monitor, her fingers typing faster than Rebecca could follow.

A series of digital sound bars flowed onto the screens and Rebecca's pulse kicked up a notch. She'd never known Sloan to be wrong about a cyber lead.

"Okay," Sloan said, leaning back with a satisfied cat-versus-canary expression. "Bianca pulled this out from Zamora's office line early this morning, and we've been working to authenticate the speakers."

"Is it him?"

"Patience," Sloan said, clearly enjoying her show. "One of his boys finally got sloppy and called his office line."

Sloan hit a key, and after a brief run of static, a surprisingly clear voice came out of the speakers.

"Carlos? What is it?"

Sloan paused the recording. "Voiceprint clearly matches Zamora."

"Nice," Rebecca murmured. He sounded impatient, a little annoyed at having his morning interrupted. Not worried.

Sloan resumed the playback.

"Sorry, Boss. Thought you should know the Spics are trying to jam us up, maybe put the feds on us. They dumped a scag whore full of bird in our territory—"

"I'm afraid I have another call," Zamora said tersely. *"Someone will be in touch."*

The call went dead. The whole conversation lasted less than a minute, a miniscule sound bite in the hundreds of calls going in and out of Zamora's offices all day long. Rebecca looked at Bianca.

"What do you make of that, Sergeant?"

Bianca straightened, a close approximation of standing at attention. Frye had that effect on everyone—she was the boss everyone wanted and loathed to disappoint. The best of the best, a cop's cop. "I wouldn't want to be Carlos right about now. He's a capo, a holdover from Zamora's father's regime."

Rebecca smiled. "Old dog, no new tricks. So he forgot about the ban on phone calls."

"Probably," Bianca said. "Or someone said they had a big problem and he wanted to make an impression with the big boss."

Sloan grunted. "He did that, all right."

"So…translation?" Rebecca said.

"The *Spic* reference is probably the Salvadorans. They're pretty well established on the East Coast now. And they're always looking to expand."

"Yes," Rebecca said. "Dell ran into them in Massachusetts not that long ago. Probably from the branch down here." She glanced at Sloan. "Are they trying to move in on Zamora?"

"They're trying to eliminate everyone," Sloan said.

"We ought to talk to OC," Bianca said, "find out who the players are."

"If the Salvadorans are trying to move in on Zamora, he may retaliate quickly to make a statement," Rebecca said. "Keep on this here. We'll needed to work the streets a little harder—find out where the border skirmishes are shaping up. What's the situation with this bird thing Carlos mentioned?"

Bianca frowned. "Never heard of it."

"Sounds like a new drug," Sloan put in.

"Let's contact the narcs, find out what they know about it." Rebecca stood. "I'll see what I can find out about this dead girl. We might be looking at a turf war here."

❖

"Don't put your hands underneath the body," Olivia said, "or anywhere else you can't see. There could be anything under there— from rats to needles to some fragile bit of evidence."

"Right," Jay muttered, trying not to think about what the rats might be doing. She carefully lifted the girl's arm, which was unexpectedly supple. "No rigor. I forget the time period for that—if I ever actually knew it."

"That will depend to some extent on the ambient temperature as well as her general muscle mass and level of activity just before death. What does her body temp tell you?"

Jay frowned and laid her palm on the girl's arm. Even through her gloves she could tell the body was warm. "She's cooling off but not cold."

"Right. Check her corneas."

Jay gently pushed on an eyelid. "Can't open her eyes. Her lids are too stiff."

"So," Olivia said, "you've got a flaccid arm, fixed lids, and a warm body temp. Early stages of rigor. She also doesn't show any signs of animal activity, and in a building like this, I'd expect the rats to have found her quickly. No insect infestation, either. All together that means she hasn't been dead very long. Three to four hours, probably."

"And she was on her back for a while right after she died," Jay said, "since the lividity is all posterior."

"Yes. Probably in the vehicle used to transport her here. Let's get a look at her back now."

As Jay started to reposition her, Olivia grasped Jay's arm.

"Wait," Olivia said. "Roll the body away from you when you want to examine beneath it. That way if there's any release of fluid or other postmortem effluents, you won't be wearing them."

"Thanks," Jay said wryly, maneuvering around so she could flip the body all the way over. The back revealed nothing they didn't already know except for one thing. Jay pointed to the spot low on the girl's back where her top had pulled free from her skirt. "Why is there lividity there if she wasn't flat on her back?"

"There shouldn't be." Olivia shone her penlight over the pale skin stained with the purple blush of death. She looked over her shoulder. "Darrel, are you getting shots of this?"

"Got it."

Olivia straightened. "I think we're done here. Bobbi, you and Darrel can transport her now."

"Okay, Doc," Bobbi said. "I'll get the gurney up here."

"Jay, anything else here?" Olivia said.

Jay appreciated Olivia treating her as if she knew what she was doing, which she definitely did not. She wished she knew what Olivia thought about her performance, and grimaced inwardly. She really was acting like a green recruit again. "Not that I can think of."

"Let's see if the police have anything else for us, then."

"Sure." Jay pushed up from her semi-kneeling position with her good leg and caught her breath when her bad knee folded. She tilted, despite planting her cane, and swayed with the wave of pain.

Olivia's hand closed around her elbow, steadying her. "Take a minute."

"I'm good," Jay said, gritting her teeth. She carefully flexed her knee a couple of times and gingerly put weight on it. Thankfully, it held. "Back in working order."

Olivia lowered her voice. "Just let me know if you need a break. Fieldwork is rigorous, I know."

"It's fine." Jay knew she sounded brusque but she was determined not to appear any less capable then Olivia already thought she was. "Really."

Olivia nodded. "I'm sure you know your limits."

The blond officer who they'd talked with earlier leaned against the wall just outside the room. When she saw Olivia, she straightened eagerly. "Done in there?"

"Yes."

"Do you have a TOD?"

Olivia shook her head. "Very approximate at this stage. Once we do the post—"

"Ballpark—less than twenty-four hours, more?"

"I'm afraid I can't say. If I speculate and later find I'm wrong, your whole investigation could be a waste of time. Check with me tonight."

"I will," Sandy said. "Anything jump out at you that says this *isn't* an OD?"

"Our preliminary findings—*very* preliminary—do not show any evidence of blunt or sharp trauma. There are no chronic signs of drug injection, but a single needle mark may not be evident at this point."

Sandy looked frustrated. "So she might have OD'd."

"Very possibly, but not here," Olivia said.

"Someone moved her here?" Sandy's eyes lit up.

"Yes."

"Huh." Sandy glanced toward the room where Bobbi and Darrell were just wheeling out the gurney with the black vinyl body bag strapped to it. "Why not just dump her in a lot somewhere. Why bother bringing her inside?"

She'd been musing aloud, and probably didn't expect an answer.

Olivia said, "Maybe he wanted her found here. Maybe it's the building that matters."

"Or where the building is. Nice." Sandy grinned, looking younger and decidedly hot. "Want a job at the PPD, Doc?"

Olivia laughed, her beauty outshining the blonde's youthful glow. "Definitely not. What about the drug you mentioned? What do you know about it?"

"Next to nothing. We haven't seen it around here yet, but there have been a few cases in NYC and Chicago. Very potent synthetic heroin. High OD rate. And other nasty side effects—coma and organ failure."

"Hmm. Sounds toxic or maybe cut with a toxin." Olivia glanced at Jay. "We'll have to check the liver for signs of infiltration or inflammation."

"My partner and I will be working this case." Sandy handed Olivia a card. "Can you call me when you get to the post?"

"You want to observe?"

"Yes, if you're cool with that."

"Certainly, but do you mind telling me why?"

Sandy hesitated. "Because it reminds me they're more than statistics, I guess."

Olivia regarded her thoughtfully. "All right, Officer Sullivan. We'll be sure to contact you."

"Thanks."

As the officer strode away, Olivia turned to Jay. "Would you mind if we postponed your official orientation for another day?"

Jay laughed. "Didn't we just do that?"

Olivia grinned. "I was thinking the same thing."

"Then I'll just stick with you," Jay said, finding that idea unexpectedly exciting.

CHAPTER SEVEN

When do we start her post?" Jay asked as Olivia pulled away from the crime scene and circled the block to head west, back to the ME complex.

"We've got another one who's been waiting since last night. I want to finish him first." Olivia flicked on the windshield wipers for a few seconds, the blades cutting through the light mist that had followed on the rain. Heading into late afternoon, the clouds had reformed and the day was gray. Still, the warm showers promised that spring was around the corner.

"How do you decide who has priority?" Jay resisted the urge to scratch the itch on the back of her neck, pretty sure if she did, she'd be chasing the irritating sensation all day. She'd tried telling herself the Tyvek suit was no hotter than standing under the OR lights for hours gowned and gloved. Sweat was sweat, after all—but somehow, she couldn't shake the feeling she'd carried something away from that desperate scene in her pores.

"Do you want the AC on?" Olivia asked. "Those suits take some getting used to."

"No, I'm good." Jay flushed. Was she that obviously rattled?

"You did fine back there. Nothing you've done so far in your training really prepares you for a crime scene. It can be unsettling."

Jay groaned. "It shows, huh?"

"A little." Olivia lifted a shoulder. "Nothing every first-year resident hasn't experienced."

"I'm not a first...I guess I am." Jay grimaced, appreciating Olivia not making a big deal out of her discomfort. If she'd had a resident who couldn't take the heat, or anything else, she'd have ridden him—or her—a bit harder. For as much as Olivia came off as aloof and remote, she was unexpectedly understanding. Surprising. Jay wasn't often surprised by people. "It's a change."

"Is it possible you're not quite ready to work full-time?" Olivia couldn't ignore the subject, even though Jay was clearly sensitive about her physical condition. Fieldwork was strenuous, and Jay was pale. "You might be asking a lot of yourself for the first day."

Jay's gut reaction was to fire back at the implied criticism, but the careful tone in Olivia's voice softened the barb. "I've been sitting on my ass for almost three months, presumably to work on getting my strength back. I'm probably as close as I'm gonna get."

"I'll tell you what," Olivia said. "I'll trust you to monitor your own limits if you agree not to play the tough guy."

Jay grinned. "Who, me?"

"Uh-huh."

"Deal."

"Good." Olivia nodded, just as happy as Jay probably was to leave the personal behind. Under different circumstances, Jay would be ready to accept a staff position at a university hospital. She wasn't an ordinary resident, but a very qualified, fully trained surgeon, and the fairest approach was to treat Jay like a junior associate, as much as possible, while still being sure she received appropriate training. "So, about the posts. Ordinarily, we would try to take the cases chronologically, but most of the time it doesn't work out that way. If there's a high-profile case, that may get bumped ahead of others."

Grateful to no longer be under the spotlight, Jay asked, "Such as?"

Olivia glanced over at her. "Have you really decided to take this fellowship seriously?"

Jay straightened, caught off guard by the question. She wasn't used to having her motivation or her dedication questioned. She got it, though, why Olivia might not take her completely seriously, and she didn't like it. She didn't like anyone wondering about her capabilities or her sense of responsibility. "I could give you the answer you want to hear, which would be yes, of course, there's nothing else I ever wanted to do, but you already know that's not true. The only thing I ever wanted to be was a trauma surgeon."

"Why is that?" Olivia asked, her eyes back on the road now.

"It's complicated—well, maybe not. My older sister is a trauma surgeon. My older sister's best friend, practically another sister, is a trauma surgeon. It's either in the genes, or maybe just fated, that I would be too."

"Or maybe a little hero worship?" Olivia asked softly.

"I'm not offended by that possibility. They've always been my heroes, along with my parents, I guess. But Ali and Vic—Victoria, my older sister—have always been a huge influence in my life, always going ahead of me, always setting the benchmark."

"And have you always exceeded it?"

She grunted. "Not hardly. If I matched it, I was happy."

"Ali—is that Dr. Torveau, the trauma surgeon at University Hospital?"

"That's right."

"Is your sister there too?"

"No, she has a staff position at Chicago General. I did my general surgery residency there and then came here for the trauma fellowship with Ali."

"How was that, working for your heroes?"

"It inspired me. Like a boot in the butt every morning when I woke up."

Olivia nodded. "It can be a powerful motivator, trying to meet the goals set by someone you admire."

"It sounds like you know."

"You never considered anything else? Or asked yourself if you were doing it for them or for yourself?"

Jay thought she probably should be offended by the question, but she wasn't. It was an honest and reasonable question. Something about the way Olivia phrased it, or maybe the pensive quality of her voice, suggested she had some firsthand knowledge of living up to someone else's standards. Maybe more than just understood it, maybe resented it just a little. Jay didn't miss how neatly Olivia had deflected conversation from herself, either. "What about you? Do you do what you do because someone inspired you?"

"Sometimes it's hard to tell where or how the germ of an idea was planted, don't you think? I can't remember a time when I didn't know I would do this."

"Seems like an odd thing to choose without having much exposure to it. I mean, how old were you when you decided?"

"Hmm," Olivia said, making a quick turn onto the expressway to cut around the beginning rush-hour clog coming out of Center City, "Eight, I would say."

"Right. So why does an eight-year-old decide they want to be a doctor to the dead?"

"I guess I've always had a fascination with dead things."

"Okay, now that sounds a little weird."

Olivia laughed. "You have no idea."

"There's gotta be a reason, don't you think? Something that pulls us in a certain direction?"

"Oh," Olivia said, "there's a reason. My mother is a physical anthropologist and an archaeologist. The dead have always been part of my life."

"That sounds pretty fascinating. Does she do a lot of fieldwork?"

"Yes. You might have heard of her. Daphne Price. Her specialty is ancient South American civilizations."

"Wasn't there a *National Geographic* special a few years back—that's your mother?"

"Mmm."

"Wow. That's pretty special. Don't those expeditions take years, sometimes?"

"They can. She was a member of some of the early teams working at Machu Picchu and related Incan sites. I grew up living in a tent for a large part of my childhood."

"Really. What about school?"

"I was homeschooled until I was a teenager, then boarding school."

"So what made you decide to study contemporary bodies and not—you know, long-ago dead, like your mom?"

"The difference between you and me"—Olivia clicked on her blinker and turned in to the drive that ran along the side of the ME building to the lot behind—"is that I had no desire to compete with my inspiration. Practicing forensic pathology, even though I study the dead, is very much a part of the present world. I am accountable to the living, the ones who need answers. Besides, I have no desire to lose myself in the past."

"Does your mother approve?"

"I don't know. It's not something we talk about."

"What about your father?"

"My parents divorced when I was small. He's remarried, and I am not close to him." Olivia pulled into a place in the first row reserved for the Medical Examiner. She shut off the engine and shut down the topic just as neatly.

Jay wanted to ask more, but she'd already trod dangerously close to an interest that was decidedly unwise. Olivia was fascinating, and far, far more complicated than she'd originally thought. The last thing she needed in her life was another complication.

"I imagine you're ready for a break," Olivia said casually, gathering her briefcase and keys. "Why don't we meet tomorrow at seven thirty, and we'll—"

"Didn't you say you have another post to do? And when are you going to start on the—on the girl we just examined?"

"I hope to get at least one done today, but it's not necessary that you keep the same hours I do."

"One thing you learn in surgery, you don't get to do the good cases if you aren't there when they come in. I'm not going home to sit in my apartment when there's work to do. If you're working, I'm working."

"You may change your mind—I tend to keep long and erratic hours."

"Don't worry about me," Jay said. "I can take it if you can."

Olivia laughed, that brief sun-shattering instant of pleasure coursing over her face. "Well then, we should test that theory. First, something to eat."

"Can I treat you to a street dog?" Jay, like most of her fellow surgeons, often ate lunch on the run, and the sidewalk vendors were the go-to place for something quick.

Olivia hesitated. "Why not."

"Excellent. I'll only be a minute."

"Meet me in my office. We'll go over the field reports while we eat."

"Sure thing." Jay headed for the line of vendors crowded in front of the medical complex, feeling almost like her old self again. She knew the feeling wouldn't last, but for now, she'd take it.

❖

"Hey," Harvey White, one of the senior members of the narcotics squad called as Sandy and Oz walked back into the bullpen, "the lieutenant is looking for you two."

"Thanks," Oz said, glancing at Sandy with an elevated eyebrow.

She shrugged. They probably weren't in any kind of trouble, considering they had the same number of open cases as all the other teams, and their clearance rate was better than most. Their lieutenant wasn't one of the desk jockeys passed up through administrative channels, but an honest-to-God street cop like Rebecca Frye who had advanced based on experience and merit. He was a tough commander, but he stood up for them, no matter what. Knowing someone had your back made all the difference. She smiled to herself as they trooped through the haphazard aisles between desks, chairs, and wastebaskets toward the lieutenant's cubbyhole office in the far corner of the room. Before she'd met Dell, the girls she'd worked with had been the ones to cover her back, and Frye too. But even then, there'd been plenty of times when she'd gone it alone. Now she never had to worry about facing anything alone. Dell was always there for her. Knowing that made it easy to face anything.

Oz rapped on the glass door, the vibration rattling the half-opened blinds that hung on the inside of the window.

"Yeah," the lieutenant called.

Oz opened the door, and he and Sandy squeezed in and pulled chairs over in front of the lieutenant's desk. The three of them, the big gray metal desk, and their chairs took up most of the room. A computer, a tall file cabinet, and a lopsided bookcase filled up the rest of the available space. The place smelled like coffee and oranges. A squat candle burned in a shallow dish on top of the bookcase—the source of the orange-blossom odor.

"My wife says it's good for my blood pressure," the lieutenant said, following Sandy's gaze.

"Yes, sir," Sandy said, smothering a smile.

"Yeah, well." Will Ramos was square jawed and blocky, his caramel face always neatly shaved and adorned with a trim mustache. His jet-black hair was cut close on the sidewalls and left a bit longer on top. An ex Marine, an ex-street cop, and solid squad leader. "I got a call from Frye, asking about anything that looks like street-level skirmishes over territory or product. Everything quiet out there?"

"Has been for the last couple months," Oz said, taking the lead.

"Everybody sticking to their corners? No sudden influx of product driving down prices and making the distributors antsy?" Ramos asked.

"Not that we're hearing." Oz glanced at Sandy. She still had plenty of her street contacts, especially among the girls who still worked them, and when she wasn't in uniform, she made the rounds, listening, keeping an eye out for trouble, watching for changes in the pattern of life on the streets.

"Nothing that anyone has noticed, Loo," Sandy said. "Maybe now that it's getting warmer there'll be more activity, but everyone seems to be sticking to their own turf."

"What about the Salvadorans? Have they been throwing their muscle around?"

"Here and there, a few excursions with them trying to gain a toehold in Center City and North," Oz said, "but nothing that looks like a major campaign."

Sandy asked, "Did Frye—Lieutenant Frye—give any indication of what she was looking at?"

"No, just general information gathering." Ramos shrugged. "Keep your eyes open. If anything changes, let me know."

Sandy glanced at Oz. He was the senior partner, and rank required she let him brief the loo. He gave her a half nod, reading her mind.

"We did get a case today, Loo, that might turn into something," Oz said. "Maybe an OD, and that part looks pretty routine. But we could have a new product we haven't seen before, and no idea where it's coming from."

Ramos frowned. "New product, like what?"

"Bird," Sandy said. "The one—"

"Yeah, I know the one. I read the reports. You think it's here now?"

"Maybe. We're waiting on chemistries and tox," Sandy said.

"The ME on it?"

"That's what they said."

Ramos tapped his fingers on the desk. "Could be nothing, but could be the beginning of something. Keep after the ME. Let me know as soon as you get a report."

"We're on it, Loo," Oz said.

When they got back to their desks, Sandy said, "The ME's gonna call me when she starts the post. You want to come?"

"Hell, no. I hate that shit. It's all yours, partner."

Sandy nodded. "Then I guess I'll leave you to the typing."

His brows rose. "Hey, I don't remember—"

She grinned and grabbed her jacket. Absolutely anything was better than the laborious job of writing up the scene reports, entering witness interviews, and setting up the case log. "Fair trade. I'll catch you later."

"Where you going?" Oz called as she beat a path to the exit.

"To take some friends to breakfast."

CHAPTER EIGHT

Jay rapped on Olivia's open door, hefting the paper bag with the street dogs as she leaned inside. "Ready for these?"

Olivia checked her watch as she motioned Jay in. "We ought to be in time to catch the last half of the afternoon review if we eat fast."

"What's that?" Jay asked, snagging her two loaded dogs out of the bag and passing the rest to Olivia. "M and M?"

As soon as she said it, she realized she'd just sent up a big flag announcing she really wasn't tuned in to what she was supposed to be doing but stuck somewhere back in the world she'd supposedly left behind. Morbidity and mortality was a standard internal review process for all the medical specialties, where clinicians presented active cases that were problematic or of special interest. The idea was to keep everyone accountable for their decisions and to ensure that standard of care was met. There wouldn't be any morbidity where the ME cases were concerned. Only mortality. "Sorry. Still catching up."

"Similar principle." Olivia spread a paper napkin from the sack out on her desk and arranged her street dogs in a neat row. She pulled a plastic fork in a clear plastic sleeve out of her desk drawer, unwrapped it, and smoothed the chili evenly over the surface of each hot dog. Once things were arranged to her apparent satisfaction, she lifted the closest one and took a healthy bite. "It helps to think of a clinical diagnosis being the parallel to our cause of death."

"Same process, you mean," Jay said.

"Mm-hmm."

If Olivia was annoyed at Jay's lack of experience, she didn't show it. She was tough to read, which kept Jay teetering between intrigued and wary. The combination was oddly compelling, and unexpectedly attractive. Usually Jay didn't go in for complicated women—she liked easy, straightforward connections that didn't require a lot of maintenance. Her schedule never allowed for a relationship that needed much attention—she just wasn't that available, emotionally or physically. Fortunately, she'd never had too much trouble finding like-minded women. The high-pressure, fast-paced world of emergency medicine was full of them. Olivia was exactly the kind of woman she avoided—driven, demanding, intense.

All she needed to do was satisfy Olivia's standards for the fellowship—that was her only goal, and she'd never failed at that kind of challenge in her life. As long as she focused on the job and didn't worry about what kind of personal impression she made, she'd survive.

"So everyone attends for case presentations?"

"That's right," Olivia said. "The process serves the same purpose as M and M. First, it keeps everyone up to date on what cases have been handled and dispensed. It also provides the benefit of groupthink for those cases still open—when something seems problematic, more heads are often better than one. It's a learning experience for the residents and fellows, and it keeps everyone sharp."

"Yeah, there's nothing quite like standing up in front of your peers and defending what you've done," Jay said. "Especially when there's a complication."

"I've always found that policing our own is the best way to go."

"As long as you have someone who's willing to make the hard choices sometimes."

Olivia smiled. "That's what being in charge means, don't you think?"

"I do." Jay shrugged. "I don't believe in excuses. If you've screwed up, you own it."

"Agreed." Olivia managed to polish off her lunch as quickly as Jay. "Ready?"

"Sure." Jay wiped her hands on a napkin and tossed the trash as she followed Olivia down the hall.

"Tomorrow you'll present our case from this afternoon." Olivia stopped just outside the rear doors to the auditorium.

"Okay—I'll take notes."

"I'm sure you'll manage." Olivia cut her a glance, smiling at her sarcasm. "Sit anywhere. I'm going down front."

"Your show?" Jay reached the door first and held it open for Olivia.

"I try to keep it on track." Olivia slipped past her, leaving the faint scent of citrus and spring in her wake.

"I'll bet," Jay murmured as Olivia strode down the center aisle. The room lights were dimmed but she could see well enough to make out the people in the first few rows. Greenly might be the chief, but Olivia seemed to be the one actually running the day-to-day business of the department. No surprise there. Department heads often got caught up in the politics of the institution and ended up removed from the clinical practice of medicine. Ali was an exception—she led from the front. Her personal involvement in resident training was a big reason why the fellowships with her were so sought after. Jay remembered the day she'd gotten accepted—she and Vic had celebrated with a rare night out together when neither of them was on call. She'd thought she had her whole life figured out back then—training with Ali, then a position at one of the big trauma centers, maybe even back in Chicago with Vic. Anything was possible—she'd cleared the last hurdle with the best trauma fellowship in the country.

Jay slipped into an aisle seat a few rows behind everyone else. She didn't know any of them. Her life had come unmoored the night she'd stopped on a rain-slick highway behind a stalled vehicle, its emergency flashers nearly obscured by the torrential downpour. She had to forge a new path, create a new picture of the future, find a new image of herself to believe in and she didn't have a clue where to start.

Ali and Vic both thought this was her chance. They believed in her. She took a deep breath. For the first time in her life she wasn't following in their footsteps. She'd never realized until now how much safety there'd been in knowing just what to expect every step of the way. She'd still had to work like a dog, had to prove herself—especially being Vic's kid sister, but she'd had the best role models to live up to.

Jay watched Olivia take the stage after a resident finished presenting a case. She strode to the podium and looked out over the audience, seeming to zero in on Jay for just an instant. "Forgive me for being late." She scanned a printout she picked up from the lectern. "Dr. Kalahari. I believe you're next."

Olivia commenced to pepper the presenters with questions, especially anyone in training, and within moments Jay's sense of being a stranger in a strange land dissipated. Olivia was fast and sharp and supremely confident. Jay liked watching her work. She appreciated anyone who commanded their field with skill, and Olivia was clearly that. Not so very different from the surgeons she admired. She listened with half an ear to the cases, only half surprised that there wasn't all that much difference between the kinds of reviews she was used to and these. Sure, these patients started out dead, rather than ending up that way, which was often the case in the M&M conferences at the hospital, but the disease processes and the workups were strikingly similar. Any clinician would likely be intrigued, and she was.

If her body hadn't been aching and her head spinning with the changes that twelve hours had brought her life, she probably would have been even more engaged. But she hadn't done any strenuous physical labor in months, and the aches and twinges in her body were dragging at her mind. She needed to get back in shape. She needed to get back on top of her game if she was going to survive in this new arena. And watching and listening to Olivia, she realized that she wanted to do more than survive. She wanted to make an impression. Hell, she wanted to impress her. Maybe just because she was so impressive herself.

"It's already getting too complicated," she muttered. All the same, she felt a twinge of life returning, a challenge to prove herself, and she'd never been better than when she was challenged.

When the session ended, people dispersed, a few scrutinizing her as they passed. Everyone seemed to have a destination except her, another foreign experience she could do without. She waited in the hall until Olivia came out, relieved when Olivia headed for her as if their meeting was planned.

"What did you think?" Olivia asked.

"I liked the 3-D reconstructions as part of determining mechanism of injury. The imaging software is amazing."

"Wait until you run your first one from a scene you've worked up yourself. You'll want to go back and look at everything again, just to compare the projections to the physical findings."

"How soon is that going to happen?" Jay asked.

Olivia laughed. "In a hurry?"

Jay grinned. "Never saw the point in going slow."

"No, I bet you didn't." Olivia unlocked her office door. "You can leave your jacket in here if you still want to stay for the first post."

Jay piled her field kit and windbreaker on a chair. "I'm staying until we're done."

Olivia gave her a long, piercing look. "How long has it been since you've been on your feet for four hours straight?"

Jay flushed. "About nine months."

"If you get fatigued or cramped, you will say so. Agreed?"

Jay calculated the odds of being able to hide her physical discomfort from Olivia and didn't like the numbers. She unclenched her jaws. "Absolutely."

Olivia's slow smile suggested she'd been reading Jay's mind. "Good. Follow me."

The brief scrub-up in the small antechamber was nothing like what Jay was used to in the OR—they didn't need to be sterile, and there was no one to infect in the next room. They just pulled on cover gowns and face shields for their own protection and headed inside. The autopsy table didn't look all that much different than an OR table except for the drain pan underneath. The instruments Olivia spread out on a towel-draped stainless steel stand while a skinny guy in scrubs removed a body bag from a big refrigerated cubicle looked familiar too, with the exception of a long-handled snipper that looked like it belonged in a garden shed.

"Is that a hedge clipper?" Jay asked.

Olivia nodded. "It's easier to remove the sternum with that—the surgical rib cutters take too long."

"*Ookay,*" Jay muttered.

"Ready, for him, Doc?" the skinny guy asked Olivia.

"Yes, thank you."

The attendant unzipped the bag, and he and Olivia swiftly lifted the body of a teenage boy onto the table. Jay looked at the penetrating wound on his chest, mentally tracing the path the bullet probably took, seeing in her mind's eye what she would have done if he'd landed in the trauma unit with that wound, still alive.

"No one even cracked his chest," Jay said softly.

"No. He was DOA."

"So we're it for him," Jay said.

"That's right. We're his doctors now." Olivia held a scalpel out to Jay. "Are you ready to start?"

Jay hesitated, then took the blade in her left hand. "Just tell me where."

❖

"Hey, Rookie," Sandy said when Dell answered her cell. "You home yet?"

"That's *detective* rookie to you, Officer," Dell said, a smile in her voice. "No, the lieutenant just called us all in for a meeting. I'm on my way to Sloan's place now."

"Something breaking?" Sandy wended her way through the crowd on the stairs down to the Broad Street subway line, moving on auto, watching everyone around her with the sixth sense she'd learned on the streets and honed as a cop.

"Don't know," Dell said. "I hope so—it's been quiet for too long."

"Yeah." Sandy knew Dell loved being part of Frye's elite squad, partly because Dell hero-worshiped Frye like most every other cop except probably Watts, and even an old half-burned-out dickhead like Watts respected her. Maybe even had a soft spot for the lieutenant, though he'd never let it show. But Dell loved the action too—loved being out on the edge on her own, undercover, making things happen. Scared the crap out of her, but she'd never let Dell know that. Dell needed her strong, just like she needed Dell steady. "So you'll let me know, if you can?"

"Sure, baby. You on your way home?"

"Just a quick stop. I'm gonna be a little late."

"You catch a hot lead?"

"I don't know, maybe. I want to talk to some of the girls. Get a read on what's happening out there."

"Okay. You turn up anything, give me a shout."

"I will."

"Be careful, huh."

Sandy smiled. Dell always said that, every time they parted. "Always. And don't be a hero."

Dell laughed. "Love you."

"Love you too."

She jumped off the subway two stops later and hurried to their apartment. She needed to change before she made the rounds. Otherwise, she might as well hang a sign around her neck that screamed *I'm a cop*. Plus, she wouldn't be caught dead going anywhere in her work clothes when she wasn't on duty. Sexy they were not, and when she met up with Dell later she definitely wanted sexy. That way she'd be ready for anything.

Smiling to herself, she shed her cop regalia and slipped into a tan leather skirt that stopped a few inches above her knees, a forest-green silk shirt that Dell had picked out for her, and a short-waisted leopard-patterned jacket. She slid into two-inch platforms that looked hot but let her actually run in them if she had to, and checked herself out in the mirror. The outfit didn't exactly shout hooker, but it didn't shout cop, either. She pulled the pins that held her hair back when she was working and shook it out. She kept it three or four inches shorter than she used to, but it was still long enough to catch Dell's eye, and that's all that mattered.

She checked her weapon and secured it in the inside pocket of her shoulder bag along with her badge, and slung the funky sequined bag over her shoulder. Funny, how quickly she could step back into the old life just by changing her clothes. She knew she wasn't really going back, but she felt herself sliding from one reality to another, from the hard blue line of the cop universe into a world of shadows and shifting allegiances that hardly anyone she knew could understand, except Dell and Frye and the others. The only ones she trusted, the only ones she'd ever let see her completely.

She stopped just inside the door, grabbed the pad where they left each other notes, and wrote, *I love you, Rookie. Get ready.* Smiling to herself, she locked up and headed back to the subway to look up some old friends.

CHAPTER NINE

"This is exactly the opposite of what you're used to doing," Olivia said as she stepped up to the autopsy table opposite Jay. "Examination of the critical anatomy is still key, but how you get there is reversed."

"I understand," Jay said, trying to get used to the feel of the scalpel in her nondominant hand. She was happy to see it wasn't shaking. They were alone in the big room, and the only sound, the hum of the air filtration unit, rose and fell like a quiet wind. Jay was used to music—Ali preferred country, she liked rock when she had the choice—and the tumble of a half dozen other voices in the background punctuated by the beep of monitors and the blare of alarms.

The silence here was oddly intimate, enclosing her in the cone of overhead light with Olivia and the boy. When she rested her right hand on his shoulder, the coolness penetrated the latex covering her fingertips. Her reflexes signaled an alarm until her mind clicked over into the new reality. She wondered if she'd ever get used to the absence of living warmth in her hands.

Olivia slipped a thin, flexible metal probe into the circular hole in his chest and gently fed it forward into the thorax until only a few inches protruded. "The goal here is maximal exposure in the most efficient manner. We're not worried about the aesthetics of the wound healing or preserving superficial anatomical planes unrelated to areas of trauma."

"Should we x-ray the tract?" Jay asked.

"We could, but given the obvious nature of this wound, it's really not necessary. We should be able to visualize and map the path of the projectile without any difficulty. If there were multiple wounds, we'd need to trace each one individually. With any kind of explosive damage where we expected widespread contamination from foreign matter, imaging would be indicated."

"Right." Jay flashed on the bombing during the Boston Marathon and realized that those kinds of mass causalities didn't just occur on the battlefield any longer.

Olivia outlined a V starting at each shoulder and ending at the upper abdomen. "Go ahead. Full thickness."

Jay had more or less anticipated where the incisions were supposed to go, everyone having heard of the Y incision, even though she'd never actually witnessed an autopsy before. She made a deeper incision than she would have in the OR and was instantly struck by the absence of blood. The tissue felt different too, thicker and more resistant to her blade, but not the rubbery consistency she remembered from her first-year gross anatomy dissections either. "It's different."

Olivia reflected the tissues to either side as Jay deepened the incisions from collarbone down to the lower aspect of the chest, one on each side, exposing the sternum and the ribs.

"These tissues are unlike anything you've encountered before," Olivia said, "still fragile but no longer responsive—fixed, if you will, at the moment of death or shortly thereafter. Technique still matters, and you have the advantage over almost every other trainee. Your surgical skill gives you an affinity for the dissection that is unique."

Good hands. Jay had always known she'd had good hands. Maybe it still mattered a little. "So what's our goal here?"

"Good question. We want to document the injuries and rule out other contributing factors. So in addition to the obvious trauma, we'll examine the rest of the internal organs, run routine tox screens, and submit tissue samples for histo." Olivia grabbed the hedge clippers. "Now you'll see why the big shears work so well." With a few deft turns of her wrist, Olivia neatly snapped through the junction of the ribs and the broad bony plate of the sternum, quickly and efficiently. "Go ahead and lift that off."

Jay carefully worked the sternum loose from the underlying tissues and placed it in the stainless steel pan Olivia held out for her. When she looked down into the wide-open chest cavity, both lungs and the heart were clearly exposed. She whistled low. "Wow, that's a lot of damage. The heart's just flopping around in there."

"Yes," Olivia murmured, gently moving some of the clotted blood away from the heart and the great vessels. "See here—the root of the aorta is shredded. The probe passes right through the juncture of the vessel with the heart and out the exit wound on the back. No ricochet."

"He must've bled out quickly."

"Possibly," Olivia said. "This massive wound might have caused enough electrical trauma to the heart muscle that the heart simply stopped beating. Note there's very little blood in the chest cavity. If his heart had continued pumping blood with the aorta severed, I would expect to see some collection in the thorax."

"I see what you mean." Jay resisted the urge to press her hand over the scar on her chest left by the defib paddle. She wasn't even upset she'd gotten a burn when some paramedic shocked her before she was grounded properly. They'd jump-started her heart, and she was alive. A scar was nothing.

"Let's weigh the heart"—Olivia pointed out where Jay should make the incisions to remove the organ—"and then we'll section the muscle in a few places. That will tell us if there's primary tissue damage."

Jay weighed the fist-sized organ on the scale at the end of the table.

"290 grams. Slightly low for a male, but he's on the small side in general." Olivia set the heart on a plastic cutting board and sliced it in half, exposing the inner chambers. "Empty—not even a clot. Conclusion?"

"He bled out from the bullet wound. Most likely his body fell in such a way the blood drained out quickly and nothing accumulated in his chest." Jay wasn't positive, but better wrong than uncertain. She smiled to herself. Surgery had taught her to be fearless. She was just remembering that.

"Mmm." Olivia dropped a small section of muscle into a labeled vial. "Possible. We'll check the scene photos when we're done. Let's move on to the abdomen."

"Do you sample all the organs in every autopsy?" Jay asked.

Olivia nodded as if the question were a good one. "Not necessarily, no, especially not if we don't suspect a chemical or toxic component contributing to death. We'll do a gross exam of all the abdominal contents and section anything that looks abnormal."

"Okay."

Olivia indicated where to extend the incision, and once the abdomen was opened completely, Jay removed each of the internal organs, weighed it, and placed it in a labeled container.

"There's no reason to do a cranial examination in this case," Olivia said. "We have clear evidence for cause of death. What would you call it?"

If Jay had been filling out a death certificate in the hospital, she'd probably say cardiac arrest, which *was* the final event, after all. But that wasn't how Olivia had explained things to her earlier, so she took a stab at the cause and mechanism. "Exsanguination due to gunshot wound."

Olivia nodded. "Good. Cause is the GSW, the mechanism is hypovolemic shock leading to cardiac arrest. According to the police report, this boy was shot from a passing vehicle, by all witness reports intentionally, making the manner of death clearly a homicide."

"Got it," Jay said, experiencing the kind of satisfaction she was used to feeling at the end of a successful case. Not the same, but still, a job done right. Better than she'd imagined feeling doing something like this.

"Why don't you dictate the final report, and we'll go over it together before you present it tomorrow." Olivia stripped off her gloves. "There are forms in the top drawer over there. They're pretty self-explanatory. Not much different than what you're used to doing with a routine discharge summary."

"Okay, I'll give it a shot." Jay hesitated. "Can I see your dictation of the external exam?"

Olivia nodded. "I'll print it out for you. You can pick it up along with the rest of the file in my office."

Jay glanced down at the body of the boy. "What about him?"

"The night attendant will close the incisions and take care of him now." Olivia rinsed out the collection tray under the table and hung up the hose. "I think you've had a pretty full first day. Let's meet tomorrow at seven."

"What about…are you done for the day?"

"I have some paperwork to do. I'll be here for a while."

Jay followed her into the scrub room and pulled off her cover gown. "What time are you going to start tomorrow?"

Olivia smiled. "Early."

"What kind of coffee do you drink?"

Olivia gave her a long look and laughed. "Black, strong."

"What time should I be here?"

"Is that a bribe?" Olivia countered.

"Absolutely."

"Five thirty."

"Great. I can sleep in."

Olivia shook her head and held the door for Jay. "All right then, Dr. Reynolds. I'll see you in the morning."

"Night," Jay called when she'd collected her jacket and the file Olivia pulled for her.

"Good night." When the door to her office closed, Olivia settled at her desk and pulled up the department's open cases on the computer and quickly scanned the status updates. No problems other than the usual backlog of lab reports waiting to come in. Finally, she reviewed the field notes Bobbi and Darrell had entered on the case that afternoon. Still no ID. They'd need dental records and DNA if nothing turned up in the police, DMV, and NCIC databases in the morning.

Finally she opened Jay's report from the scene—she'd been thorough in noting standard data and had added some on-scene observations without having been told to. Jay had also done a very nice job on the post. She had a natural affinity for the work, although she might never let herself acknowledge it. Pain had a way of blinding one to the truth.

Olivia sighed, closed the case files, and rose to study the Go array in the corner for a minute, having made up her mind when she'd walked into the office fifteen hours earlier what her move would be. Still satisfied with the strategy, she moved a single stone, took a photo with her phone, and emailed the image.

A minute later an email reply with a familiar avatar appeared, a dragon with jeweled eyes and an oddly mischievous smile. A text message followed. *A daring move.*

Olivia smiled, knowing her nameless opponent had been baiting her for the last few moves to push her advantage. Now she was ready.

She typed *Challenge accepted* and turned off her computer. Tomorrow's response should be interesting.

As she shut off the lights, she thought of Jay's promise of early-morning coffee—an altogether different sort of challenge, as if Jay was daring her to prove this new direction in her life could match what she'd lost. She wondered if Jay was really ready to find out, and to her surprise, found herself hoping she was.

❖

Jay had never been so glad she'd decided on a bare-bones efficiency apartment a block from the University Hospital, sacrificing amenities for expedience. Walking home, more like dragging her ass home, she was more tired than she could remember being after sixty hours straight on call. As much as she hated her cane, she was glad to have it, and glad for the dark that kept anyone she might know from noticing her leaning heavily on it. Her leg throbbed like a mother, and the headache that had been her constant companion for most of the last few months was threatening to bloom behind her eyes. As tired as she was, a buzz she hadn't experienced in a long time sizzled in the pit of her stomach. She wasn't ready to go dancing, metaphorically, since dancing probably wasn't in her future ever again, but the heavy curtain of despair that had clouded every waking moment was lighter tonight. She'd worked, with her hands and with her mind. Even her body, such as it was now, had held up well enough not to embarrass her too much.

She let herself into the tiny foyer with its cracked vinyl floor tiles and tired green-painted walls, checked her mailbox and found it empty, and slowly climbed the worn brown carpeted stairs to the second-floor rear apartment. The place was not much bigger than the room she'd had as a medical student a dozen years before. The hall door opened directly into an afterthought kitchen with just enough room for a narrow pine table and two chairs, a sink, a two-burner stove, and a narrow refrigerator with a freezer barely big enough for two frozen dinners. Beyond that, the single room held a sofa bed pushed up against the windows that looked out onto a postage-stamp yard between the rear of her building and the rear of the ones on the opposite block. The bathroom had a stall shower, a pint-sized corner sink, and a toilet. And that was it. But she didn't need anything more than that. When she'd moved from Chicago, she hadn't anticipated spending any time in her apartment, other than to sleep when she wasn't on call, and even then she knew she'd be sleeping in the hospital most of the time. She had one short year to get every possible experience under her belt, to learn everything Ali Torveau had to teach her, everything the three a.m. trauma calls could challenge her to do. The hospital was the only world she wanted, the place she knew her purpose, where she proved her value, and where she found her greatest satisfaction.

She propped her cane against the kitchen table and draped her jacket over the back of the chair. When she pulled her phone from her pocket and checked the screen, the phone icon indicated a message.

Shower first. She found a yogurt in the back of the refrigerator and ate it while she stripped in the bathroom and threw her clothes into the corner. The hot water beat on her skin like a thousand angry drummers, and she gritted her teeth while she waited for the heat to work its way into her abused tissues. When she finally stepped out and toweled dry, she figured she had ten minutes before she was asleep. The phone rang as she approached the bed, and she dropped down onto the sheets naked.

"Hello."

"I have to find out from Ali," Vic said, "that you've gone back to work? And why aren't you answering your voice mail?"

"Because I was working." Jay covered her eyes against the light coming in the window from someone's rear porch light and smiled in the dark. "Good to hear you too, sis."

"So? You decided to be a pathologist?"

"I thought you and Ali decided that for me."

Vic snorted. "Yeah, right, like we could ever talk you into anything you didn't want to do." She paused. "*Is* it what you want to do?"

"Good question," Jay muttered. "People have been asking me that all day."

"Because, listen, I can get you a radiology spot here starting in July."

"Radiology." Jay shook her head. "Can you see me spending my life staring at films?"

"There's always interventional—"

"Vic," Jay said gently, "I'm not gonna be able to do that kind of work. My hand—"

"You don't know that," Vic said adamantly.

"No, you're right, I don't. But even if I could, it's still not what I want to do. They're technicians—someone else makes all the calls."

"You don't have to decide now, you know."

"I thought you were all for this?"

"I just want you to be…happy."

Jay didn't have the heart to say that happy was way down her list. "How about I start with useful. Because I haven't felt that way in a long time."

"You don't have to *do* anything to be worth something."

"Hey. You need to stop worrying about me. I'm on the mend. And I had a pretty good day, except I'm beat to shit right now."

"What do you mean? You okay?"

"Yeah, just a long day," Jay said. "We had a case in the field, it was…different. Interesting."

"Yeah?" For the first time, Vic's voice held a lightness Jay hadn't heard in a long time. "You serious?"

"Yeah, I mean it," Jay said. "It's only the first day, but it was better than I thought."

"Ali says it's a good program—one of the best."

"I haven't met everyone yet, but Olivia—Olivia Price is the assistant chief medical examiner…I'll be working with her a lot, I think. She's good. Really good."

"You'll let me know how it's going, right?" Vic said. "Don't make me chase you down again."

"Yeah, sure. I promise."

"Okay, I gotta go. The OR's calling."

A swift pang shot through her chest, but Jay swallowed it down. "Right. Have fun."

"Always. Love you."

"Love you," Jay whispered.

She had meant pretty much everything she'd said—she'd had a good day, better than she'd expected. She still couldn't see herself in this new life, like trying on a suit of clothes belonging to someone else. When she thought about standing across from Olivia at the table, working with her to get the job done, that part felt right. That was more than enough for now, and maybe she could actually go to sleep looking forward to the morning for a change.

CHAPTER TEN

S andy exited the subway just south of City Hall and walked a few blocks from the business district into the border zone between the commercial and residential areas. The bars, diners, and adult entertainment centers that clustered in the five or six square blocks south of Walnut and east of Broad had resisted gentrification along with the insistent demands of adjacent upscale neighbors for the police to eliminate them. Not many of the street cops had much enthusiasm for rousting working girls or closing down porn shops when the girls would be out on bail by morning and the shops open at sundown the next night, and no one was really sure there was a victim in the picture. As long as the corners were clear of dealers and the alleys weren't being used to turn tricks, beat cops and narcotics officers had bigger crimes to worry about.

Turning the corner onto Locust and heading toward Twelfth, Sandy slipped her hand into her front pocket and curled her fingers around her badge—more to ward off johns than identify herself to fellow cops. She wasn't worried about being hassled by uniforms, but she might get some unwanted attention from the hopefuls cruising by. She figured most of the cops she had contact with knew she'd once worked these corners, but the few comments and curious looks she'd gotten in the academy had pretty much stopped. The cutting remarks couched in fake good-natured teasing never bothered her much. She'd never have survived to make it as far as she had if she'd let the opinions of other people shape her own view of herself. Having Frye for a rabbi hadn't hurt, and she wasn't too proud to acknowledge it. The cops were a fraternity as old as the Romans, and patronage was part of the tradition. She was lucky to have had Frye and Dell to lend her credibility at the beginning, and she'd earned her place now. She was as solidly blue as any cop on the force.

But no matter how far she'd come, she'd never forget where she'd started, or the women who'd been her first family. In the time she'd been gone, new faces had appeared, but she always knew where to find her friends. Seven p.m. They'd just be emerging from their shared flops and four-to-a-bedroom apartments. They'd be putting on their makeup, doing their hair, sorting through their wardrobe for something to help them stand out, something showy and flashy and skimpy to catch the eye of the johns trolling the streets in their darkened cars, slowing at the corners to look over the merchandise, but something that would keep them halfway warm and let them run if they had to. They'd be thinking about how much they needed to make for the rent, for the food, for the kids, and some of them would be thinking about how much they'd have to give their pimps and how much they might be able to hide away without giving up a cut and risking a black eye or split lip or worse. A dangerous game, played night after night, with no real way to win, but only, with luck, to break even. She knew she'd been lucky—lucky to trust Frye, lucky to find Dell, lucky to risk loving one more time.

She pushed through the revolving door of Stuie's Diner, the heat and the grease and the noise a familiar slap in the face. Stuie, big belly made wider by his smeared white apron, was behind the grill, his florid face framed in the pass-through as he kept an eye on the waitresses and the register. Gert, one of the regular waitresses, worked the counter, busily sliding heavy white plates heaped with burgers and fries and gravy and mashed potatoes in front of the customers lined up on the stools along the chipped and discolored Formica counter.

Sandy waved hi and made her way to the last booth in the long, narrow diner and stopped beside the three young women crowded around the skinny red-topped table. She knew two of them. Lola, a brassy blonde with sun-kissed skin and old eyes, and Marie, a thin brunette in her late thirties with just about the best legs Sandy had ever seen. The third was young, as young as she'd been once, maybe. The new girl, a pale redhead with a smattering of freckles and a deep blue gaze that vacillated between fear and suspicion, eyed her suspiciously.

"Buy you girls some breakfast?" Sandy said.

"You're just in time, sugar. How you been?" Lola pointed to the free spot beside the new girl, across from Marie.

Sandy slid in, nodded to the young redhead. "Hi, I'm Sandy."

The girl said nothing and averted her gaze.

"Couldn't stay away, huh? Knew you'd be missing us," Marie said, a teasing note in her voice, but a question in her eyes.

Sandy understood. Almost no one left for good, unless they were *really* gone for good, like never coming back—anywhere. Those who tried to leave the life were met with mixed hopes and cynicism.

"I'm always around if you want me for anything," Sandy said, sidestepping the unspoken question. They all knew she'd crossed the line to the opposite side. Most of them had known she was getting friendly with Dell, but none of them knew about her relationship with Frye. That had been a secret that would've gotten her killed, and she couldn't afford even those she considered her friends to know about it.

"How is your handsome stud?" Lola asked.

Sandy grinned. "I keep her busy."

Lola and Marie made whooping sounds and raised their brows.

Sandy laughed. "What's new?"

Silence fell as Gert plodded over to them with her order pad and pen at the ready.

"The regulars for all youse girls?"

Lola, Marie, and the nameless newcomer all said yes. Sandy said, "I'll have a burger and fries, thanks, Gert."

"No breakfast for you, honey?" Gert said as she scribbled.

"Not this time around," Sandy said.

Gert disappeared and Sandy waited. She could ask, but it was up to them whether they would tell her anything or not. Her relationship with her old friends had changed, although none of them had ever talked about it. She wasn't one of them any longer, but she was someone they still trusted—at least for now. She would use whatever she learned to try and make their lives a little safer. The last thing she wanted to do was endanger them.

"Not much has changed," Lola said. "The weather is getting warmer, so business is better."

Marie snorted. "That's one way of putting it."

"Trouble from anyone?" Sandy asked.

Lola shook her head. "No more than usual. What you looking at?"

Sandy reached into the pocket of her jacket and took out a copy of the headshot of the dead girl the crime scene techs had taken. She put it on the table. "I don't know her. Do any of you?"

"Uh-uh." The laughter went out of Lola's eyes.

Marie's face was a mask as she studied the picture. She was the unofficial head of the local girls, keeping an eye on everyone, making sure the strays ended up with a place to stay at night, putting out the word if there was trouble with certain johns or certain officers, calling the bail bondsman if it came to that. "Not one of ours," she said at last.

"Thanks."

Lola turned the picture this way and that with her index finger. "She doesn't look like one of us at all. You sure?"

Sandy pocketed the picture. "No, not really. We don't know who she is."

"OD?" Lola asked.

"Yes."

"Around here?" Marie asked.

"No, a few blocks north of Market."

"Huh," Lola said musingly. "I would've bet south of Bainbridge." MS-13 territory. The Salvadorans.

"Why?" Sandy asked.

Gert brought their food, and after she passed plates around and left again, Lola replied, "Word is they're not too fussy who they sell to, or what they sell. They're getting popular with the car hoppers from the suburbs."

"Not so north of Market?" Sandy asked. Zamora's territory.

Lola shrugged. "Maybe not yet."

"Have you heard anything about bad stuff? Maybe something new?"

"Should we have?" Marie said.

"Possibly. Let everyone know to be careful of anything new, especially coming from out of state."

"Got a name?" Lola asked.

Sandy nodded. "They're calling it bird."

She finished her meal and left the girls to relax before they had to go to work. She hadn't learned much, except that her dead girl might only be the first.

❖

Dell parked her Harley under the overhang adjacent to the double garage doors opening into the first floor of Sloan's building in Old City, locked her helmet to the back, and climbed the brick steps to the small porch in front of the unmarked brown door. No sign, just a small square window a little too high to see through. She glanced up at the security camera tucked into the corner beneath the short roof and waved. The door lock buzzed open, and she walked through into a hallway with a polished wood floor that led back into the cavernous garage where Sloan kept her Porsche and the field-equipped utility vehicles the team used on surveillance. The service elevator, one of the old-fashioned kind with the fold-back metal grate and an interior big enough to accommodate dollies loaded with equipment and supplies from when the building had been a working warehouse, stood open in the back corner. She stepped in, pushed a button, and it rose noiselessly on the new hydraulics, opening on the third floor where Sloan and Jason had their private offices. The space also served as the High Profile Crime Unit's operations center.

Frye had an office she never used at Police Plaza and Sloan worked there as a consultant helping the department upgrade its cyber security division, but this was where the heart of their operation resided—in the banks of computers, monitoring devices, and surveillance equipment that rivaled anything in Virginia. Of course, both Sloan and Jason had started out in Virginia and still had contacts there—as well as the coolest toys.

Jason, lithe and blond and androgynously beautiful, swiveled in his chair and waved.

"Am I the first one here?" Dell walked over and lifted the baby from the carrier resting on the workbench next to Jason. "Hey, Mr. Timmy. How's your day been?"

Jason smiled. "His day's been just dandy. He had applesauce for lunch, his favorite."

The baby smiled as only four-month-old babies could do, wide and innocent and delighted with everything, and Dell settled him back in the carrier. "How's Dad doing?"

"Dad would like very much to get a full night's sleep, which he fervently hopes will be happening soon."

"What else is happening?"

Jason's face settled back into work mode. "Nobody's entirely sure, but there's drumbeats in the air."

Dell hitched a hip onto the counter and shed her leather jacket onto a nearby stool. "Yeah. It's been way too quiet. Zamora coming out of the woodwork?"

"He's still being cautious, but we're starting to see some cracks in the shell. Keeping an organization his size muzzled is practically impossible."

"Good. Maybe the troops are getting restless." She knew she was.

Building cases against sophisticated crime organizations took time, and she was lucky she got to spend most of her time on the streets and in the clubs, but she could do with some action.

"Well, the lieutenant will be here soon," Jason said. "Must be something heating up."

Dell nodded. "You want coffee?"

"Are you buying?"

"Sure." Dell sauntered back to the full kitchen in the rear and put on a fresh pot of coffee. She checked her watch, mentally calculating what Sandy would be doing right about now. Where she might be. A little kernel of unease always resided in the center of her chest when Sandy was working. She guessed Sandy probably felt the same way about her. Neither of them would change anything, and she knew Sandy was more than capable of taking care of herself under any circumstances—on the street, in the squad, on the job. Her girl was just about the most capable person she'd ever met—resilient, resourceful, smart as anything. But still, she was Dell's girl—beautiful, delicate in her own way, and the single thing that made Dell's heart beat every minute of every day. She blew out a breath, put the worry aside. They'd both be home in a few hours, and Sandy had promised she'd be getting a surprise. Surprises always meant hot sex.

Smiling to herself, she carried the coffee back to Jason just as Sloan and the lieutenant walked in. Frye, tall and lean and cool, looked sharp as always in her tailored dark trousers and pearl-gray shirt, the cuffs rolled back, black cashmere topcoat draped over her arm. The one she hardly ever wore but carried around because her wife wanted her to. Dell smiled to herself. She knew how that went.

Watts shambled along behind Frye and Sloan, although his step was quicker and lighter than it used to be, now that he'd shed a lot of the extra weight he'd been carrying around. She even thought his suit might be less than five years old, a distinct change for the detective who had joined the group reluctantly and now was a pivotal part of the team. Watts was a seasoned cop who knew his way around the city and the department and had acquired years of invaluable contacts. Bianca Cormey followed close behind Watts, and Dell's blood buzzed with anticipation. If Bianca was there, they must have gotten something from the tap. At last.

"I'll try to make this quick," Frye said without slowing. "Let's all go back to the conference room."

Watts stopped to grab coffee, Sloan got a bottle of water, and they convened around the big table, everyone taking their customary seats as they had done dozens of times before. The lieutenant sat at the head of the table.

"Sergeant Cormey," Frye said, nodding toward the brunette, "picked up a little snippet this morning that I want to chase down. Why don't you go ahead and play it for everyone, Sergeant."

Bianca set a small computer on the table, rapidly keyed in commands, and turned it so the speakers faced the group. A conversation between Zamora and one of his capos about a dead girl who might have been dumped in their territory played.

Watts grunted. "I'd be covering my balls with a steel jock if I was that guy. Zamora probably knows we're listening."

"He certainly assumes so," Sloan said.

Watts lifted a still-beefy shoulder, but his florid complexion had settled down into a healthier tone, and even the bags under his eyes seemed shallower. "So what do we think—is anyone smart enough to try to put the squeeze on Zamora by pointing us at him?"

Dell said, "Seems pretty sophisticated for the Salvadorans, and they're his biggest competition."

"What about someone inside his organization?" Frye said.

"A takeover, you mean?" Sloan waggled her hand. "Unless it's a faction loyal to Gregor looking for revenge, I don't see it. And Gregor is dead, so there's no percentage in it."

"I agree," Frye said. "I'm more inclined to think it's just a message—spit in your face kind of thing. Or maybe somebody just wanted to get rid of a body and didn't want it on their home turf."

"That's not how the Salvadorans usually handle things," Dell pointed out. "They're not particularly concerned about crapping in their own backyard."

Watts said, "Maybe they're getting tired of stepping in their own shit. Maybe somebody with brains instead of balls is in charge."

"We haven't heard anything like that on the streets," Dell said.

"I want to up the surveillance on the border zones," Frye said. "If a territory skirmish is coming, it's going to start there. In the meantime, we follow up on this conversation—let's talk to the homicide guys, see what they've got on this." She looked at Dell. "Chase down the ID and the rest of the details."

"Sure, Lieutenant. No problem."

"Watts," Frye said, "things have been quiet on the docks. Alert them to be on the lookout for any change in manifests—we don't want to miss a new distribution pipeline. You've got some people you can talk to there, right?"

"Can do, Loo." Watts very nearly smiled, which on him looked a little bit like he had gas. He'd kept his new relationship with the port commandant under pretty close wraps, but he'd shown up for work a few times with a new spring in his step. Plus, he'd been getting regular haircuts.

"Sloan, Cormey, if we've gotten one break from the wire, there'll be more. Keep on it."

Cormey smiled. "Absolutely."

Frye stood. "All right then. Daily roll call here, seven a.m. starting now."

Watts winced. Sloan, who never seemed to sleep anyhow, grinned.

Dell thought about Sandy on the streets, the friends they both had out there. When a street war started, the innocent often became the first victims.

CHAPTER ELEVEN

Sandy let herself into the apartment a little after nine p.m. The lamp by the living room sofa was turned down low. Dell sprawled in the corner of the couch, her head back, her eyes closed. Sandy gently closed the door behind her and took off her jacket.

"Hey, baby," Dell murmured, a grin breaking across her face.

"Hi." Sandy leaned back against the door to take in the view. Dell's thick dark hair was tousled, and her loose-limbed slouch looked sexy as hell. So did her tight dark T-shirt, black jeans, and scuffed motocross boots. "You just get home?"

"A little bit ago."

"You tired?"

Dell shook her head. "Not really."

Sandy stopped in front of the sofa and kicked off her shoes. "Been thinking about me?"

"Always." Dell settled back on the sofa, her legs spread, her expression just this side of a smirk, like she knew what she wanted and knew she'd be getting it.

"Are you ready?" Sandy let her eyes drift down Dell's body, checking to see just how ready and just what Dell might be in the mood for. A faint bulge lifted the fly of her button jeans, and she smiled. "Looks like you might be."

Dell brushed a hand over the front of her pants. "You did tell me to be prepared, and I try to always do what you want."

Sandy pulled up her tight skirt, giving her room to spread her thighs as she straddled Dell's legs. She wiggled until the narrow swatch of silk panties that barely covered the delta between her thighs settled onto the ridge in Dell's jeans. She murmured in approval as the pressure flooded her clit. Her breath came faster as she rocked. "And you always follow my instructions so well."

"Try to." Dell grasped Sandy's hips, pulling her down as she lifted up, easing Sandy back and forth over the cock tucked along her thigh. "And what would you like tonight, huh, baby?"

"You know what I want?" Sandy braced her arm on Dell's chest and tugged Dell's shirt from her jeans, sliding her hand underneath. Dell's chest was free tonight and her small, firm breast filled Sandy's hand, the nipple tight against her palm. She liked Dell in this halfway state, a little bit her and a little bit Mitch. She liked Dell and Mitch any way they came to her, and she especially liked knowing Dell could be whoever she needed to be with her. She squeezed Dell's breast, brushing the nipple with her thumb, and Dell arched her back, her lids dropping low for an instant. Sandy caught Dell's lip between her teeth and tugged a little bit, sliding her tongue over the soft inner surface of Dell's lower lip. "I've been thinking about you fucking me all day."

Dell's breath whooshed out and her hips surged. "That's good, because I've been thinking about fucking you all day."

Sandy kissed her, toying with her tongue, probing and stroking, sucking, nipping every now and then, smoothing her palms over the muscles in Dell's chest, cupping the soft lift of her breasts, tracing the tight ridge of her belly, getting tighter all the time. When she turned her hand and pushed her fingers below the waistband of Dell's jeans, Dell groaned.

Sandy laughed. She loved making Dell wait, knowing every minute she was getting wetter and harder for her, feeling her thighs tremble and the sculpted planes of her shoulders and arms shudder. Dell was powerful, beautiful, and hers. Never more hers than in these moments when they both demanded and offered, gave and took, commanded and surrendered until they moved as one to the edge. Dell swept her hands up the backs of Sandy's thighs, pushing the skirt even higher, and clasped her ass, massaging her as she rotated her cock deeper into the cleft between Sandy's legs.

"I'm gonna get come all over your jeans if you keep doing that," Sandy murmured.

Dell laughed. "You know that makes me hot."

Sandy forced her racing heart to slow, ignoring the pulsing need coalescing between her thighs. "I don't plan on coming until you're inside me, so don't think you're getting off easy."

Dell slid one hand over Sandy's thigh and cupped between her legs, flicking the thin strand of silk aside. She teased a fingertip through the wetness and circled her clit. "Oh, I don't mind working for it."

Sandy gasped at the swift rise of need in her pelvis. Her clit twitched under Dell's fingers, and her vision dimmed.

"It looks like I'm gonna have to take what I want, then," Sandy whispered, her voice sounding strange to her ears, a wire stretched to the breaking point. She snapped the buttons open on Dell's fly and pushed her hand inside. Finding the smooth, warm length of her, she drew her out, clasped the base of the cock in her palm, and lifted up. "You ready?"

Dell gritted her teeth, fingers gripping the arch of Sandy's hips. "Fuck, yes."

Sandy worked the head of Dell's cock to move her panties aside and guided her to her opening. She settled down, taking her all the way in until her clit pressed against the base of Dell's cock and the cock pressed into Dell's clit beneath her. When she rocked slowly forward, rising an inch or two and dropping back down, Dell moaned. Making Dell come like this was more exciting than coming herself. "I'm going to take my time, and I'm going to make you come first."

"You won't have to wait very long," Dell muttered, her neck straining, her back arched off the sofa. "Just watching you on top of me like that is enough to make me come."

"Don't rush me, Rookie. I feel like riding you for a long time." She meant to go slow, meant to drive Dell crazy, meant to pound Dell's clit until she came all over herself, but her body disagreed. Every stroke made her clit tingle and the fire spread inside her, down the inside of her thighs, deep in her core. One stroke, another. "Oh God!"

"Yeah," Dell cried, and the floodgates opened.

Sandy fell and Dell caught her, just like she knew she would. When the aftershocks ebbed, she shifted until the cock slipped out and she snuggled closer, her cheek tucked into the curve of Dell's neck. Somehow they'd ended up mostly stretched out on the sofa, her leg thrown over Dell's hip.

"I'm thinking we should try making it to the bedroom," Dell muttered, "as soon as I can walk."

"What's the matter, wear you out?"

Dell chuckled, the rumble of her laughter beneath Sandy's ear a familiar and comforting sound. "Totally. You waste me, baby."

Sandy propped her head up on her bent elbow and grinned. "That's because you're so easy." She kissed Dell lightly. "For a stud, you're kind of a pushover."

Dell stroked Sandy's back and cupped her bare ass. Somehow, her panties had disappeared. "It's not my fault you're so hot. You'd make stone melt."

"Mmm, smart too." Sandy sighed and curled up again, one hand stroking Dell's belly. "I love you."

"I love you too, baby." Dell kissed the top of her head. "Glad I got home in time."

"What did Frye want with your meeting? Something breaking?"

Dell sighed. "Maybe. We finally got something over the wire. Just a little rumble, but if it turns into something, we might be seeing some repercussions on the street."

"Zamora and the Salvadorans?"

"Maybe, it's a little soon to tell."

"I should tell the girls to be careful."

"Yeah, I would," Dell said. "How about you? Anything cooking out there?"

"No, not so you'd notice." Sandy chewed her lip. "But it doesn't feel right, you know? Like maybe there's something right there we're not seeing. Just a feeling, like a storm coming."

"I know what you mean. Maybe it's just because it's been too quiet for a while."

"Maybe."

"Frye has us back on alert," Dell said. "Seven o'clock roll call again."

"Ouch. That's rough for you if you're working the clubs."

"Yeah, good thing I'm young and tough."

Sandy rolled on top of her, tugged on her T-shirt, and when Dell lifted her arms, stripped it off. She pushed down on the couch, unbuttoned the waistband of Dell's jeans, and tugged them off along with her briefs and gear. "Let's see how tough you are."

"I don't know, baby," Dell said. "I might be wiped out."

Smiling, Sandy settled between her thighs and licked her. Dell groaned.

"*I* know," Sandy murmured.

Sometime later they stumbled to bed. Dell curled up behind her, an arm around her waist, her face against the back of Sandy's neck. Sandy found Dell's hand and drew it between her breasts, their fingers intertwined. She loved sleeping in the curve of Dell's body, not just because she felt sexy and wanted. She felt safe too.

❖

Jay opened her eyes in the still-dark room, still naked, and turned on her side. She pulled her watch off the charger and checked the time. Four a.m. Time to get up. She always woke up fast, habituated after years of being on call to be thinking before her feet hit the floor. She didn't bother with a light, but headed for the bathroom to wash up, and pulled fresh jeans and a V-neck maroon cotton pullover from the dresser that had come in the furnished apartment. Furnished being a generous word, but she didn't need much. She found her ankle-high boots in the bottom of the closet and grabbed her windbreaker. The day before, Olivia had been dressed in designer pants and shirt, and boots that were admittedly practical looking but also screamed chic and expensive. Jay decided she was going to be herself if this was going to be her job, at least for a while. That meant comfortable and casual. If there was a dress code, she didn't care about it.

She checked the refrigerator, found the last lone yogurt, and spooned it up while standing in front of the sink checking her mail on her phone. Five minutes later, she trashed the container and collected her wallet and keys. Altogether, under twenty-five minutes.

When she reached the street, she was the only one walking on her block, a narrow one-way street that backed up to the vet school. Three- and four-story houses converted to apartments lined each side. When she turned onto Baltimore Avenue, the trolley chugged past and suddenly a few more people appeared. Some of them, maybe a lot of them, were headed for the OR at this hour. Her chest tightened and she thought about what she would have been doing if she was on her way to the hospital and not the morgue. Preparing for Ali to show up at six for walk rounds—checking patients' vital signs, collecting labs taken during the night, chasing down X-rays, reading the nurses' reports, getting sign-out from the in-house residents. Moving from bed to bed in the intensive care unit, reviewing respiratory status, pressor levels, wound healing, chest tube drainage. All the things that went into caring for living patients.

But she didn't turn left to walk down the pedestrian lane between the medical school and the two-hundred-year-old brick quadrangle, where medical students and undergraduates lived, to the medical complex at the far end. Instead, she continued around the curve of University Avenue, past the Veterans Administration Hospital to the utilitarian building that housed the medical examiner's office. Her favorite street vendor was there, a lone light casting a bright patch onto the dark sidewalk.

"What time do you get here?" She stepped up to the little window of the cart. "I don't think I've ever gotten out here before you."

The vendor, a middle-aged Middle Eastern man, grinned. "It is good to be the first, no?"

"Yeah, it is. A couple cups of coffee. One black, one with cream." When he turned to pour them, she added, "And two of those apple fritters."

He passed her the coffees on a cardboard tray with the bag in the middle, and she handed him ten dollars. "Have a good one."

"You too."

She was going to be early, but like he'd said, it was always best to be first. She used the ID swipe card she'd gotten in her truncated orientation the day before and let herself in through the side door. The main hall on her right led to the administration and the public spaces toward the front of the building. She turned left in the direction of the staff offices in the rear of the building. As soon as she turned the corner into the dim corridor, she saw the light shining under Olivia's door.

Ten of five. Yep, best to be first.

Shaking her head, Jay knocked softly.

"Who is it?" Olivia asked.

"Jay."

"Just a moment." A second later Olivia opened the door and held it wide. "You're early."

"So are you."

"Not really. Come on in."

Jay deposited the container with the black coffee on Olivia's side of the desk and sat down opposite her, balancing her own cup on her knee. Today Olivia wore a dark green shirt and tailored pants the color of the interior of oyster shells, not exactly gray, not green, but something in between. Her only jewelry was a large, round stone—an opal, it looked like—set in a wide gold band on her right hand. Jay wondered if she was involved and couldn't figure out a way to ask. Of course, there wasn't any reason she really needed to know. Idle curiosity, that's all. She opened the bag and held it out. "Apple fritter?"

Olivia's brow arched. "Those things are evil."

"True." Jay continued to hold out the bag.

Olivia laughed, took it from her, and dug out one of the fritters. She pulled a napkin out after it and set the fritter in the center of it on her desk. "Thank you for both."

"My pleasure." Jay sipped her coffee and glanced at the game board in the corner. "Who are you playing with?"

"Sorry?"

"The game. Who do you play with?"

"How do you know I'm playing with anyone? It might just be a decoration."

"True. But you changed the stones."

Olivia sat back in her chair, her coffee balanced on the arm, studying Jay the way she had studied the crime scene the day before, calm and focused, analyzing her. Jay fought not to blush under the scrutiny. She didn't mind being looked at by a beautiful woman, and she never really worried too much about what kind of impression she was making. Right now, she cared.

"How do you know that?" Olivia asked.

"I noticed yesterday. It's interesting—the three-dimensional thing. I've seen that with chess boards before."

"How do you know I've moved a stone? Two, in fact."

"Oh—that red one on the top by the edge wasn't there yesterday."

"You can remember that?"

"I have a good memory for physical spatial things, but actually, I noticed the color." Jay shrugged. "My math is lousy, but I can remember the order of books on the shelves if I've seen them once, or the position of pieces on a board. Not a really useful skill."

"So do you play?" Olivia asked. "Chess or Go?"

"You'd think so, but I don't. I used to play chess with my older sister, but she always beat me and it frustrated the hell out of me. I'm too impatient. Well, not really impatient, but I have a plan and I tend to be a little inflexible, at least according to Vic." She laughed to herself and sipped her coffee. "I probably shouldn't be admitting that."

Olivia shook her head. "No, sometimes our faults are also our greatest strengths. As long as you are aware that you sometimes develop tunnel vision, and correct for it consciously, it's a good trait. You need to be focused for the kind of work we do."

The work we do. When had it become *we*? Funny, but Jay liked the sound of that. "Well obviously, you're a pretty serious player." She frowned. "Greenly?"

Olivia laughed, hearing the disbelief in Jay's voice. "No. No one here. In fact, no one I know. He...or she...is anonymous. We play on the internet."

"Seriously. And you don't know each other?"

"Oh," Olivia said softly, "we know each other very well. We've just never met."

"Right," Jay said, fascinated by the faraway look in Olivia's eyes that was quickly extinguished. She wondered where Olivia went on those mental journeys and what Olivia would do with someone who wanted to play face-to-face.

"Well," Olivia said, retreating after revealing more than she had intended. She hadn't told anyone about the game, and certainly not about how she played. Somehow, Jay managed to engage her, made her forget to be cautious. Interesting. And something to be wary of. "Let's go over your fieldwork from yesterday, and then we'll go see to her."

"Right," Jay said. "Absolutely."

The moment of connection, of two people getting to know each other, was over. Jay felt the distance widen between them, and she didn't like it.

❖

An insistent beeping pulled Sandy awake.

"Fuck," she muttered and glanced at the clock. Six a.m. She'd forgotten to set the alarm, so what...? Her phone was going off. Dell snored lightly behind her. Dell swore she didn't snore, and every time Sandy teased her about it, she blushed.

Easing from beneath Dell's grasp, Sandy stumbled into the living room and dug around in her bag. The text was from dispatch. Fuck. She called the number and it was picked up after a half dozen rings.

"Sullivan," she said, coughing the sleep from her voice.

"Got a message for you," the dispatcher said laconically, as if it were noon instead of the ass-crack of dawn.

"What, we catch a case?"

"If it is, it's the easiest one you're gonna have today. Somebody... hold on a minute...a Dr. Price called, said you wanted to be notified about an autopsy."

"Who?" Sandy's brain finally engaged. "Yeah, right. So when?"

The dispatcher chuckled. "Seven thirty."

"Fuck."

Chapter Twelve

Is this from Hasim's truck?" Olivia asked as she attacked the apple fritter with the enthusiasm worthy of a surgeon who'd just finished an all-night case.

"The one right at the corner?" Jay mainlined the first hit of caffeine of the day as quickly as the temperature allowed.

Olivia nodded. "That's the one. I wish I knew where he got his beans. Tastes like real Colombian, but that's hard to come by when they haven't been adulterated with chemicals or roasted beyond recognition."

"Coffee aficionado?"

"Snob is probably more accurate." Olivia smiled, a faint blush highlighting her angled cheekbones. "I grew up drinking coffee in South America right off the trees. The beans the locals use are so fresh they could jump-start a mummy."

Jay grinned, mesmerized by the playful note in Olivia's voice. Aware of her heart racing, she enjoyed the nearly forgotten sensation of her body responding to a beautiful woman. Not just garden-variety beautiful either. Olivia was a spectacular combination of physical attractiveness and fascinating temperament—a cool exterior hiding a multitude of deeper layers. "What was your favorite part of growing up like that?"

"The flowers," Olivia said instantly.

"Uh—?"

Olivia laughed. "Have you ever been to the rain forest, Jay?"

Jay's throat tightened. How dumb was that, getting a rush just because Olivia used her name. She shook her head.

"The most gorgeous, sensual, unforgettable plants you could

imagine, everywhere—hanging from the tree limbs, climbing the trunks, tangled among the vines. Each more exquisite than the next."

"So do you grow things like that now?" Jay tried to picture Olivia in a greenhouse, tending captive plants, and couldn't quite make it work. Olivia carried a hint of the untamed, of unfettered nature, subtle and rich and free. Jay had the sudden, inexplicable urge to immerse herself in that earthy freedom. What kind of magic did Olivia possess to turn her into someone she barely recognized? She didn't know, but she sure as hell wanted to find out.

"No, I'm no horticulturalist," Olivia said. "Somehow I think their essence is lost when we take them from the wild."

"Like the animals?"

"Exactly." Olivia smiled at her, a little chagrined. How had their conversation strayed so far from the professional? And when was the last time she'd shared coffee and conversation with a colleague in her office? Exactly never. And she hardly knew Jay—she shouldn't be so comfortable with her, or so easily disarmed. Striving for lightness, she added, "Seems a little mystical, I suppose."

"No, it doesn't. A little surprising at first, but then it shouldn't be."

Olivia's gaze narrowed, that focus again. Not critical, not angry, just appraising. "How so?"

"You. You're surprising. First the secret Go opponent, now the scientist with the heart of an artist."

"Flowers as art?"

"Sure, why not? Don't you think of the human body as an art form?"

"Oh," Olivia said softly, "I certainly do." She smiled. "And it appears I'm not the only one who's surprising."

Jay tried not to blush and failed. Jeez, you'd think she'd never flirted with a woman before. She caught herself before she could suck in a breath. Flirting with Olivia—bad idea, but she couldn't remember why. Of all the moments she'd spent with women she admired, or desired, these came most naturally. Olivia turned the key to a place somewhere deep inside she hadn't known she harbored—a place of barely restrained anticipation, waiting for the storm to be unleashed. Olivia excited her on some fundamental level that needed no explaining. "You're not wearing a wedding ring."

Olivia stared at her. The silence grew. Jay would have cursed her stupidity if she'd been rational, but she didn't care about reason. Instincts drove her now, and her instincts demanded she know everything about the woman sitting across from her.

"I'm divorced," Olivia said.

A surge of jealousy blazed across Jay's brain. "Should I say I'm sorry?"

Olivia grimaced. "I was unhappy at the time, but I was young and naïve. So no—sympathy is not required."

"Okay. Good. I wouldn't have meant it." The tightness in Jay's chest relaxed a little. "Thank you."

Olivia shook her head. "Conversations with you have a way of wandering into strange territory. We would be wise to return to business."

"Are you always wise?"

"Not always. Witness my recent admission." She knew better, but for a moment Olivia gave in to the utter fascination of watching the unbridled emotions play across Jay's face. Flashes of anger, possessiveness, humor, and desire—directed at her and so intense, so addicting. So very, very dangerous. She hadn't thought herself susceptible to that kind of intense attention again, but she'd been wrong. Right at that moment, Jay reminded her far too much of Marcos—or perhaps what she was remembering was her own attraction to the attention. She had learned that lesson once and did not intend to repeat it. "We should get to work."

"Right," Jay said thickly, her brain blazing with a wash of adrenaline and hormones. "Do you mind if I get another cup of coffee?"

Olivia sat back. "Of course not. Go ahead."

Jay pushed up so fast her right leg nearly buckled. She grabbed her cane with a curse.

"Are you all right?" Olivia rose.

"Fine," Jay said between clenched teeth. Fine, except for the ripping pain in her knee and the fire tearing through the pit of her stomach that had nothing to do with her injuries. "I'll just be a minute."

❖

Once outside, Jay took a few deep breaths of cold morning air. What the hell had she just done? If there hadn't been a desk between them, she would have been all over Olivia. She could almost taste her right now. Like one of those fucking exotic flowers that had started the whole damn conversation. She wanted to kiss her. She wanted to unbutton her and expose the mystery underneath the careful exterior. She wanted her. And she had about five minutes to douse her libido and get her head back in the game. The other game—the one she actually knew how to play.

"Great," she muttered. "Brilliant move, Reynolds."

"You know you're mumbling to yourself, right?" Ali said.

Jay jumped. Ali wore scrubs and a white lab coat with *Trauma Chief* stitched above the pocket.

"Hey," Jay said. "Where you headed?"

"Rounds at the VA. You getting coffee?"

"Yeah." Jay got in line with Ali. "You staffing there this month?"

"Yep." Ali ordered two coffees and handed one to Jay. "How are things at the ME's?"

"They're letting me work on cases, so that's good. Otherwise, too soon to tell." *Especially considering I just tried to put the move on the assistant chief.*

"You're starting pretty early." Ali moved away from the line, cracked her coffee, and took a sip. "Ah. Better."

"Olivia keeps surgeon's hours."

"She keeping you busy for real?"

"Busy enough." Jay kept her expression blank. She sure as hell did not want Ali to get wind of her obsession with the assistant ME, especially not when her sister would know by the end of the day.

Ali grinned. "Good. Don't want you getting slow and lazy."

"Ha ha."

"Listen—I have to go, but I'll call you about dinner soon."

"Sure." Jay waved and hustled back inside as fast as her leg would carry her. Olivia's door was ajar, and she slipped through and returned to her chair. "Thanks."

"You did a good job with this field report." Olivia handed Jay a copy of the report as if they'd been discussing it all along, no hint of discomfort or concern in her voice. "The next question is, how do you interpret what's in here?"

Jay struggled to get her mind in gear—in work gear, at least. Fortunately, the problem interested her. "While I was dictating the initial findings, it reminded me of doing the initial H and P."

"Excellent analogy." Olivia's smile was like a reward. "When a new patient presents in the ER, for example, you'd follow an established and reliable routine—you'd ascertain the patient's problem in their own words, elicit the history pertinent to that problem, review their medical history for associated or potentially causative problems, examine their family history for similar problems, and once all that information gathering had been completed, you'd perform a physical examination. How do things differ for us?"

Jay liked problems. She liked solving them mentally as well as physically. She wouldn't have become a surgeon if she didn't want to treat a problem directly by applying what she knew in tandem with her intrinsic technical skills. She didn't want to prescribe a drug or provide an opinion so someone else could deliver treatment. She wanted to be the one to fix the problem, and the first step in treatment was understanding the disease. Death was the final common denominator, after all. Captivated by where Olivia was going, she sat forward. She liked games too, and Olivia was challenging her to play. "First problem, the patient can't provide any kind of information. So no history, at least."

Olivia held up a finger. "Are you sure? Think about that for a minute. What did you know from looking at that girl yesterday before you touched her, before anyone told you anything. What did her body tell you?"

Jay blew out a breath. "I knew her general state of health, at least in the sense that she wasn't visibly malnourished or chronically ill in some way—no jaundice, unusual skin lesions, or hair loss. I could tell in rough terms how long she'd been dead. Certainly not for a week. Her clothes were expensive, probably off the rack, but still designer." She laughed. "I'm not exactly a clotheshorse."

"You dress to suit."

For a second, Jay's brain misfired again. Dress to suit what? The job, her personality, her sexuality? Did Olivia notice anything personal about her? Did she like what she saw? Jay grabbed the reins and tugged her runaway thoughts back into line. "Uh—anyhow, I get what you're saying. There were things, or at least impressions, that I got from looking at her. But observations aren't the same as facts, right? I thought the whole point of what we do is that only the facts mattered."

"If only the facts mattered, then almost anyone could do the job." Olivia's eyes took on a predatory glint and Jay recognized the alpha wolf hiding behind the reserve. "A reasonably informed layman could take what was known and fit it into some kind of algorithm and come up with an answer. That's not what we do. We go where the facts lead

us, but we also interpret evidence, which may not be clearly factual.
Does that make sense?"

Jay nodded. "That's a thin line to walk."

Olivia smiled. "Exactly. And that's why experience matters. And
discipline. And that tunnel vision you're so worried about. I'd far rather
have someone who focuses narrowly than someone who wanders off
following a pretty hypothesis. We don't get paid to hypothesize. We
get paid to apply expertise and specific knowledge to identifiable
problems."

"Okay. What do we know?" Jay glanced down at her copy of the
field report, reviewing the observations she'd made. She looked at the
other information that didn't have specifically to do with the deceased
herself. A picture formed in her mind, a scenario. She glanced at Olivia.
"We know she didn't die there."

"How?"

"She was moved, and from all reports, no one moved her. The
lividity indicates she was on her back for at least an hour before she
was left on her side."

"Yes, unless there was someone else on scene before any officials
arrived," Olivia said. "In which case we would have to reevaluate our
conclusions."

"The best interpretation of the evidence *right now* is that someone
moved her intentionally."

"Yes."

"So we're drawing conclusions," Jay said, "working outward from
the facts that we know, rather than eliminating from a list of potential
possibilities, which is how traditionally one makes a diagnosis."

"Exactly. The mind-set is different."

"It's gonna take me a while to make that adjustment."

Olivia shrugged. "Of course it is. All your training teaches you to
approach a problem by considering the potential causes of a particular
constellation of signs and symptoms. But that's true for everyone in this
field. You're not behind."

"I'm glad to hear that," Jay muttered.

Olivia glanced at her watch. "Are you ready to put some more
facts together?"

"Definitely."

"By the time the police officer arrives, we'll have the external
exam almost done. If she shows up."

"But we don't wait."

Olivia met her gaze, the spark glinting again. "No. We don't wait."
Jay had been totally wrong about her first impression of Olivia. She was anything but cool. Heart pounding, Jay rose, steady this time. "So let's go."

❖

"Where you going, babe?" Dell said as she pulled on her jeans and slicked back hair still wet from the shower.

"The morgue." Sandy gave her the once-over. "You might want to put a shirt on, stud."

Dell shot her a raised eyebrow. "Why to both?"

Sandy wrapped her arms around Dell's waist and kissed her, purring lightly at the press of Dell's breasts against hers. "Because I have to go to work. Because you look hot. Because last night was hours ago and I'm ready again."

Dell grinned and kissed her. "So I'll see you tonight, and maybe we'll have a repeat."

"Maybe?"

"For sure." Dell nuzzled her neck. "You're going to get a damp spot on your shirt."

"You could try drying off once in a while instead of air drying," Sandy said, exaggerating her sigh. "Although you do look hot."

"Now you know why I hate to dry off."

Sandy squeezed her ass and backed away. "You should still put a shirt on because I don't want to be thinking about your naked body where I'm going."

"True." Dell pulled on a T-shirt. "What are you doing at the morgue anyhow? Shouldn't that be homicide's turf?"

"Usually, but this looks like an OD, and if that's what the ME's calling it, it'll be accidental and not homicide."

Dell stuffed in her shirttail and slid her holster onto her belt. "So why is it yours?"

"It's not the death as much as how she got that way. There was a weird drug bag with her body. Might be something new. That's what we're looking into."

"Huh. Okay. You'll be on the streets later tracking it down?"

"Yeah." Sandy sat on the sofa and zipped her ankle-high boots. "Asking around, trying to find out if there's a source for this stuff, or, who knows, maybe it was a one-off."

"Yeah, what are the chances of that," Dell muttered.

"You're right. That's what we're worried about too."

"Okay." Dell kissed the top of her head and grabbed her leather jacket. "Text me when you can, okay?"

Sandy slipped her badge into her bag and her gun into the special inner pocket. "I will, you too."

❖

Twenty-five minutes later, Sandy jumped off the subway in West Philadelphia and hurried the two blocks to the ME's office. Seven thirty. Right on time. She'd actually never been to the morgue before and had to ask someone in the hall how to find where the autopsies were done when she got inside. She took the elevator to the basement, of course, because where else would you put it, and followed the signs along a surprisingly well-lit generic institutional hallway to the morgue. When she got there and peered into the little room marked No Entrance, she wasn't quite sure what to do.

A woman in a lab coat and casual street clothes asked in passing, "Help you?"

"Officer Sullivan, PPD. I'm supposed to be observing an autopsy?"

The tech pointed to the door to the little room. "You want to go right through there. Just slip on booties and one of those green gowns from the stack by the inner door. You can hang your jacket on a peg right inside there."

"Thanks."

"Have fun."

"Sure. Thanks." Sandy wasn't squeamish, and she'd seen plenty of DBs before. She did as she was instructed and, once she'd gotten the gown tied up and the booties on, opened the inner door. A bright light on a swivel arm illuminated the table closest to her, and women in scrubs stood on either side of it. All she could make out of the body were the legs. She cleared her throat.

The woman nearest her looked over her shoulder. Early thirties, blond hair, green eyes. The one across from her, about the same height and age but broader in the shoulders, gray eyes, dark hair visible around the edges of her surgical cap.

"I'm Officer Sullivan. Looking for Dr. Price."

The blonde nodded. "Right on time, Officer. If you'd like to come over here, we've just completed the external examination and are about to start the internal." Dr. Price looked at the other woman. "Go ahead, Dr. Reynolds."

Sandy got as close as she needed to see what they were doing. She recognized the victim from the day before, although she looked different on the table, more dead, if that were even possible. It looked like her hair had been washed and was a lustrous blond even now. That seemed wrong somehow, as if beauty belonged to the living. She looked young. Her breasts were full, her abdomen slightly rounded, her legs toned. This was not a street girl. Even the young ones tended to be stringy—a lot of walking, not a lot of optimal nutrition—and usually plenty of scars. This girl looked like she'd just stepped out of the sorority house. Sandy's stomach tightened. How long would it take a missing student to be missed?

"Do you have an ID yet?" Dr. Price said.

"Nothing yet. DMV didn't turn up anything. Neither did missing persons. We ought to have results from CODIS and the national databases late morning."

"We have dental X-rays if you need them. A scan showed no other fractures that might have been of value in identifying her."

"What about DNA?" Sandy asked.

"Your CSU people bagged her hands, so your lab will run anything under her nails along with whatever else they found externally on her person, but that will take days at least."

"Thanks. Anything interesting turn up so far?" Sandy asked.

"She's pretty much as you see." The dark-haired doctor—Reynolds, the other one had called her—spoke for the first time. "Well-nourished female, estimated age twenty, no external wounds, no evidence of a struggle that we could see."

As they talked, the dark-haired doctor made an incision angled across the girl's chest from her shoulders to her breastbone, skirting her breasts. Sandy had a quick thought it was a violation of a beautiful body, and then the filters clicked in. Not a girl, not a young woman, but the victim. She hadn't forgotten that the dead girl was someone's daughter or someone's sister or someone's lover, but that wasn't how she needed to think of her. She was also someone's victim, at least she might be, and it was Sandy's job to find out if she was, then who.

"Track marks?" Sandy asked.

"None."

"Then whatever it was she took, she snorted or ingested it."

"Yes," Dr. Price said, looking at her with a speculative expression of appreciation.

Sandy smiled inwardly. She knew how she came off: young, blond, and potentially naïve. She couldn't change her age, but she was more seasoned than cops with twice as much experience and two decades on her. But that didn't matter. All that mattered to her was information that she needed. "How long for tox?"

"We should have something for you tomorrow," Dr. Price said, "unless we get a backlog, which can happen."

Sandy laughed. "Yeah, I know how that is."

Over the next hour, she watched them remove organs, weigh things, and pretty much find nothing other than what they already suspected.

"Dr. Reynolds," Dr. Price said when they appeared to be finished, "would you dictate the post, please."

"Sure."

Price walked to a big hamper by the door, stripped off her gown, removed her gloves and booties, and tossed things in various receptacles. "At this point, there appears to be no evidence of external trauma or significant disease. The tox will tell us more."

"So this is likely accidental?" Sandy deposited her gown and booties in the same bins.

"We'll know when we get the results of the tox," Dr. Price said.

Sandy mentally rolled her eyes. Sometimes, these lab types were really anal. But then, that's what they were supposed to be. "Okay, will you call me as soon as you hear something?"

"I'll do that." Dr. Price walked Sandy out to the hall. "What can you tell me about this new drug you're worried about?"

"I don't know too much about it." Sandy pulled her jacket on. "We're not even sure that's what this is all about. Our lab will be analyzing the contents of the glassine envelope found by the body today."

"Then it seems we'll need to share our findings. You'll call me on that?"

"I'll ask our chief CSI—her name is Flanagan—to call you with whatever she gets."

"That would be good. I appreciate it."

"I'll let you know on the ID too."

"Then it appears we've gone as far as we can for her. For the time being."

Sandy glanced back through the windows where the other doctor was covering the body. "I've still got some avenues to investigate."

The doctor cocked her head. "Literally, I'm assuming."

Huh. Sharp as well as hot. Sandy held out her hand. "Thanks, Dr. Price."

"Sandy, isn't it?" The doctor took her hand.

"That's right."

"Call me Olivia."

CHAPTER THIRTEEN

Jay didn't get performance anxiety, at least not since she was forced to recite a poem in second grade on Parents' Day, and her mother was in the audience. That was pretty terrifying, especially because Ali and Vic were five years ahead of her and nowhere around. She couldn't remember too many times in her life when they hadn't been around to support her—they'd been her cheering squad in intramural soccer, her sounding board when she was figuring out she liked girls the way most of her friends liked boys, and her mentors and toughest critics in college and med school. She wondered who she'd be today if it hadn't been for them. Maybe she wouldn't be standing up at this podium in front of an audience of people she didn't know, except for the woman in the pristine lab coat standing in the center aisle, one hip resting lightly against the end seat in the first row, asking her questions.

Olivia.

The woman she wanted to impress for a whole lot of reasons, most of which had more to do with the persistent tug of desire every time she looked at her than any professional goal, and none of which she should be thinking about right now in the middle of her presentation. She was acquainted with almost everyone else in the room, at least by name, now. Olivia had taken her on a midmorning tour of the facilities to complete her orientation and, at the conclusion, had shown her to the lounge where the investigators and fellows fielded incoming calls and divvied up new cases.

Adjacent to the pit, as one of the techs called the place that looked a lot like an OR lounge, was a little warren of cubicles loosely considered offices. Olivia told her to claim any empty cubbyhole for her own. After Olivia left her with an entirely appropriate and impersonal good-bye, Jay had spent the next few hours preparing the case presentation

Olivia had assigned her. Most of the time she'd actually been able to concentrate. She only thought about Olivia every ten minutes or so.

Olivia asked another question.

Jay wasn't sweating. She never sweated under pressure. Fortunately, the stage lights were low enough that any discomfort was pretty well hidden in the shadows. Not that she was uncomfortable. Hell, no. This was nothing compared to the two days of grilling she'd weathered when she'd taken her general surgery boards. She might be a newbie here, but she was far from being green and unseasoned. She walked everyone through the specifics of the scene, reviewing the photographs of the deceased and her field report along with Bobbi and Darrell's. She finished with a summary of the post, which was pretty much negative.

"Toxicology is pending, as is the identification of the deceased," she said as she cut off the slides.

Greenly cleared his throat somewhat impatiently. "So this appears to be an overdose and will be signed out as accidental." He glanced at his watch. "What else do we have on the list?"

Jay glanced at Olivia while waiting for a question or comment or something from someone. Olivia raised a brow a fraction of an inch— or it might just have been a trick of the dim auditorium lighting. No one said anything.

Okay then. Game time. Jay rested her forearms on the podium and lightly gripped the raised edge. Her right hand had an annoying habit of trembling when she wasn't using it, which might appear to others as nerves. And she wasn't nervous. Greenly was a poseur.

"Actually, Dr. Greenly," Jay said, letting her voice carry but keeping it nice and cool and even, "that remains to be seen. The position of the body relative to the pattern of lividity, as I noted earlier in the field scenes, indicates her body was moved at least once after death. The reason for that remains unknown, as does the identity of whoever moved her, so we cannot say at this time the manner of death is accidental."

"Are you suggesting this could be a homicide?" He sounded as if she'd just proposed the girl had died from Ebola.

"I'm not *suggesting* anything," Jay said. "But I am pointing out that presently the evidence is incomplete and the final COD remains in question."

"Let's not forget the old aphorism about zebras," Dr. Greenly said, sounding as officious as he appeared.

"Absolutely not," Jay said amiably. "In this case, however, the hoofbeats are certainly related to some kind of horse. I'm just not willing to speculate which kind. I'd rather let the facts determine if we've got a Thoroughbred or a plow horse."

Several people laughed, including some staff members. Out of the corner of her eye, Jay saw Olivia smile.

"Thank you, Dr. Reynolds," Olivia said. "You can update us when the toxicology and the police examinations are compete. Dr. Inouye—I believe you're next."

Jay collected her notes, slipped to the back of the stage, and stepped carefully down to floor level, annoyed she still needed her cane, but since remaining upright was preferable to toppling over, she used it. She settled into the third row and glanced over at Olivia. Olivia's attention was on the stage, and when the presentations were finally over, she disappeared before Jay had a chance to speak with her. She tried to come up with some reason to drop around Olivia's office and couldn't fabricate anything that wouldn't look like she was stalking her. Which she wasn't. She was just healthily obsessed with a beautiful, smart, sexy woman, a welcome state after feeling more than half dead for months.

She'd have to settle for seeing Olivia when they had cases together or during the thrice-weekly seminars. Her orientation period was over, and she'd been relegated to the pit. She'd gotten spoiled working directly with Olivia, and her frustration at not seeing her until tomorrow, if then, left her edgy and distracted. Since nothing was required of her for the rest of the day and she was too keyed up to read anything, she called the operators, gave them her cell number, and left. A little fresh air would help clear her head.

The sun was just going down at a little after five, and it wasn't dark yet. She couldn't remember ever finishing up before seven, and often didn't leave the hospital even when she wasn't on call until ten or later. Walking home in the dark and going to work in the dark was so routine, the fading daylight was foreign and disorienting. The night stretched out ahead of her in a long line of interminable, monotonous hours.

"Hey, Jay!" A familiar-looking guy about her age in khakis and a pullover with a sports logo on the chest stepped up beside her. "Nice comeback with Greenly this afternoon."

"You're Archie, right?" Jay hoped she fit the right name to the face. He'd been passing through the pit when she'd been there earlier.

"I couldn't tell if Greenly was baiting me or not, but what the hell. I didn't see any point in looking stupid."

"Good call. Archie Cohen, by the way." The short, faintly balding guy with horn-rim glasses grinned. "I'm finishing up in a couple months."

"What then?"

"I've got a job lined up at KSU. My wife's from there and is doing another year in GYN ONC, so it worked out great."

Kansas State University. A medical school appointment. Nice. "That sounds terrific. Congrats."

"One of the best things about being here," he said with obvious enthusiasm, "is we can pretty much get whatever job we want."

"Uh, yeah. That is...terrific." Jay hadn't thought past the next day and wasn't even close to imagining a job as a pathologist. Where, doing what, exactly? She tried to make the picture with herself in the center, the way she'd done since she was twenty, seeing herself standing in the middle of the trauma unit, waiting for the paramedics to bring in the patient, eager, ready, charged up for battle. Everything in this new picture seemed too quiet, too controlled, too calm.

"So listen," Archie said, "my wife's on call tonight. And I don't cook. You want to grab a burger at Smokes?"

Smokey Joe's, the residents' preferred after-hours place for a brew and a burger and maybe a little flirtation that might lead to a night's company. She hadn't been there since before the accident. She'd run into some of the surgery residents there, for sure, if she went tonight. Hell, any night. Maybe even a couple who'd been on call the night they brought her in. Not that she remembered any of that, but quite a few people, including Ali, had seen her at her most vulnerable and helpless. They'd saved her life but she still felt exposed, even a little embarrassed. Made no sense, but there it was. *No* was on the tip of her tongue, and then she thought about her empty refrigerator, her empty apartment. Archie was offering her a few hours with someone who didn't know her and with whom she could leave the past behind, at least until she got home again.

"Sure. Let's do it," Jay said.

"My car's around back. We can drive over—"

"Thanks, but I can walk. Actually"—she tapped her calf with her cane—"it's good for me since I've sort of been skipping out on physical therapy. As long as you don't mind going a little bit slow."

"Hey, no problem."

They'd just started walking when a woman called out, "Hey, Archie? You going to Smokes?"

Jay and Archie paused to let a petite African American in jeans, a dark gold V-neck sweater, and a short dusty-gray leather jacket catch up.

"Yep," Archie said. "You coming?"

"I'm on call, so it's Coke for me, but I'm starving." She smiled at Jay and held out her hand. "Tasha Clark. I'm the other fellow."

"Jay Reynolds. I'm the new guy."

Archie and Tasha laughed, and a layer of loneliness Jay hadn't realized she'd been wearing like a second coat slid away. She didn't know them, or they her, but they all knew each other on a certain level—what it took to get where they were, what it took to survive, what it said about each of them.

"I'll stand you to the first round of brews," Jay said.

"You're on," Tasha replied.

Archie led the way. "Let's go before the surgeons take all the booths."

The pain was a little less this time as Jay said, "Good idea."

❖

Rebecca hung her topcoat on the wooden clothes tree just inside the front door of the town house. She removed her weapon and locked it in the antique sideboard in the foyer before walking down the center hall toward the kitchen and something that smelled amazing. The kitchen took up the entire width of the rear of the house and was lit by several frosted amber globes suspended from brushed bronze ceiling fixtures that captured the historic feel of the Victorian twin so popular in the neighborhood surrounding the medical center. Catherine, in soft earth-toned cotton pants, a dark umber boatneck sweater, and a loose red-striped apron, worked at a double stove, sautéing something in a big cast-iron frying pan. The table was set for two, and a candle in a pewter holder resembling a frog, one of Catherine's favorite animals, flickered in the center.

Rebecca's stomach clenched, a response she never experienced even when facing a perp with a gun. "I forgot something important, didn't I. Whatever it is, I'm sorry and I love you very much."

Catherine glanced over her shoulder, the warmth in her green eyes all the welcome home Rebecca needed. "You're safe this time, Detective. My last patient canceled, so I decided to cook. Tell me you don't have anything going on that you have to go back out for right away."

Rebecca held up both hands. "I'm all yours."

"I like hearing that. Are you hungry?"

Rebecca slid an arm around Catherine's waist and kissed her before leaning over to survey the stir-fry. "Starving."

"Good. Would you open a bottle of wine for me?"

"What's your pleasure, red or white?"

"I think the spices in this can handle a red. There's a Merlot over there somewhere, I think."

Rebecca found the bottle, opened it, and poured a glass, setting the wine by Catherine's plate. She opened a bottle of sparkling water for herself and set it by her plate. After Catherine dished out their dinner, they sat beside each other at the oak plank table. Rebecca leaned over and kissed Catherine again. "Thank you for dinner. I love you."

Catherine brushed Rebecca's jaw with the tips of her fingers. "I love you too."

"This is great," Rebecca said after a minute. "I have to say I'm very glad you got home early."

Catherine sipped her wine. "You're home early too. Is it quiet out there?"

Rebecca winced. "Yes and no. It feels like something's brewing, but we can't zero in on it."

"That always worries me. Your instincts are usually very accurate." Catherine set her glass down and leaned back. "Is it Zamora?"

"Maybe. I hope so."

"What do you mean?"

Catherine, one of the department's psych consultants, had profiled for Rebecca's unit in the past, often adding valuable insight into the criminals Rebecca's team hunted. She was also a great sounding board. "Zamora knows we're trying to build a RICO case against him. The feds have been trying for a decade and getting nowhere, but we're halfway there with the links to human trafficking we uncovered in his organization. We just can't link them to him directly yet, and he's been very careful pulling in his net."

"Mmm, so you can't get close to him unless someone slips up somewhere."

"Exactly." Rebecca stabbed a piece of chicken and, reminding herself to enjoy the meal and the company, set her frustration aside. "But we maybe have a break with something over the wire—a homicide that might be the first move into Zamora's territory."

"One of his people got killed?" Catherine got up to add the rest of the food to Rebecca's plate. "Finish that—I know what you usually eat."

Rebecca smiled. Catherine was the only person she'd ever let take care of her, and it always felt good. "We're not sure of anything right now. Dell couldn't turn up much when she checked with homicide today."

"So what next?"

"We keep watching for someone to make the next move," Rebecca said. "If there is a move on his territory, the people will begin to talk. Discipline breaks down. People make mistakes."

"Who's behind it?"

"That we do know—or at least, we have a pretty good idea." Rebecca blew out a breath and drank half a glass of water. "The Salvadorans. MS-13."

Catherine nodded. "It seems like they're becoming a force everywhere. DC, New York, here."

"The problem is the organization is decentralized with fairly autonomous local factions. It's tough to identify who's at the top. They're almost impossible to infiltrate, and even with our excellent street sources, we're mostly chasing shadows."

"Dell's contacts, you mean?"

"And Sandy's."

"Your team isn't frontline, though, is it," Catherine said carefully. "That would be organized crime? Or the gang squad?"

Rebecca took Catherine's hand. Catherine was very good at hiding her worry. Once upon a time, she would have tried to soften the truth to spare her the fear, but not now. Catherine deserved more than that from her. "The HPCU can cross departmental lines whenever we need to. We coordinate as best as we can, but whatever impacts our investigation is fair game for us."

"Of course. I knew that." Catherine smiled softly. "Which is why you love it."

"It gives me the freedom to run my investigations pretty much as I see fit."

"And that's what makes you so very good too."

"Something will break soon." Rebecca kissed Catherine's palm. "But for now, let's not talk about work for the rest of the night."

Catherine slipped her fingers through Rebecca's. "I was thinking we wouldn't do too much talking at all."

Rebecca grinned. "Since you cooked, let me clear the dishes, and I'll meet you in the bedroom."

Catherine tugged Rebecca's hand, pulling her to her feet. "The dishes can wait."

❖

Olivia stared at the image on her computer of the Go board her opponent had sent her late in the afternoon. She studied the new position of the black stone with a mixture of surprise, admiration, and irritation. She hadn't expected that particular move, and she should have. Worse, she couldn't conjure a response. She couldn't even mentally visualize the next two or three moves, and usually she had no problem planning the next half dozen. But every time she postulated a potential response and tried to anticipate her opponent's countermove, her mind went blank.

Not blank, exactly.

She kept coming back to her conversation with Jay over coffee. As soon as she pictured Jay with her windblown hair and just this side of too-good-looking-for-her-own-good grin, heard her playful, teasing words and the way she offered up an apple fritter like it was a bouquet of roses, her mind flooded with more images and thoughts and sensations than she could keep track of. She couldn't recall any one particular exchange that had sent her off in this unanticipated and unexpectedly uncomfortable direction, which only confused her more. She would have liked to blame her confusion on Jay, but she couldn't. She knew the problem, which probably explained her unsettled state. Jay's intensity hadn't made her uncomfortable.

She was uncomfortable with the way Jay made her feel.

Jay made her feel a good many things she'd felt before and had learned through painful experience to distrust—excitement, anticipation, sexual interest. Jay awakened her senses and her sensual curiosity. Marcos had done that too, and she'd been willing to cast aside her better judgment and her pride to keep the feelings alive. Jay was even more dangerous, all the more compelling, because she'd been so certain she'd never experience the same things again. Even worse, she welcomed them. She welcomed the rush of heat and pleasure and the eager anticipation of seeing Jay again.

Fortunately, she recognized what was happening. This time, she could keep things from going any further. This time, she was in control. Firmly in control.

CHAPTER FOURTEEN

Olivia told herself she was staying late in the office waiting for her Go opponent to send his next move, even though she knew he wouldn't until after midnight. She knew very well she was working late to occupy her mind and avoid thinking about Jay. When she found herself actually considering calling Jay under the pretense of reviewing her perfectly acceptable case presentation from earlier that day, she packed up her belongings and went home. At least she wouldn't be tempted to do anything foolish there. She even managed to stop thinking about what Jay might be doing right then and wondering if Jay even gave their exchange a second thought. She'd been replaying every word like an endless loop of YouTube video. Unlike her. For heaven's sake, she could be inflating the whole encounter in her own overheated imagination. Jay likely hadn't even noticed the turn their conversation had taken into the personal.

She read journals in bed until she was tired enough to sleep. When she woke at twenty to five, her eyes were still scratchy from a restless night. A quick shower helped revive her, and after an even quicker cup of coffee, she walked the half block to the narrow lot squeezed between two town houses on Twenty-Fifth Street where she rented a parking space. Ten minutes later she pulled in to her customary spot behind the ME's office.

Hasim was just opening his food truck when she reached him.

"Morning, Doctor," Hasim said with his usual energetic good humor as he arranged cardboard trays of pastries on the shelf below the service window.

"Morning, Hasim. An extra-large this morning when you can."

"Sure thing." He entered the four-by-six-foot truck where he spent fifteen hours a day and poured a steaming cup of coffee into a large cardboard container with a generic blue logo on the side and placed a lid on top. "Something to eat to go with it?"

Olivia glanced at the apple fritters, thought of Jay, and firmly glanced away. "I'll have one of the plain bagels and a container of cream cheese. Thanks."

She handed him the money, he passed her the food, and she walked back to the medical examiner's office through mostly empty streets. She was looking for Jay, and when she realized it, berated herself for the lapse. They didn't have a meeting scheduled, and there was no reason for Jay to show up before morning review. Most of the residents and staff came rushing in a minute before the meeting started unless they had cases to present. She didn't blame the residents for taking every spare moment for themselves they could. Once their training was over, they would have years of long demanding days, nights on call when their social and family lives would be disrupted at a moment's notice. They'd all chosen to do it, as had she, but that didn't mean the work was without sacrifice. As she expected, the halls were empty and still. Jay was not waiting by her door, and she hadn't realized how much she'd hoped she would be until the spurt of disappointment washed over her. Foolish, as she'd been saying.

She unlocked her office, hung her raincoat in the small closet inside, and sat behind her desk. She spread the cream cheese on the bagel and sipped her coffee, all the while staring at the empty chair Jay had occupied the day before. Since she couldn't stop thinking about her, maybe if she actually analyzed her feelings she could impose a little reason on her irrational reactions. She'd simply approach the problem as she would any other clinical challenge.

Jay was remarkable, true, but no more so than many other women she'd met. Supremely confident, accomplished, intelligent. Capable. The university was full of women just like her. Some who might even be as attractive and intriguing and…

Olivia shook her head, unwilling to be party to her own ridiculous self-delusion. Yes, Jay was all those things, but what made her truly exceptional, what intrigued and captivated Olivia as no woman ever had, was Jay's refusal to be broken by devastating loss or physical injury even as she struggled with her anger and frustration. Jay probably thought she hid that, or that only her stubborn resolve showed through, but Olivia knew something about loss and how difficult the pain was to hide. She admired Jay for her determination to recover, no matter the cost. Jay was a warrior in the classic sense of the word—unwilling to surrender despite fearsome odds. Olivia could see her at the head of a tribe of Amazons, her ferocious charisma compelling all to follow.

"Mother would be proud," Olivia muttered, pressing her fingertips to her eyes. She'd finally learned to see the present as a mere reconfiguration of the past. "But not just yet. I still have some willpower left."

No matter how she felt about Jay, she didn't intend for it to show. She wouldn't make excuses for her or treat her any differently than she would have if she had been an ordinary trainee. She wasn't grading her, for which she was thankful. That wasn't her job. Her job was to teach, to share her knowledge, and to ensure Jay met the basic standards of their training program. When Jay's fellowship was over, she would have to pass her boards in order to practice, and that wasn't Olivia's decision. In that sense, Olivia had no power over Jay's future. This wasn't college, or anything even close to it. Postgraduate medical training was like no other training in the world—an apprenticeship of sorts, some would argue, more akin to indentured servitude.

Archaic, perhaps. *Yes, Mother, I hear you.* History again. Well, she wouldn't be letting her history repeat itself. One disastrous love affair was quite enough. As if that were even a possibility. Her world was right here in this building. She had made the life she wanted already.

With a relieved sigh, Olivia turned on the computer and scanned her email. One message halfway down the screen caught her eye, the header indicating the lab report on her unidentified female. She clicked to open the file and skimmed it. Frowning, she scrolled down to the mass spectrographic results of the blood chemistry. A large spike appeared labeled *unidentified substance*. The computer-generated summary below that indicated the compound matched nothing in the database, which contained literally hundreds of thousands of drugs. She went on to read the analysis.

This substance most closely resembles synthetic opioid compounds such as fentanyl in chemical composition, but matches no registered pharmaceutical compounds presently available in the United States.

An unregistered synthetic opioid. Olivia sat back. Well, Sandy Sullivan had said there was a possibility they were dealing with a new street drug. That would explain this kind of result. Olivia pulled out the top drawer of her desk, checked the phone list of commonly called numbers she kept inside, and dialed Police Plaza.

"Can you connect me to the CSU, please," Olivia asked when the operator picked up.

"Normal working hours are seven a.m. to five p.m.," the operator helpfully informed her.

"Thank you," Olivia said. "If you connect me, please, I'll leave a message."

"Certainly."

Olivia continued to read her mail, waiting for the computerized menu to come on.

"Flanagan," a woman with a determined Irish accent said after the third ring.

"This is Dr. Olivia Price, assistant chief medical examiner for the county. Good morning. I didn't expect to reach anyone."

"Dee Flanagan here, Doctor. How can I help you?"

"I'm following up on an open case, female victim, possible OD." Olivia read off the case number. "Officer Sandy Sullivan informed me you would be analyzing the evidence."

"We're working that case, but I don't know we have much of anything for you. It's been a busy week. Let me pull it up."

"Thanks. I was wondering if you've identified the drug in question. Sandy thought there might've been some remnants in the packages found at the scene."

"Hold on for a second. Yeah, we've got something," Flanagan said, "but I'll be damned if I know what it is."

"Unknown spike on the mass spec?"

Flanagan laughed. "I guess you got the same thing. I was rather hoping you'd have something more specific on your end."

"It looks like a synthetic opioid, but not a registered legal pharmaceutical."

"That fits with what we're seeing too."

"What does that mean, exactly? From a practical point of view?" Olivia asked.

"You mean as pertaining to cause of death?"

Olivia smiled. Flanagan was sharp. "That and what I might be seeing more of."

"How much time do you have?"

"About a cup of coffee's worth?"

"That makes two of us. Give me another second," Flanagan said and Olivia could hear her pouring something in the background. "So back in the seventies and eighties, Upjohn and a couple of other pharmaceutical biggies were in a race to find the perfect analgesic, one that alleviated pain but didn't cause addiction. And they wanted high potency as a side benefit."

"Sounds like a devil's bargain to me," Olivia said, making a quick note to dig out the references.

"Yep," Flanagan said. "The Holy Grail of opioids. The perfect heroin without the poppies or the side effects. So anyhow they started cranking out drugs and systematically altering them in an attempt to defang them, for want of a better analogy."

"I take it that didn't work?"

"Oh, they made some mighty fine drugs," Flanagan said sarcastically. "The only problem was they were so potent they tended to be lethal to just about every animal tested. No clinical trials ever got started because all the lab animals were dying."

"So they were never released?" Olivia stared at the spike on the mass spec.

"No, most of them were patented but never marketed in any way."

"Okay," Olivia said, nibbling on the bagel. "So there's precedent for this kind of lab research. I'm not sure—"

"See, the thing is, the patents had the chemical formulations and, in a lot of instances, fairly specific instructions on how to manufacture them."

"Ah. And now all those filings are available on the internet if you know how to look for them."

"Exactly."

"Does anyone know who's making the current versions?"

Flanagan grunted. "China for one, and in large quantities for the last year at least, but it hasn't been a major problem here in the States. Some sporadic outbreaks, but the outbreaks are becoming more common and closer together."

"What about narcotic antagonists? How effective are they?"

"Not at all. Unlike with standard heroin compounds, if an EMT is standing by while someone snorts one of these drugs and goes into cardiac arrest, there's nothing they can give them to counteract the drug."

Olivia's chest tightened. Flanagan had just described what could be an epidemic if this drug showed up in quantity. "I hope very much this is an isolated instance. For now, the case will remain open until we identify her and know more about the circumstances of her death."

"I'm going to call around to some of my counterparts in New York and DC and see if they're seeing any of this," Flanagan said. "If I get anything further, I'll let you know."

"Thanks, I appreciate it."

"Have a good one," Flanagan said.

"You too." Olivia disconnected. The victim still needed to be identified, and she needed to know a lot more about the agent that killed her in case she wasn't the last.

❖

"Morning," Tasha called as Jay arrived at the pit a little after seven. Tasha wore pale blue scrubs and had her running shoes propped up on the coffee table, a half-eaten sandwich balanced on the arm of a dark green vinyl chair. She sipped from a mug with an image of the Statue of Liberty and looked surprisingly rested after a night on call.

"How was your night?" Jay rinsed out a mug from the communal stash on the counter and poured some coffee. Tasha had left Smokey Joe's right after dinner while Archie and Jay stayed for another beer.

"Quiet. A couple death reports from the hospital, but no callouts. I got about six hours."

"That *is* nice." Jay tried to remember a night on call when she'd actually been able to sleep and couldn't think of one. She'd learned to get by on an hour or two in between cases or floor emergencies. Even now, when she had the opportunity to sleep straight through the night, she rarely could. Last night hadn't been any different. After she'd gotten home, she'd read a book until almost midnight and still only catnapped until six. "So what's on the agenda?"

"The rotation list is over there on the bulletin board," Tasha said. "Basically, we take calls in the order posted up there as they come in, unless we all get busy at once, and then we pretty much try to back up as needed. You're on phone duty today."

"Okay, what's that? Since I'm the new guy, I'm assuming it sucks."

"Not so much. Okay, maybe it's really boring." Tasha grinned. "You get to triage the calls that come in to us from the hospitals and emergency services. You'll decide if a body needs to come here or can be released to family."

"Okay." Jay sipped her coffee. "I don't have any idea how to do that."

"I didn't figure you did. Archie and I will give you a hand. We both have posts to do, but we'll be around if you need us."

"Thanks, but I don't want to interrupt you if you're in the middle of a post—"

Tasha waved her off. "Hey, it's no problem. They're not going anywhere."

Remember, to call for help is a sign of weakness.

Jay shook her head. She sure as hell wasn't in Kansas anymore. "All right, you want to give me a quick rundown of how I'll know what I don't know?"

"Absolutely. When the police call, it's usually straightforward—they've got a DB and you need to determine if it's a scene we need to roll out on. Violent deaths—suspected homicides or suicides, ODs, accidents—they're all rollouts for the investigators and one of us. Pretty much anything they get, we roll on it unless it's somebody who dies at home after a long illness. Then the body will need to come here, but we don't need to go out on it."

"Okay, so if it's anything other than clear natural causes, we go."

"Yup. The hospital calls are almost always the opposite. They're calling to tell you they've lost the patient."

"Yeah, been there a few times."

"The thing is, most docs don't actually understand how to distinguish between cause of death and the final event. They all want to say—"

"Cardiac arrest."

Tasha laughed. "You got it. So you'll have to take a history to figure out what the presenting symptoms were, what the underlying disease process was, and kind of walk them through it until you come to the appropriate cause of death. Then if you're comfortable with the course of events, you can call it natural causes and release the body to the family."

"Wow, I really don't want to fuck that up."

"You won't. You've got plenty of clinical experience, so you'll recognize the red flags. But like I said, just give one of us a yell."

"Okay, sure. Thanks."

"No problem." Tasha stretched, her breasts straining against her scrub shirt as she arched her back. "I'm not complaining about getting a full night's sleep, but I sure as hell wish the beds here were a little more comfortable."

Jay had spent so many nights sleeping on sofas in the OR lounge or worse than that, anything that resembled an actual bed was a bonus for her, but she made agreeable noises.

Tasha rolled her shoulders, sat up straight, and glanced over at Jay. "So are you seeing anyone?"

Jay was good at not showing her feelings, and she managed to keep her mouth from dropping open. "Uh, not at the moment."

"Am I reading you wrong or would I be out of line asking you out to dinner or something?"

"Your radar's good," Jay said slowly. "I've been out of commission for a while, though."

"Is that a no or a maybe?"

"That's thanks and can I think about it?"

Tasha grinned. "Sure. You let me know. And if it makes any difference to you, I'm bi."

"Nope. It doesn't."

Tasha bounced up. "Good, I'm going to take a shower. Want to come?"

"Uh—"

"Just kidding." Tasha's smile was infectious and Jay relaxed, grinning back.

"All right, thanks anyhow," Jay said.

"See you later."

Jay leaned back against the counter and watched her go. She hadn't had a date in over nine months, and she sure as hell hadn't been thinking about one. She'd been thinking about a woman, though, and one she probably shouldn't be. Olivia Price was complicated and interesting as hell, and anything with her would be intense. For a minute the image of Tasha in the shower teased at her senses. Tasha was attractive and easygoing and obviously not shy. Maybe something light and easy was a much better idea.

When her phone buzzed, she jumped. She'd gotten out of the habit of taking calls since the accident. The only calls she'd gotten before were about patients or emergencies, and she didn't do that any longer. Well, maybe now she did. "Reynolds."

"It's Olivia."

"Hi." Jay's heart rate spiked and she forgot all about naked women in showers.

"Can you drop by my office before morning review?"

"I'm on my way."

CHAPTER FIFTEEN

Jay arrived at Olivia's door, breathless, and took a second to catch her wind before knocking. She didn't want to look like she'd just raced through the building, or at least her facsimile of racing considering her gimpy leg, which she had. Fortunately she hadn't run into anyone who might have noticed her rush. Too early still for most people. She glanced at her watch. Forty-five minutes until morning review. That was good. Forty-five minutes with Olivia if she was lucky. She rapped on the door and concentrated on getting her game face on in the next second. "It's Jay."

"Come in," Olivia called, and Jay figured her game, such as it was, was a losing proposition. Just the sound of Olivia's voice made her grin. She opened the door and stepped inside.

"I wasn't sure you'd be here this early." Olivia smiled at her from across the desk.

"I would have been waiting outside your door, but you know, stalkerish."

Olivia laughed. "That would not have occurred to me."

"Good." Jay mentally rolled her eyes. Stalkerish? Could she be any less smooth? And now Olivia probably thought she'd been having X-rated fantasies about her. And she hadn't. She didn't need a fantasy when just being in the same space with her was a turn-on.

"I see you're settling in."

Jay stopped halfway to the chair, confused, and then realized what she'd done. When she'd arrived that morning, she'd automatically changed into scrubs and grabbed a cover gown from a metal shelf filled with them in the pit. "Oh. Habit. Sorry, I don't have a lab coat yet. I have to order a couple plain ones."

"You can take one of mine that doesn't have my name on it. It might be a little bit short on you, but we're almost the same size." Olivia frowned and her gaze drifted over Jay's body. "Might be a little tight in the shoulders too. Do you row?"

Jay had that feeling of being studied again, the way Olivia measured her with her eyes. She'd never worried so much about measuring up to a woman's speculation before, or liked the prospect of having a woman check her out so much. When she realized the silence stretched on between them and Olivia merely continued to watch her, heat rose in her face. "Ah, I did row, a long time ago it seems like now. I rowed crew in college, and some in med school. But once my residency started—" She shrugged. "You know how it is. There wasn't time for anything except that."

"Nothing?" Olivia asked quietly.

Was she asking about a relationship? She could hope. Jay shrugged. If she was wrong, what would she lose. She wasn't raised to be a coward. "Nothing except the OR and the trauma unit and the gym sometimes. No hobbies. And nobody even halfway serious."

"Ever?"

Jay shook her head sheepishly. "Nope. One-track mind, and everything else was just a distraction."

"Ah." Olivia pursed her lips. "I can see where that might have been a deterrent on the personal front."

"I didn't see it that way then," Jay said honestly. She'd never wanted for anything, or if she had, she'd been too busy to think about it for more than a minute when the next crisis came down the pike. She'd occasionally envied Ali her relationship with Beau, but figured one day—a long time in the future—she'd have time. "I ran out of time, I guess."

"How so?"

"You know the question everyone asks you every time you apply for a position—med school, residency, fellowships—where do you see yourself in ten years?" Jay shrugged. "I guess I just figured once I hit the ten-year mark, I'd have time to think about other things."

"It's a long hard road for everyone, and even longer in surgery with a sub-specialty added on. I'm so sorry that your previous path ended the way it did."

Your previous path. Your old life. The one that was over now.

The wind left Jay's lungs, and for just an instant, she swayed unsteadily. She caught her breath and sat down in the chair across from Olivia's desk. "It was kind of my fault."

Olivia leaned forward and laced her hands together, her gaze never leaving Jay's face. "How is that?"

Jay hadn't talked about it with anyone, not even Vic or Ali. For a long time after she'd come to in the trauma ICU she couldn't remember all the details, and then she hadn't wanted to remember. Ali and Vic both knew the details from the EMTs, and they sure as hell knew what happened here in the hospital, but they didn't know her story. Her memories and her nightmares. All of a sudden, she wanted someone to know. She wanted Olivia to know. "It was late May, almost a year ago, and I'd been on call the night before and left the hospital pretty late. Midnight maybe. I was alone driving west on the expressway. I had a week of vacation coming, believe it or not, and had rented a place in the Adirondacks. Figured I'd sit around and do nothing for a week, no internet, not much cell service. Maybe hike a bit. It was raining pretty good."

She still remembered the feeling of excitement, of freedom, as she left the city and the hospital behind. She loved what she did, but the pace could wear you down to a stub before you knew it was happening. A week away was just what she needed to recharge. Even the rain hadn't dulled her spirits.

"Traffic was light, even though it was a Friday night, and visibility was pretty crappy. I saw emergency flashers up ahead of me and slowed down. The wipers were going at top speed, and I could still barely see through a wash of water on the windshield." She laughed ruefully, all the way back in that car in that freak rainstorm, feeling like she was escaping for just a little while from the nonstop pressure and relentless pace. Man. Had she been wrong. "I slowed down when I made out a woman with the trunk of an SUV open, trying to drag a tire out and looking like she wasn't gonna manage it alone. At least that's how it looked in the quick glimpse I had. So I pulled over as much as I could and got out to give her a hand. I think maybe I forgot to put my flashers on and maybe that's why the guy in the tow truck didn't see me. He took off the door of the rental car and me along with it."

Olivia wanted to close her eyes, if only for a second, but she kept her gaze on Jay's pain-filled, haunted face. She did not want to envision Jay crushed and bleeding on some dark, rain-soaked highway, but let the image come. She owed her that. She'd asked her to share the horror, after all. "You survived. I'm so glad."

Jay snorted. "I spent three months more or less out of it in the ICU and then rehab, and well"—she gestured to her body—"some of this is permanent. I took a helluva bang on my head, and the nerve damage is central. Rehab won't undo that."

"You might yet see improvement. The brain is remarkably resilient."

"I'm not waiting around to find out." Jay shrugged. "I'm not one to live on hope."

"No," Olivia said. "I suspect you prefer to forge your own reality."

"Not doing so great with that."

"Oh, I don't know. You're here."

"Maybe I'm starting to wise up."

Olivia smiled. "How is it you think the accident's your fault?"

"Stupid thing to do," Jay muttered. "Everybody knows stopping on the highway, in a storm, no less, is a setup for an accident. Hell, I've taken care of half a dozen people run down during the same scenario. But what do I do? I hop out of my car like fucking Sir Galahad."

"Did someone accuse you of being foolhardy?" Olivia demanded.

"Not to my face."

"I should hope not. You stopped to help someone who needed help. I know the expressway pretty well, and none of the sections are so dark that you would have been completely invisible even without your flashers, if that was even the case. But a rainy night, late at night, I can see how someone wouldn't see you. But that's not your fault."

"Well, it's not the guy driving the truck's, either."

"No, that's what makes it so hard. There's no one to blame. That's why we call those things accidents. And I'm not the least bit surprised you stopped that night. I'm just sorry about the way it turned out."

Jay blew out a breath. "I'm still pissed at myself."

Olivia nodded. "I know how that is. It's hard not to blame yourself for the things you would do differently if you had the chance. In your case, I would say you are completely guiltless, and you should absolve yourself. You're the only one who can."

"In my case?"

"Yes," she said softly.

"You don't feel the same?"

"I'm sorry?"

"About your past, and I'm guessing the guilt has something to do with the guy you divorced. It is a guy, right?"

"Yes. How did you know?"

Jay lifted a shoulder. "I'm betting you were a lot younger and probably weren't very experienced and bought in to some romantic picture before you really asked yourself what you wanted."

Olivia shook her head. "I appreciate your attempt to exonerate me, but I was never a romantic. True, I never asked myself what I wanted—I was a little too busy trying to be who my mother wanted." She let out an aggravated breath. "And that's a story too old and too clichéd to repeat. We should do our jobs and deal with the present."

"All right." Jay hid her disappointment. She knew from experience some revelations couldn't be rushed. "But I'd like to hear it sometime, when you feel like you can tell me."

"It doesn't make for very interesting listening."

"I disagree. Anything you tell me is interesting."

Olivia blushed, such a rare occurrence, Jay wished she could freeze the moment in time. She wished to hell they were somewhere else. Anywhere else. If the desk, the damn desk again, hadn't been between them, she could have reached out, she could have brushed the loose strand of hair off Olivia's cheek, could've run her thumb along the angle of her jaw, could've leaned down just a little and pressed her mouth over Olivia's. The image made her groan softly.

"Jay," Olivia murmured, her voice as hazy as Jay's vision, "wherever you just went might be a very dangerous place to go."

"I don't think so." Jay's voice came out as if she'd strained it through gravel. "I don't think so at all."

Olivia leaned back and busied herself with her computer, a clear signal they needed to change lanes and get back on track. "Yes, well, I wanted your input on something."

Jay lassoed her libido and tied it down. "Right—one of the cases?"

"I've got the lab report on our suspected OD."

"What do we have?"

Olivia turned her monitor ninety degrees and gestured to Jay. "Come see."

Jay rose, walked just the slightest bit unsteadily around the desk, and stood beside Olivia's chair. A series of numbers, percentages, and chemical compounds ran down the page on the screen. Her curiosity kicked in along with her focus. "Blood chemistry?"

"That's right," Olivia said. "Nothing unusual showed up in her blood except a very high concentration of this substance right here." She tapped the screen with a stylus. "Unidentified."

"Could they at least narrow down the class of drugs?"

Olivia tilted her head and smiled. "You're good at this, you know that?"

The appreciation in Olivia's gaze hit Jay like an auditorium full of applause. Pleasure at pleasing Olivia bubbled through her blood. That look right there, the spark in Olivia's eyes that said she had done well was more addictive than any drug. Jay wanted more of that, a lot more. Waiting, along with hope, just wasn't in her nature.

"Tell me if I'm good at this," Jay murmured as she leaned down and kissed her.

Olivia's lips were cool and firm beneath hers, unmoving for an instant and then parting to admit the tip of Jay's tongue, just enough for her to slide her mouth over Olivia's, to tease the inner surface of her lip, to taste her heat. She groaned again, a sound in her chest that would've been pain if it hadn't been such pleasure. Lightly, ever so lightly, she rested her fingertips on the edge of Olivia's jaw. Her skin was soft, the scent of her hair a teasing hint of oranges. She kept her eyes open, and Olivia gazed back, her lids partly lowered, the gray-green a hazy morning's promise of heat to come. Jay didn't breathe, she didn't need to, but when she shifted to take the kiss deeper, Olivia slowly pushed her chair back until the distance broke their connection. Jay's hand slowly fell through the void to her side.

"Jay…" Olivia's emotions swirled out of control—desire a swift blade in her depths, sweetness more intense than mere pleasure, and heat everywhere. Jay's breath rasped sharply in the quiet room, and Olivia sensed the effort Jay made to hold back. Another touch and they would both break. The cold hand of reason clamped Olivia in a vise. She'd been the one to say yes, now she had to be the one to say no. She took a deep breath. "You are an excellent kisser."

Jay looked stunned, and then she laughed, a wild sound that dared Olivia to leave logic behind. "That's not what I expected you to say."

"What did you think?" Olivia whispered.

"I thought you'd say no."

"I already have, haven't I?"

"Maybe." Jay didn't move, didn't close the space between them, but didn't back away either. "Is that no more ever, or no more right now?"

The look on Jay's face, the need she didn't even bother to hide, pulled at Olivia like fingers on the strings of a harp, achingly beautiful music and dark warning all tangled together. "Aren't you afraid of anything?"

"A week ago I was afraid of everything," Jay whispered. "I was afraid of this body I lived in, I was afraid of the future, I was afraid of myself. I'm not afraid now."

"You should be. I am."

"Why?"

"Because I've been here before," Olivia said. "Because I know the cost of what a kiss can be."

"I'm not him."

"I know, but I'm still me."

Jay's jaw tensed. "Every time I look at you I want to kiss you."

"We have a meeting in fifteen minutes."

"Uh-huh." Jay shrugged. "I don't suppose you'd let me kiss you for fifteen more minutes."

Olivia shook her head. "No, I don't think so."

"Then I'd better not be close enough to touch you right now." Jay stepped back around the desk.

Olivia's relief was bittersweet. Longing simmered in her depths, an old ache tinged with loneliness and need, but at least she was familiar with that. She sat for a minute behind her desk in the silence. "We're going to have to work together, and it might be best if we not repeat that."

"Is that what you want?" Jay asked.

"It's what I think."

"I understand." Jay buried the kiss the way she buried everything else that mattered except the case, just as she'd done for years the moment she'd walked into the OR. The reflex was so ingrained, she didn't even have to think about it. Olivia had set the boundaries, at least for now. Jay had a job to do, and she intended to do it. Wanted to do it for herself, and because Olivia would accept nothing less.

Olivia expected the disappointment and didn't let it show. Her reason had never completely ruled her senses, but she'd learned to live with that. What she couldn't bear to repeat was the surrender of her willpower and her dignity, her very self, to some primitive hunger she couldn't control. This was a far better course to follow. She cleared her throat. "So, this drug. I spoke to Flanagan in the crime scene unit about it this morning."

Jay laughed, a hard-edged laugh that might have masked frustration. "Does everybody in the death business start work at five?"

"Only some of us," Olivia said. "At any rate, best guess is this is a manufactured opioid, probably illegally produced and distributed. It's not a regulation pharmaceutical."

"Which means untraceable?"

"Yes," Olivia said. "Apparently no one knows where it's coming from, or how much of it is already available on the streets. This may be an isolated incident."

"It would certainly help if they knew who she was and how she got it," Jay said.

"You're right, it would. Unfortunately, that's not our responsibility or our job. She would be a clear accidental death if it weren't for the fact she'd been moved." Olivia rubbed a spot between her brows, a rare sign of irritation. "That complicates the picture. We'll leave the case open at least until the police have a chance to investigate further."

"And what if we never know?"

"I hate signing cases out as undetermined." Olivia met Jay's gaze and her eyes clouded with regret. "But sometimes we have to do the things we don't want to do, just because they make the most sense."

CHAPTER SIXTEEN

So, how's it going at the new place?" Beau slid a plate of grilled chicken onto the dining room table. The afternoon had been warm, and the three of them sat outside in the narrow yard behind Ali's town house until the sun started to go down and the air turned cool. A flagstone patio took up half the space, and the rest was casually landscaped with hostas and other hardy perennials. The wooden fences on each side, hung with planters that would soon be overflowing with flowers, divided the runway yard from the adjacent ones and made the space into a little oasis amidst the city stone and steel.

Jay caught Ali's glance of concern at Beau's question. Although she appreciated Ali still worried over her, she didn't need her to. She wasn't recovering any longer—she was back to living. Funny how shedding the label helped improve her mood and a lot of other things, including her libido. She would have smiled if she'd actually been able to do anything about that particular reawakened part of herself. Jay speared some chicken, baked potato, and the broccoli that Ali had placed next to the chicken. "Well, I haven't killed anyone yet."

Beau laughed. Ali arched an eyebrow as she filled Jay's wineglass and sat between Jay and Beau at one end of the table.

"Not that I was in the habit of doing that in the trauma unit," Jay hastened to add with a sideways grin at Ali.

"I'm really glad to hear I hadn't somehow missed a run of unexplained complications," Ali said dryly.

"Still tough to lose one," Beau murmured, "especially when you're just a few minutes late."

"Yeah," Jay said, thinking of a recent callout when the teen driver of a vehicle involved in an expressway pileup was still warm when they'd arrived, looking as if she had just closed her eyes to nap for a minute. Except for the deceleration injury that had severed her aorta and caused her to bleed out in under a minute, she didn't have a mark on her. "Sometimes it feels like if we could just turn the clock back a couple of minutes, we could change everything."

"Fine line between living and dying," Beau said softly. Dressed casually in jeans and a T-shirt that displayed the emblem of the Philadelphia Fire Department, she was muscled through the shoulders and chest and lean in the hips. She was a bit younger than Jay and slightly tanned even in the middle of spring from all the time she spent outside working fire rescue. The gold ring on her left hand matched the one on Ali's.

Ali covered Beau's hand and squeezed. "A lot more stay this side of the line because of you and your team."

Beau smiled, although her gaze was fixed on some image only she saw. "I know—and you and yours."

Ali cast an almost apologetic look at Jay. Ali was still worried about her, thinking she was still mourning, still fragile. Time for her to fix that. Ali had no reason to feel guilty.

"It's only been a few weeks, but it's going good so far." When she saw Ali's look of mild disbelief, she shook her head. "No, really, I'm serious. It's not what I expected at all. There's a lot more action than you realize."

"Well, *I* know that." Beau sipped a beer and glanced at Ali, the look in her eyes mischievous and smoky at the same time. "You trauma types think all the excitement happens in trauma admitting and the OR, but we get plenty of excitement out on the streets. Even when there's nothing for me to do, the crime scene guys and the morgue techs get some action."

"We like to call our techs medicolegal investigators," Jay said with a straight face.

Beau grinned. "Uh-huh."

"And I agree," Jay said. "I thought I'd be sitting at a desk all day looking through a microscope or something. Most of the time I'm not even in the building. I do a lot of phone rotations, sure, triaging stuff and talking to house docs from all the hospitals in our county, but I roll out plenty."

"Are they letting you do anything?" Ali asked carefully.

"Oh yeah." Jay laughed. "I get to take notes and pretend that I'm actually filling out the reports myself—Olivia calls it being a scribe.

Then she or one of the other MEs goes over them with me. The usual kind of review for newbies."

"Who's Olivia?" Beau asked, helping herself to more chicken.

"Olivia Price, she's the assistant chief medical examiner. She's pretty much the head of the training program, although the title actually belongs to Dr. Greenly. He's the chief medical examiner, but as near as I can tell he spends all day in meetings."

"So this Olivia is your boss," Beau said.

"Well, as much as Ali was my boss."

Ali rolled her eyes. "I feel sorry for her if she's riding herd on you."

"Ha." Jay appreciated the banter, appreciated being treated like she wasn't still in recovery, even though she pretty much was still improving. She'd jettisoned her regular therapy sessions since she was spending so much more time on callouts walking, bending down, standing up, and using her hands. Her right hand still wasn't much good for fine motor functions, but her left worked just fine. "Olivia doesn't need to rein me in—I'm a model fellow."

Ali groaned. "Now I know you're BS-ing."

"Okay—maybe I'm finessing a bit."

"Hey, I like that," Beau said. "Finessing. A classier way of saying bullshitting."

Jay snorted. "I learn fast—years of Ali and Vic beating on me. And I know what Olivia expects—she is very...precise."

Ali pinned her with a look. "Oh, and I'm not?"

"Surgery is different, that's all. More unknowns, for one thing, which means more risk in the short term. In our line of work, there's no theorizing. You can't substitute instinct for evidence. We have no margin for uncertainty."

"You mean," Beau said, "no challenge?"

"Not at all," Jay said, not in the least offended by Beau's questions. Hell, she hadn't known anything about forensic pathology, so why should Beau? "We've got plenty of questions and plenty of challenges with every case. Every death needs an explanation, but the answers are all there to be found, like hidden images in a puzzle. The pieces have to be fit together, but you can't make up new ones, you can't fill in any blanks. You have to find the proof for every answer."

"Almost sounds like you like it," Ali said quietly.

"I do." Jay settled back to finish the meal, a little surprised at all she'd said. She hadn't put into words the reason for the slowly evolving sense of satisfaction she'd noticed since she'd started back to work. At first she'd figured it was just the high from being back to doing anything, but now she realized it wasn't just that, but the actual work itself. Ali was right—she did like the work. Seeing Olivia every day was the bonus she hadn't counted on—the best and worst parts of her new reality.

Everyone had finished and Jay stood, suddenly inexplicably restless. "I'll bus the table since you guys cooked."

"You don't have to do that," Ali said.

"I know." Jay stacked plates into her left hand with her right. "But I want to, and it's good therapy."

Beau relaxed and sipped her beer. "Works for me. Thanks."

Ali leaned down and kissed her. "The chef does not need to clear the table." She picked up the platters of unfinished food and followed Jay into the kitchen. "Sorry about the third degree."

"Hey, it's fine," Jay said.

"So how much of that was BS?"

"Honestly, none of it." Jay laughed. "Except, you know, the part about you not being a demanding—er, precise—chief."

"I'm glad to hear it's working out."

Jay set the dishes on the counter and Ali started to rinse them. She retrieved her wine from the other room and helped Ali load the dishwasher. "I'd appreciate it if you'd tell Vic not to worry about me next time you talk to her. That you got me over here for dinner and I'm doing okay."

"I will, as long as you're up front with me. I know damn well it can't be easy to adjust."

"I miss surgery," Jay said quietly, "but not what I thought I would. I miss being in the OR where no matter what happens in the rest of the world, we're free for a while. I miss the light right above my head shining like our own sun, how close everyone stands around the table with shoulders touching, hands crossing with instruments passing, everyone working together. I miss the beauty of it."

"Yeah, I can see that." Ali's voice was tight, strained.

"I miss *you*," Jay said softly.

Ali dried her hands and grasped Jay's shoulders. "I miss you every damn day." Her eyes glistened with tears. "I'm just so damn glad you're okay."

Ali'd never said anything before, never been anything but upbeat and positive. She'd never admitted she was worried or scared or sad.

Jay let out a breath and rested her head on Ali's shoulder for the briefest moment. "I would never have made it without you."

Ali stroked her hair. "Well, you did. Vic and me and you. The Three Musketeers, right?"

Jay nodded, her heart full. "Yeah, that's us. Except now there's like four, because there's Beau."

"True."

Jay sucked in a breath and straightened. "It's never going to be the same, but that doesn't mean it can't be as good."

"I know. Life changes, and we change too." Ali glanced toward the dining room. Beau was still at the table, phone to her ear, maybe taking a call from the department. "I never expected her."

"Yeah, I know what you mean."

Ali, sharp as always, narrowed her gaze. "Are you trying to tell me some woman actually made an impression on you for more than sixty minutes?"

"Hey," Jay protested. "I'm not a horndog."

"True. You never ran wild, but I can't remember you with anybody that lasted more than six weeks. And quite a lot of mornings you looked like you showed up in the same clothes—"

"That's just called being honest about my intentions."

"All right, you're an honorable short-termer," Ali said. "You're also avoiding the question."

Jay retreated to the safety of her wineglass and took another sip. The last few weeks she'd been busy learning the triage routines, taking her turn on the callout rotations, attending the catch-up histology seminars, and assisting at posts. She'd spent a lot of time working with Olivia, but somehow they never ended up alone together for very long. She had a feeling that was Olivia's doing. They rode to scenes together, but their conversations were all about work or none at all. She didn't mind the silences and sensed none of the awkwardness or tension that often accompanied unresolved sexual interests. Or misplaced ones.

She'd been happy with whatever chance she had to see Olivia, but the contact only made the hunger worse. Joining her in the Graveyard or in the field, watching her work, learning her rhythms the way she'd once known Ali's, was a pleasure in itself. A short sweet pleasure that left her wanting more. She wanted more with Olivia than she'd ever wanted with another woman. She wanted more of those moments of intense intimate contact, not just the physical excitement of a kiss or a caress, but the emotional ecstasy of being known. Whenever she thought of how easy it had been to share her pain with Olivia, how the acceptance in Olivia's steady gaze had shone like a light calling her home, she wanted those moments of connection again. She wanted her.

"Uh-oh," Ali whispered. "Somebody's gotten under your skin."

"More than that," Jay muttered.

"Who, what's going on? Come on, details."

Jay finished the wine in a long swallow and dangled the glass between her fingers. Interesting, the tremor in her hand barely registered with her any longer when a month ago she'd wanted the whole hand gone. "Nothing's going on. And everything."

"Well, let's start with the simple part. Who?"

"Olivia."

"Whoa. Olivia Price, the assistant chief medical examiner?"

Jay grinned. "The very one."

"Okay. That's…interesting. We haven't met but I've seen her once or twice—tall, kind of willowy, shoulder-length blond hair. Gorgeous. That the one?"

"That's her."

"I got the impression when we talked she was sharp and pretty much no-nonsense."

"She's brilliant," Jay said, "and I'm not exaggerating. She's excellent at her job, and a really good teacher."

"Somehow, I don't think that's exactly what's got you twisted up, though." Ali leaned a hip against the counter. "I think it might be more the blond and hot side of things."

"Well, it's all of it. She's also incredibly intense and sexy as hell, and she can hear the hard stuff and never blink."

"Sounds pretty phenomenal."

"I kissed her," Jay said in a rush.

"Holy hell," Ali said with a mixture of surprise and admiration. "You're not losing any time. So the two of you are…" She waggled a hand.

Jay shook her head. "No. One kiss. Then she shut me down."

"Ouch. Is it causing problems?"

"Not that way. She was totally straightforward about putting on the brakes, and she doesn't play games." Jay grinned. "She did tell me I was an excellent kisser."

"Huh—how long was the kiss?"

"Not nearly long enough." Jay sighed. "My timing was probably bad. I kind of just went with it."

"In my experience," Ali said musingly, "when someone tells you you're an excellent kisser and then says no more the next minute, they are not really certain about that."

"Olivia is always certain," Jay said. "But I'm hoping this time, she changes her mind."

"You'll be careful, right?"

"Not to worry, it's not a problem at work. You know all of us can keep personal things like this separate when we need to. That and just about everything else. Otherwise, how could any of us do what we do?"

"I'm not worried about your love life getting in the way of your job. You're both adults, and it's nothing new for people who work together around here to have a fling. I'm talking about here." Ali tapped Jay's chest. "You've had a rough year. You need to take care of yourself."

"We can't control when these things happen, can we?"

Ali sighed as Beau appeared in the doorway. "Hell, no. I should know that as well as anyone. But I still get to worry about you."

"I'll be careful." Jay said what Ali needed to hear, but she wasn't interested in being careful.

What she wanted was another kiss.

CHAPTER SEVENTEEN

Jay's phone rang at the same time as Beau's. They looked at each other, eyebrows raised in the universal expression of *oh crap*, and answered simultaneously.

"Reynolds," Jay said, turning slightly away from Beau's side of the table to hear.

"It's Olivia. I'm sorry to interrupt your evening, but we've got a situation. I know you're third call, but I thought you'd like to know about it. We'll need backup and I thought you might be free. If you're not…"

"No, I'm good. Free. Whatever you need. What is it?"

"First reports are of multiple victims at a nightclub on Arch. At least three unsubstantiated fatalities. If you're home, I can pick you up on my way in."

"Uh, no, I'm not, but I can get a cab—"

"Listen, it's your night off. Really, I'll just call Tasha to come in."

"No," Jay said quickly. "I'm on it. I'm not that far from Arch. I'm at St. James Place."

Olivia laughed. "Well, you're probably down the block from me, then."

"You're kidding. I'm at 2022." Jay wasn't all that surprised. Being within twenty minutes of the hospital, the neighborhood was popular with the medical personnel who could afford it. The four-square-block enclave of three-story brownstone town houses was pricey, but given what Jay knew of Olivia's family background, she suspected Olivia probably had some independent means. Her mother was, after all, one of the world's experts in her field and internationally renowned. From what Olivia had told Jay, she'd lived an unusual but privileged childhood. Maybe. What looked like privilege from the outside was often a prison on the inside, or at least not something of a child's choosing, and Olivia was pretty vague about the details. Jay tried to respect everyone's secrets, but with Olivia, she hungered to know more. Everything. She sighed. Not making much progress on that front. Maybe patience wasn't the right approach.

"Then you're only three doors away," Olivia said. "I keep my car around the corner. If you want to meet me out front—"

"That's good. Yes." Just the thought of Olivia being that close made Jay's heart jump. Maybe Ali was right and she really did have a serious case of the *must have this woman soon*s. And she'd just have to worry about that some other time. Work first, unrestrained libido later. "I'll be down in two minutes."

Olivia laughed again, that low throaty laugh Jay imagined was accompanied by the rare sunburst expression of heat and beauty she hadn't seen for a while.

"You don't have to rush quite that much," Olivia said. "CSU is on scene, and there's no telling when they'll be ready for us. It could be several hours, but I want to get there as soon as possible. We need to get a better idea of what's happening. Apparently the police have already locked down the establishment, so there may be potential witnesses who won't be there for long. If there are any, we may have a fair amount of interviewing to do."

"Look, whatever you need, I'm there. I just need to grab my coat."

"Again, I'm sorry about this."

"Why would you be. It's our job, right? See you in a minute."

"All right, yes."

Jay disconnected and glanced over at Beau, who was just hanging up. "You too? Something big going down in a club on Arch?"

"Yep. Not sure there's much for us to do, but they want us on standby in case there are more casualties."

"What's going on?" Ali said.

"Nobody's sure. Could be a gas leak or some ventilation problem with carbon monoxide toxicity. We're rolling to secure the building and the street."

Jay stood, the familiar high of handling an emergency making her feel like her old self. "So much for boring jobs, huh."

Beau laughed. "I think you just like all the flashing lights."

Jay grinned. Okay, yeah, maybe a little. Hell, going out on a field call was fun.

"I'd better call the unit," Ali said, "just to put them on standby in case we've got a mass casualty situation."

"Good idea. I'll call you as soon as I know what's what." Beau kissed her, pulled her jacket with *Fire Rescue* stamped across the back in tall yellow letters off the hook by the door, and shrugged it on. "I love you. See you later."

"See you soon," Ali called, watching her go.

"I gotta get me one of those jackets," Jay muttered.

Ali gave her a look like the old days, one of fondness, exasperation, and a little bit of pride. "You really are getting into it, aren't you."

"I meant what I said." Jay halted, wanting to make sure Ali believed her. "I can either move on or give up. I choose not to quit."

"I always knew that. I was trying not to eavesdrop, but it didn't sound like you needed a ride. If you do—"

"Oh, no, thanks. Olivia's right up the street. I'm meeting her."

"She's a neighbor?" Ali said.

"Yeah."

Ali shook her head. "I love the city—you can live next to someone for years and never run into them."

"Gotta go." Jay squeezed Ali's arm. "Thanks for tonight. Hell, thanks for my whole damn life."

"Oh, shut up." Ali gave her a quick hug. "Be safe out there."

"Don't think I can get into too much trouble—I'm just the scribe." Happy to be useful, or maybe just happy to be seeing Olivia, Jay collected her jacket and cane and headed downstairs. She hadn't realized how late it had gotten as they'd all sat around talking, but the air was twenty degrees cooler than it had been that afternoon when the teasing hint of early spring had lulled her into thinking warm weather was upon them. She hunched her shoulders in her thin nylon jacket and looked up and down the street, checking addresses. She'd been so psyched at the thought of seeing Olivia, she'd forgotten to get her address. She could always go door to door if she had to. She didn't have to search long. Olivia exited a brownstone a few doors away and waved as she descended the curving stone steps with their gracious scrolled wrought-iron railing.

Jay hurried in her direction. "Hi."

"Hi." Olivia heard the breathlessness in her voice and swallowed hard. She'd thought of Jay the instant she was contacted about the crisis, but she'd hesitated to call. First, Jay wasn't technically on call, second, it was a Saturday night and she was probably enjoying her personal life, and third, because she really wanted to see her. Maintaining professional distance hadn't been as easy as she'd expected. She hadn't had any trouble working with her. They both had plenty of practice separating the personal from the professional, but every time they weren't actually working together, she was thinking about her. Despite her resolve, and Jay's apparent willingness to accept the distance between them, the very palpable barrier between them hadn't gotten any easier to tolerate as time had passed. Being in the same space with her was a mixture of pleasure and frustration, although at just that moment the pleasure was definitely winning.

Jay looked great in dark tapered pants, a V-neck sweater, and an expression that said she was very glad to see Olivia. As Jay drew closer, Olivia read excitement and undisguised desire in her eyes. For a brief instant, she feasted on the sight of her.

"Hi," Olivia repeated. She really had to get ahold of herself.

Jay grinned. "Hi. You look great."

"Thanks. Ah…so do you." Olivia hesitated and lost the inner battle. "Date?"

Jay laughed. "No way. I had dinner with Ali Torveau and her wife."

"Oh. Good. I mean, that's nice." Olivia shook her head and started to walk. She had stopped to change out of her shapeless sit-around-the-house pants and pullover into tailored pants and a linen shirt, but that was just work attire. This wasn't a date. Why did she almost feel as if it were?

"Where are we headed?" Jay asked.

"A place called Galaxy," Olivia said.

"How many victims?"

"Not sure. First reports were three, then five. We may be looking at a lot more." Olivia glanced at Jay. "Do you know the place?"

"I've never heard of it, but I don't have much experience with nightclubs."

"That surprises me a little."

"When would I have time for nightlife?" Jay laughed.

"It's just that…" Olivia clamped her teeth together before she could finish the thought. *You're so attractive, you must have plenty of dates.*

"Sorry?" Jay said.

"Nothing. My car's down here." Olivia led Jay down the narrow alley that opened into a gated parking lot behind a closed business establishment.

Jay looked around. "You come down here alone at night?"

"It's well lit, and I've never had any problems."

Jay gritted her teeth. "Still, it's not a very good idea."

Olivia unlocked the doors. "I'm always careful. I learned to maneuver through some pretty treacherous territory growing up, geographically speaking."

Jay stopped, her door partly open. "I don't doubt you can take care of yourself, but I wouldn't want anything to happen to you."

"I'll exercise extreme caution," Olivia said, her throat tightening. One of the things she found most attractive about Jay was her willingness to expose her feelings. She was terrible at that herself, had learned to hide her fears or her desires or her needs. All of them sooner or later brought her pain. She slid into the driver's seat and looked over at Jay. "I don't want you to worry, but I...appreciate that you do."

"Fair enough," Jay said as Olivia backed out and headed north across Market. "So what's the plan when we get there?"

Comfortable now that they were back on safe ground, Olivia sped through the mostly empty streets. The area was still mostly residential until north of Market, when the landscape changed abruptly to warehouses, gas stations, seedy-looking bars, and clubs that tried for trendy but mostly looked trashy. "As the senior member on scene, I'll be the incident commander. First task is to find the police officer in charge and get a report so we know what we're dealing with. Then I'll make assignments."

"How many of us?" Jay asked.

"Right now, me, you, Darrell, and Archie. If we need more hands, we'll call in Bobbi and one of the other MEs."

"I noticed the other MEs don't go out much."

Olivia laughed, not really bothered by the other MEs' preference for waiting for the dead to come to them. "Strictly speaking, the investigators can handle almost every scene, but I find that teaching in the field is invaluable for the fellows, and when one of you is going out, we should too if at all possible."

"Well, I appreciate the attention."

"You're welcome. I enjoy it, really." She enjoyed the time she spent in the field with all the trainees, although she had a special fondness for working with Jay. Not favoritism as much as indulgence, if she was being honest, and she hoped she could be at least that if not cautious.

When she turned onto Arch, the street was clogged by at least a dozen fire rescue rigs, fire trucks, and police cruisers, parked haphazardly with competing light bars flashing. Beyond the swirling cloud of emergency lights, the rest of the block looked dark and abandoned. She pulled up as close as she could and flipped down the visor with its reflective Medical Examiner sign.

"Nice neighborhood," Jay said as Olivia opened the trunk.

"Now I'm not surprised you've never heard of this place." Olivia pulled on her ME jacket, handed her backup jacket to Jay, and extracted her field kit.

Jay shrugged into the jacket and held out her hand. "I'll carry that kit for you."

Olivia hesitated for a second and then handed it over. "Thanks."

"Can I keep this jacket until I get one for myself?"

Olivia laughed. "Sure. Ask Jodi in the office to order you one. Tell her I cleared it."

Jay grinned. "Thanks. It's like getting your white coat, you know? Makes you official."

"You're on my team. You're already official."

Jay's expression in the flickering light turned suddenly serious. "I like that."

"Yes. Well." Olivia eyed her, searching for a lighter tone. "Plus that's way too small for you."

"It works," Jay said as they skirted between the haphazardly parked emergency vehicles.

First responders from multiple agencies milled about, police, paramedics, firefighters in turnout gear. A uniformed officer stopped them at a hastily constructed barricade of yellow tape. Olivia held out her identification. "Olivia Price, assistant medical examiner."

The officer nodded. "Go ahead, Docs."

"Who's in charge?"

"Right now, Detective Mitchell. She's..." He turned, looked around, and shrugged. "Last time I saw her, she was inside the club somewhere. Skinny, dark hair, leather jacket and jeans."

"Thank you." Olivia led the way under the tape and down the sidewalk to the club. No marquee, just a battered neon sign above the door marked the entrance. As they walked, she said, "The most important thing is for us to get as much accurate firsthand information as we can. That means witness statements if possible. Witnesses forget very quickly, and they'll often speak more candidly to those of us who aren't police. Doctors are much less threatening."

Jay laughed. "I've never thought of myself as being threatening when dealing with patients or anyone else. Course, I didn't have to do a lot of talking in an emergency. My role was a lot narrower then, in a way. Somehow I've become a detective as well as a doctor."

"That's one way of thinking of it." Olivia paused at the club entrance. Posters of seminude women who she supposed were meant to be dancers but looked like porn stars flanked the windowless double doors. "Are you enjoying yourself?"

"I am, in more ways than I imagined."

"Good. Let's get to work." Olivia reached for the door but Jay beat her to it, pushing it open and holding it for her to pass inside. Olivia stepped into a long, narrow room that smelled of alcohol and mold, grateful Jay wouldn't see the blush she felt coloring her cheeks in the semidarkness. She rarely took anything as innocent as Jay's statement personally, but she couldn't help but hope she was part of the reason for Jay's pleasure. Fortunately, she had work to do and could push aside the quick surge of desire Jay seemed to stir effortlessly. She recognized the feelings, knew where they led. She'd spent nearly ten years training herself to ignore them. Jay was the first one to challenge that control.

"That might be our detective." Jay pointed to a woman with a gold shield hanging on a lanyard around her neck.

The young woman in tight dark jeans, motorcycle boots, and a black T-shirt was the least likely candidate for lead detective Olivia had yet dealt with, but she headed in that direction. "Detective Mitchell?"

"That's right," the handsome young woman said.

"Olivia Price, assistant chief medical examiner. Have a minute to fill me in?"

"Sure. Dellon Mitchell," the young woman said, holding out her hand. "Dell."

"Good to meet you. This is Jay Reynolds, one of our fellows."

"Doc," Dell said, inclining her head at Jay. "I'll tell you what we know, which isn't much right now. The 9-1-1 came in about twenty-three minutes ago, anonymous, reporting an unconscious man in the men's room. Paramedics rolled on it and called us as soon as they ascertained we were dealing with a death. While they were in transit, another call came in, another victim, this one in the alley right outside the door."

"Same caller?" Jay asked.

"Unknown at the moment," Dell said. "I was in the area, caught the call, and headed over right away. By the time I got here, we had another victim inside the club. People were panicking. We weren't sure what we were dealing with—gas leak, carbon monoxide, something in the water or even the liquor. Could be almost anything."

"Were you able to contain the customers?" Olivia asked.

Dell grimaced. "We moved everyone outside as soon as we could. By the time we had uniforms for crowd control, I'd say at least half the place disappeared before we had any kind of scene management."

Olivia nodded. "I'm surprised you were able to keep that many. Where are they?"

"We moved them to the lobby of the Starlight Hotel—which is kind of being generous since it's a flophouse—across the street. Uniforms are interviewing them now along with some other members of my team."

"How far along is CSU?" Olivia asked.

"They cleared the men's room. They're still working the other two scenes, but it shouldn't be long."

"Good." Olivia waved to Darrell and Archie, who had just walked in together. "I'll get our people on the first scene and assisting with interviews."

"Anything you can tell us would be a help," Dell said. "We don't know what we're dealing with here."

Jay glanced at the bar, at the dozens of bottles behind it and the half-empty glasses covering its surface—many tipped over, probably in the rush for customers to get out once the panic started. Other upended glasses and bottles littered the tables and floor. "Is the CSU planning to wrap up everything that's open?"

Dell nodded. "Yeah, glasses and alcohol all have to be checked."

Jay grimaced. "It's gonna be a big job to analyze."

"That's what makes it fun," a woman with a distinct Irish accent said as she walked up to them.

Olivia recognized the voice and smiled. "You would be chief CSI Flanagan."

"The very one."

"Hi, Dee. We spoke on the phone recently." Olivia held out her hand and introduced herself.

Dee shook it vigorously. "Good to meet you, Doc."

"And you. Anything you can tell me right now?" Olivia asked.

"The gas company's on scene. They're going through the building with the fire department and checking the street outside. So far no sign of a leak. We're not registering any other kind of airborne chemical contaminant. Carbon monoxide levels are normal. They've got a furnace in the basement, and the air down there checks out."

"I would expect many more affected if it was something like that," Olivia said.

"Absolutely," Dee said.

"Any evidence of external trauma on the victims?" Olivia asked.

"Not that we can see." Dee grinned. "Course, we don't touch the bodies."

Olivia smiled. "Of course."

Dell chimed in. "No one heard gunshots or noted any kind of altercation, and we've got no evidence of weapons on scene. Looks like it could be bad drugs."

"We'll see." Olivia was used to other departments speculating on cause and saw no reason to correct them. In the end, the ME's conclusions were all that mattered.

"We're sampling everything we can find," Dee said.

"Good. Are we free to look at the bodies now?" Olivia asked.

"Start in the men's room," Dee said. "We'll have the alley and the third victim—he's over by the bar—ready for you within the hour."

"Thanks, we'll do that."

Someone called to Dell, and she nodded and disappeared into the crowd with Dee.

Olivia turned to Jay. "Why don't you process the scene with me, unless you'd rather interview."

Jay laughed. "Just try to get rid of me."

"I wouldn't think of it," Olivia murmured.

Jay gave her a long look. "Glad to hear it."

CHAPTER EIGHTEEN

Jay followed Olivia down a narrow hallway at the back of the club to the restrooms. The main part of the club was probably almost as crowded as during a regular night, although now all the people crowding around wore a uniform of one type or another, and most carried cameras or instrument cases or had phones pressed to their ears. Over in one corner, Dellon Mitchell and a tall, striking blonde in an expensive-looking suit were talking to a harried-looking man who waved his arms while shaking his head vigorously. The owner or possibly a bartender, disavowing all knowledge maybe. The men's room door stood open on a slant, and bright light spilled out from a halogen work light clamped to the frame and pointed down onto dirty subway tiles and the body sprawled halfway beneath one of the naked sinks clamped to one side wall. The opposite wall held a trio of urinals she didn't examine too closely, although the smell let her know the place hadn't been scrubbed down recently. Two toilet stalls next to them completed the facilities. The illumination from a single hanging fluorescent fixture with two flickering bulbs lost the competition to the bright halogens, the pale light fading into the background as if trying to go unnoticed. A mesh grate on the ten-inch-high transom window at the far end of the room had to be a fire code violation. Not her job, but she'd include it in her report.

Olivia set her case down by the door and stopped a few feet from the body, stillness surrounding her as if the very air had stopped moving. Jay halted abruptly just behind her, keeping her eyes wide despite the bright light, letting her mind empty while her vision accommodated.

He lay on his side, back to the wall, his face turned outward toward the urinals. A thin trickle of greenish fluid smeared the angle of his mouth and pooled on the floor beneath his cheek. A dusting of beard darkened the tight angle of his jaw. His chalky cheeks contrasted sharply with the gray tinge beginning in his lids and lips. His hair looked professionally barbered and clean. His shirttails were out, the shirt itself drawn up to expose his flat, flaccid abdomen. Washed denim jeans and loafers without socks completed the ensemble. Something tickled the back of her mind but she kept silent, waiting for a cue from Olivia. Observation ruled now.

The natural tendency of the untrained in any kind of emergency was to rush to action, to do *something*: stop the blood flow, get the heart beating, repair the damage. She imagined it was similar for firefighters—find the victims, rescue the injured, douse the flames. But action without direction often led to further trauma. Missing the big bleeder hidden deep in a wound because a small pumper near the surface caught your attention first was a lethal mistake. Suturing the wrong tendons together because they were obvious at first glance was a newbie error. How many times had she told her residents, *Look, don't touch. Identify, don't disturb. See the whole picture, identify the border between the healthy and the dying.* Now she had to learn the border between the living and the dead.

Jay's gaze narrowed and her focus sharpened, the sensation of hyperawareness familiar and automatic, even though circumstances had changed.

"What do you see?" Olivia asked the familiar question.

Jay had been expecting it, had answered the same question at least a dozen times before, and every time her stomach tightened just a little. A test. She liked being tested. She liked being right even more, but mostly she liked honing the sharp edge of her abilities, especially this one. This was her new domain, or would be one day. Olivia ruled here right now, and Jay was earning a place in Olivia's domain. She was familiar with the routine, the hierarchy, and the eventual outcome. She would pay her dues and one day be in charge. She'd almost been there once and would be again. She knew the game and the rules, but now there was a new and different challenge. Now there was a woman she wanted to impress. There had been others before Olivia—first her sister, then Ali, then mentors she'd respected—but none like Olivia. This was personal. Every time Olivia smiled at her for something she'd answered correctly, something she'd done right, rewarded her with a pulse of animal pleasure, was a small victory.

"I'm going to break all the rules," Jay said.

Olivia turned her head, arched a brow. "That's probably not the best way to start."

"I know, but tell me if I'm wrong."

"Oh, I most certainly will."

Olivia's tone was a dare, and Jay liked dares too. "He looks like the girl."

Olivia's expression didn't change, but her eyes glinted. "What do you mean?"

"It's not the superficial positioning with him curled on his side, because I think this time that's how he expired. He hasn't been moved. Look at the vomit. If he'd been dead when he was moved, his stomach muscles would have been denervated and he wouldn't have vomited. He vomited as he was dying, so he was in the position we see him in now prior to death. It's his overall appearance that's similar—he's clean, well nourished, with an expensive haircut and expensive clothes, at least for casual wear. He's young, about her age. I'd be willing to bet when we look at his arms, he's not a junkie. Maybe he's a casual user, maybe a first-timer. Like her. Plus, he's out of his element here. This place is a dive, but I bet it's a great place to score drugs or somewhere around here is."

"You think this is an overdose?"

"I think it might be," Jay said, avoiding the trap of assumption. "We've ruled out penetrating injury—nothing to indicate a GSW, no blood on the floor or on him, at least from what we can see now. We can't be sure there isn't some blunt trauma since we can't see the back of his head and neck completely. I suppose there could be an ice pick wound that would've left minimal blood, but that would be a very unusual form of death for someone like this in this place. I think we'll know more when we're finished with the autopsy and the toxicology comes back."

Olivia smiled, the pleased smile that set Jay's heart tapping a little faster. "I think you're right."

"To all of it?"

"He falls into the same age and apparent socioeconomic demographic as our Jane Doe. Maybe this time we'll get lucky and actually get an ID. He's got a wallet in his back pocket."

"How do you know that?"

"Easy. I can see it."

Jay squinted, and sure enough, the faint line of a slim wallet tented the lower corner of his back pocket, all that was visible from their angle. "Good eye."

"I'm surprised the CSU techs didn't try to tease it out, but they know it aggravates me when they fool with the body."

From the doorway, Dell said, "I'd be very happy if you teased it out now. I'd like to ID him so we can try to piece together what happened here."

"Give us just a moment," Olivia said without turning. "Jay, will you photograph, please."

"Absolutely." Jay opened the field kit, assembled the digital camera, and starting with the perimeter, worked her way counterclockwise around the room, ending with the body, first distant shots, then multiple close-ups. She shot over fifty photos from various angles and backed everything up to an external hard drive when she was done. "Got it."

Olivia pulled on gloves, extracted the wallet, and handed it to Dell.

Dell, also gloved, flipped open the wallet. "He's from Massachusetts. Victor Gutierrez, twenty years old."

"Visitor?" Jay mused out loud. "Weird place to be visiting."

"He could be in town for an interview, some sports event, a family visit, who knows." Dell took a digital image of the license, looked through the rest of the wallet, and dropped everything into an evidence bag. She handed the bag to Olivia to initial and then added her own, securing the chain of custody. "I'll tell Flanagan's people to come collect this."

"He could also be a student," Olivia said. "That fits."

Dell paused. "Fits with what?"

Olivia stood, a forceps in her right hand, holding a postage-stamp-sized glassine envelope with some kind of marking in black ink. "This is like the one found with our Jane Doe. I've been trying to think of reasons she hasn't been identified yet. If she's a student, she might not be missed right away, especially if her family isn't used to hearing from her regularly or they think she's on some kind of trip, or any number of reasons."

"Wait a minute," Dell said. "You have another victim related to this one?"

"We don't know that yet," Olivia said. "But we do have an unidentified female who died of a drug overdose. It's possible he did as well. I was speculating perhaps they were students. *Just* speculating."

"It's SOP to canvass all the local colleges," Dell said, "but it's also like looking for a needle in a haystack if no one's reported her missing.

Sometimes kids move off campus without telling the parents, and their dorm mates never miss them because they think they're shacked up somewhere else. If this one's a student, though, his student ID isn't with him."

"Hopefully he'll turn up in the databases," Olivia said, already kneeling again, a thin probe in her right hand. She lifted his shirt, palpated the lower edge of his right rib cage, and slid the probe into his abdomen and the liver underneath. She read out the body temp to Jay, who had started the field report without being asked. That was part of her job.

A few minutes later, Olivia said, "I think we're done here. I'll text Darrell and let him know this one's ready for transport."

"It looks like he came in here, maybe wasn't feeling very well, lost consciousness, and died," Jay said quietly.

"I agree with you." Olivia sighed. "I had hoped we wouldn't have a repeat, but this looks very much like the other case."

"Coincidences do happen," Jay said.

"Yes, they do, but I for one consider them the cause of last resort."

Jay chuckled. "Me too. Time to check out the alley?"

"Yes."

Jay picked up the field kit, and Olivia handed the evidence bag with the wallet to one of the CSU techs who appeared to collect it. A door marked exit had been propped open with a wooden chair braced under the push bar. The harsh white light just beyond was eerie and disorienting. From the depths of the club, Jay felt like she was stepping into some alternate reality. Two halogen lamps on stands fifteen feet apart spotlighted their second victim, another young white male, this one in chinos, oxfords, again with no socks, and an expensive-looking V-neck sweater. He lay on his back, staring up into the light, eyes wide and unblinking. His fly was open, but otherwise, his body seemed undisturbed. No blood, no external signs of injury, nothing around him to suggest a struggle. Jay pointed to a wide streak on the brick wall a few feet away. "I bet that is urine."

Olivia turned, followed Jay's gaze. "You think he came out here to relieve himself, and then…?"

"And then whatever he took, either inside or right after he came out, killed him."

"We need to determine the onset of action for this drug. I'm beginning to think we already know the LD50."

"You mean like everyone who takes it dies?"

"We can't know that," Olivia said, "but when we've got more than one victim in the same place, we have to assume it's highly lethal."

Jay pulled out her tablet, scrolled to a new page.

"Let me do that," Olivia said. "You do the photos and the body."

"Yes, ma'am." Jay happily handed over the tablet and took the scene photos. After measuring liver temp, she checked his pockets, removed his wallet, and almost as an afterthought, slid her fingertip into the small key pocket on the inside of his waistband. She came out with a small glassine envelope between her index and middle fingers, a thin line of white powder still coating the bottom seam. "Got a residual sample here."

"How did you know to check in there?"

"I've got a pair of pants like this," Jay said. "It's kind of a design quirk of the brand. Instead of a watch pocket, which doesn't look right on chinos, they put this small inner pocket on all their casual pants."

"I would've missed that," Olivia said, her tone distressed.

"CSU would've gotten it from the clothes. Probably."

"But now we're ahead of things. Good job."

By the time they reached the third body, the story was depressingly repetitive. Another twenty-year-old male, African American, dressed similarly to the other two, sprawled at the far end of the bar in a pool of vomit. Archie appeared as they were starting their examination and took over the scene photographs from Jay. Olivia collected specimens of the vomitus and went through his clothes. She extracted a plastic photo ID card from his shirt pocket.

"Someone should get Detective Mitchell," Olivia said as she rose. "Student ID. Schuyler College."

"I'll find her." Jay circled the club and, when she didn't see her, stepped outside to look. A pair of news vans had pulled up tight behind the police cruisers, their satellite dishes standing out above them like mini UFOs. A woman pushed a mic toward a police officer wearing a uniform with a lot of brass. Not surprisingly, Dellon Mitchell wasn't in the spotlight. She didn't look the type who lusted for publicity. Jay finally found her at the margin of the bright lights flaring from the news vans and told her about the ID.

"Excellent, thanks," Dell said, heading back toward the club. "What do you think so far?"

Jay was used to interfacing with the police in the trauma unit. She often treated crime victims or suspected offenders, and updating law enforcement was standard procedure. But in those cases, she'd been giving a medical report of changing conditions. Now she was being asked for a conclusion. "Other than all three of them being dead, nothing you don't already know."

Dell snorted. "Had to try."

"Yep. But if I know Olivia, we'll be working them all night."

"That's good, because we'll be out all night too. Maybe I'll buy you breakfast, and we can compare notes."

"Done," Jay said, "if I can."

"Good enough. Let me have your number," Dell said.

Jay extracted her phone. "Trade."

They synced their numbers and Dell entered the club. Jay was about to follow when someone called her name.

She turned and Dr. Greenly emerged from the crowd onto the sidewalk. He looked like he was ready for the office in a topcoat, suit, and tie instead of being out in the middle of the night on a trash-strewn street.

Jay hid her surprise, or at least she hoped she did. "Hello, sir."

"Doctor," Greenly said, and Jay wondered if he actually remembered her name. "Captain O'Hara, the police commander in this district, contacted me for information about the investigation, so I thought I'd best come oversee the progress. Why don't you update me."

"Ah…" Jay had a feeling what he was asking was a little above her pay grade. "Dr. Price is right inside, Dr. Greenly. I'm sure she can—"

"That's quite all right. Just give me the pertinent details for now."

"Actually, sir, I've just been taking photographs and don't really have any details. Come this way." Before he could question her again, she pushed open the door and held it for him, giving him no choice but to follow. Looking exasperated and a little reluctant, he stepped into the semidark, dank club. Jay hoped to give Olivia a heads-up before they descended on her, but Olivia saw them from across the room, said something to Archie, and strode to meet them well away from the last victim.

"Dr. Greenly, I'm sorry someone got you out of bed."

"Quite all right." He grimaced as if the situation were anything but, then replaced the discomfited expression with a forced smile. "It's the job, after all. So, what do we have?"

"Three deceased," Olivia said instantly, "all male. No positive IDs at the moment, but we're working on it and should have something reasonably soon."

"Yes. And cause of death?"

Just as smoothly, Olivia replied, "Not definitive at this moment, but we can allay the fears of the concerned members of the community. We have determined there is no risk from noxious chemicals, gas leaks, or other environmental contamination. I'm sure everyone will want to know. A brief press statement to that effect, perhaps?"

He seemed to brighten and nodded. "You're absolutely right. Good work. Thank you."

Jay stifled a laugh as Greenly hastily retreated. "That was slick."

"I'm sure I don't have any idea what you mean," Olivia deadpanned. "The trick is to provide some information that's already been released or doesn't have any direct bearing on your conclusions. That we have three male victims is probably all over the street by now, and we know from CSU and fire rescue there's no risk to any of us from airborne toxins. So I didn't actually tell him anything we don't want the news to have."

"You think that's where he's headed?"

"I know that's where he's headed. It's politics."

Jay grunted. "Can't escape it."

"No, but—"

The front door banged open and a police officer yelled, "We need you out here, Doc. ASAP."

Olivia took off on the run and Jay hurried to keep up. A circle had formed around a figure lying in the street, and it took Jay a second to realize it was Greenly and not another overdose. "What happened?"

"He just…dropped," the officer said.

Olivia knelt, felt Greenly's neck for a pulse, and shouted, "Get the paramedics. He's arrested."

CHAPTER NINETEEN

Fire rescue, coming through." Beau, an oxygen tank tucked under one arm and a red equipment box in the other hand, squatted beside Jay, who continued chest compressions in a steady, rapid rate. "What we got?"

"Sixty-year-old male," Olivia said, keeping Greenly's chin up and his airway clear. "Abrupt syncopal episode. I can't find a pulse."

Beau opened her field kit, and her partner, a big ruddy blond, cut open Greenly's shirt with heavy field scissors, exposed his chest and abdomen, and deftly attached EKG leads to Greenly's shoulders and flanks. Beau charged the defibrillator.

"Flatline," the blond grunted and fitted a breathing mask over Greenly's mouth with one hand, pumping oxygen through the bag with the other.

Beau set the paddles on Greenly's chest. "Clear."

Jay lifted her hands off Greenly's body. His body jumped with the first electrical discharge. She watched the portable monitor. Still flatline. Somewhere in the recesses of her mind, memory flared. Flashes of light, a cacophony of unintelligible voices, a burst of pain. Sweat popped out on her brow despite the cold. She shivered, shook off the animal instinct to escape the danger she sensed but couldn't see.

"Got the epi, Bobby?" Beau asked.

Bobby taped in the IV he'd just started and grabbed a prefilled syringe from the med drawer. "Got it."

"Go ahead."

The EKG stayed flat. Beau upped the current of the defibrillator. Jump-starting a flatline didn't often work, but they didn't have much else to try. "Clear!"

Again, no response. Jay resumed compressions, shutting out any other thoughts.

"Get the rig, Bobby," Beau said. "We need to transport."

"On it," Bobby said.

"Here, I'll take over there." Olivia knelt and Bobby handed over the breathing bag.

"Thanks." The big man rose and the crowd around them parted to let him through. Two police officers hurried after him and jumped into patrol cars to make room for the rescue rig.

"Do you want to intubate him?" Olivia asked. Although technically, either Jay or Olivia could have run the resuscitation, neither of them had said a word, smart enough to know that Beau and her colleague were far more adept at field resuscitation than either of them. Jay had plenty of experience in acute resuscitation in the trauma unit, but they weren't in the relatively controlled environment of the unit now. This was Beau's domain.

"O2 sats are good so far." Beau hurriedly packed gear automatically, her focus on the monitors. "I'd rather get him to the ER ASAP."

"Of course," Olivia replied.

"Does he have any heart condition that you know of?" Beau asked.

"None that I'm aware of," Olivia said. "Jay, do you want to switch with me?"

Jay's arms trembled from the strenuous compressions she hadn't performed in almost a year. Thankfully the PT had helped her preserve her upper body strength. Still, her shoulders and arms were slowly going numb. Pride had no place in this situation, and after another few seconds, she leaned back. "Yeah, you can spell me now."

"Anything?" Bobby asked as he jumped out of the rescue rig and hurried to join them.

"Still flatline," Olivia said, watching the monitor.

"Let's push another round of epi and get going," Beau said.

Bobby injected the second ampule and everyone watched the monitor. A tiny blip, then another, then nothing.

"Damn it," Beau said. "That's it. Let's roll."

Bobby pushed the gurney into position, and he and Beau swiftly transferred Greenly. As Beau strapped him down, Jay said, "Listen, you need me to ride with you? Somebody's gonna have to keep up the chest compression, or I can bag him."

"Yeah," Beau said, "that would be good. Then we don't have to pull one of the fire crew to assist. Bobby's the best driver in the whole station."

Olivia sprinted alongside the stretcher as Bobby and Beau pushed it toward the fire rescue truck. "I'll follow you there."

Jay climbed in after Beau, strapped into the jump seat at the head of the gurney, and took over cycling the breathing bag. Beau continued closed chest compression. Bobby slammed the rear doors closed, and ten seconds later they lurched forward, sirens blaring. Jay stared at the monitor so long without blinking, her eyes burned. She blinked. Blinked again.

"Got a rhythm!" Jay checked his carotid. "Weak pulse here."

Beau stopped compressions and took a quick pressure. "Got a BP too. Ninety over forty. Keep bagging him."

"On it."

Beau adjusted the IV drip, added lidocaine, and rechecked the pressure. "He's holding."

Jay stopped pumping the bag. "Spontaneous respirations."

"Let's up the volume." Beau switched him to a rebreathing mask and watched his oxygen sats. Greenly's rhythm stabilized and his O2 sats held in the midnineties. "I'll call us in."

"Nice save."

"Got a ways to go," Beau said but her eyes gleamed with triumph. "But yeah. Thanks for the assist."

"No problem." Jay's chest ached and her head swam from the adrenaline rush. She was out of practice. She really looked at Greenly for the first time, unconscious, so…mortal. That had been her. She shivered again. Maybe life was all about the luck of the draw.

Beau updated the ER by phone, and five minutes later, they pulled into the emergency zone at University Hospital and jerked to a stop. The doors swung open and Bobby reached in and Beau released the brakes on the gurney. They slid the gurney out, trundled off at top speed toward the entrance, and were met at the big sliding doors by a man and woman in ER scrubs.

Jay slowly climbed out, her legs and back stiff from tension and the unfamiliar position in the back of the rig. She hesitated in the parking lot, unsure of her next move. She had no role to play inside the hospital for the first time in a decade. She felt more than displaced. She felt lost.

Olivia's SUV pulled up beside her, and Olivia got out. The world righted itself and the disabling disorientation dissolved. She *did* have a place, although right now, she didn't have a role to play inside, and that was okay. She had other things that mattered.

Olivia hurried over. "How is he?"

"They got a rhythm and spontaneous respirations back."

"Oh, that's great." Olivia scanned Jay with that intense look that said she was really seeing her, searching past the surface. "You okay?"

"Sure," Jay said automatically.

"Good. I should get inside." Olivia glanced at her vehicle, shrugged. "I guess if they tow it, they tow it."

"They won't bother it for a while."

"Thanks for riding in with him," Olivia said.

Jay slid an arm under Olivia's elbow. "I'm staying till we see how he does."

Olivia smiled. "Thanks. You know your way around better than me."

Jay led the way inside, aware Olivia hadn't just meant geographically. It did help to be on a first-name basis with the first responders when it came to getting regular updates on patients. She led Olivia along the familiar path to ER admitting, and the few staff around in the wee hours barely gave them a glance. Trauma admitting was just down the hall in the opposite direction, and she briefly wondered who was on duty. She waved to the charge nurse behind the desk in the ER. "Hey, Claudia. We're with the guy the paramedics just brought in. I guess you know who he is."

The brunette smiled distractedly. "Should I?"

"Uh, yeah, maybe," Jay said, lowering her voice. "He's the chief medical examiner."

"Uh-oh. Okay. I'll put a lock on his chart. Thanks, Flash."

"No problem. Can we check on him?"

"Yeah, sure," Claudia said, already turning back to the computer. "I think they're down in nine. Go ahead."

"Thanks."

Olivia gave her a look. "Flash?"

Jay colored. "Old nickname."

"It helps to know the important people," Olivia murmured.

Jay chuckled briefly. "In another six months, they won't remember me."

"I bet you're wrong. *Flash*."

The warmth in her tone was like a caress, and Jay luxuriated in the near touch until the sounds of the resuscitation caught her focus. The cubicle curtain was closed, but the familiar verbal exchanges of the code team projected into the hallway. Beau giving a report of the vitals, a doctor ordering meds to be given, a nurse updating the staff in the intensive care unit about the imminent transfer. They'd only be in the way inside, and as much as a part of her clamored to be behind that curtain, in the midst of the action, she accepted she didn't belong there, even as a concerned staffer.

"We probably won't know anything for a few minutes," Jay murmured, leaning against the wall opposite the cubicle. "I'm still trying to get my head around this."

"He seemed fine when we were talking to him." Olivia's expression grew pensive. "I had no idea he was ill, only maybe I haven't been paying attention. We aren't exactly close."

"No fault there," Jay said. "He's the right age for a coronary event. Maybe he's got a preexisting condition. And even if he does have a history, no reason you should know about it."

"Thanks for making me feel a little less responsible." Olivia grimaced. "He is my chief, though, and I never made much effort to get to know him very well." She rubbed her eyes. "Someone should call his family. I've never met his wife either."

Jay resisted the urge to rub the tension from Olivia's shoulders. All she could do was stand watch with her. "Why don't we wait until they get him stabilized. The ER doc can make the call to family then and give them his status."

"Yes, of course. You're right. I'm out of practice with this sort of thing." Olivia stepped against the wall to make room for a technician pushing a portable ventilator toward the curtain. "I speak with families all the time, but the circumstances are…well, as you know…"

"Yeah, I do." Jay shrugged. "Looked like you were on the ball back there on the street."

"Well, you never forget, do you."

"No, you don't."

Olivia studied her. "Is it hard for you? Being out here instead of in there?"

The question was almost a relief. Jay could say the words out loud to someone who would believe her. Ali and Vic would probably always be a little worried she couldn't adjust, couldn't give up the excitement and the clinical highs they lived for. Olivia took her at face value—no ghosts of her past getting between them. Not even her own. "Not as hard as I thought it would be. Not as hard as it would've been even a few weeks ago. I have a different place now. Different job to do."

"I'm glad it's getting easier. I know how hard it must've been. I'm very impressed with you."

Jay shook her head. "Believe me, I'm not impressive. I spent a lot of time feeling sorry for myself and being pissed off at fate, and generally whining. Nothing to be impressed about."

Olivia shrugged. "Anyone would've done the same, and for a lot longer. You've made an incredible recovery, and if I haven't said this before, I should have. I'm glad we got you as a fellow. You have a knack for the fieldwork and you know how to handle an autopsy as well as some junior attendings."

Jay sucked in a breath. She hadn't realized how much she needed to hear that. Not just that Olivia was pleased with her, but that the assistant chief medical examiner thought she was doing a good job. Thought she would be an asset. "I hate doing anything I can't do well. I just don't see the point in it. So you'll let me know if I screw up, right?"

"You can ask me that at this point?"

Olivia's amused smile was almost as good as a kiss. Almost. Jay very much wanted another kiss. Time to stop pretending she didn't. "Okay, point taken. And thanks for the positive reinforcement."

"Anytime."

"Listen—"

Beau pulled the curtain aside and stepped out, closing it behind her. "Hey."

"How is he?" Olivia asked.

"Stable. He's flipped his T-waves, so it's definitely an MI. They're calling in the cardiologists to take him straight up to cath and possibly stent him."

"Long night," Jay murmured.

"They're pretty fast," Beau said. "You've heard of the golden hour rule."

Jay, like every other first responder, knew the value of speed. Statistics showed if the heart could be reperfused within an hour, the heart muscle suffered much less damage and the chance of recovery was much higher.

"Yeah, I know it."

"Right." Beau blushed. "Sorry. Course you would know that."

Jay waved off the reminder she was no longer viewed the way

she had been as a surgeon, even by those who knew her. "Well, you busted your asses to get him in here as quickly as we could. You did good work."

"We all did. We're wrapping up here," Beau said. "You heading back down to the other scene?"

Jay looked to Olivia. "What's the plan?"

"I'll call Archie, but as long as there are no unexpected developments, I'll stay here."

Beau glanced back toward the closed curtain. "If you have a chance, can you call tomorrow and let me know how he does? That's one of the hardest parts of our job, not knowing sometimes if we made it in time or not."

"Sure," Jay said.

Bobby joined Beau and they headed off together. Jay glanced at Olivia. "Getting Greenly squared away is probably going to take the rest of the night, you know."

"Yes." Olivia sighed. "I'll have to make a few calls to the backup staff to cover the new cases. I ought to be able to take over in the morning."

"You'll be wiped out by morning."

"It's only a few more hours. I'll be fine, but you should go."

"Uh-huh," Jay said. "Coffee, something to eat?"

Olivia smiled in defeat. "Yes to both. Something sinful if you can find it. I don't even care if it comes in a cellophane package."

"Hey, this used to be my turf, remember? I know where all the best secret stashes are." Jay pointed down the hall. "You can call from the family lounge down there. I'll be back in a few minutes."

"Thanks."

"I'll let the nurses know we're waiting for an update too. They'll keep us informed."

Olivia squeezed Jay's forearm. "I'm glad you're staying."

Jay held still to keep Olivia's hand on her arm a few seconds longer. "So am I."

CHAPTER TWENTY

*H*ow *did those Spics end up selling their junk in our territory?"* a
man with a heavy Greek accent barked.

*"Ain't no way of knowing that, Toto. We can't watch every carload
of greasers cruising north of Bainbridge."* The second man's whiny
voice came over the wire high and snuffling, like his nose was stuffed
with cotton.

"That's what we paying you to do."

"Maybe it ain't the Spics."

*"Who else, the Russians? You know the boss says they're allies
now."*

The other man snorted. *"Yeah, till they ain't no more. Then we'll
be back to cutting their supply lines again."*

*"Listen, you little weasel. This is the second time thirteen has
dumped in our backyard, and now we've got cops crawling all over
the place. They'll be shaking down our dealers and going after our
distributors now."*

"We don't know who it is," the nasal underling whined.

*"Then find out. I don't want to have to tell the big boss we were
standing around holding our dicks while they were givin' it to us up the
butt."*

"We'll find him. Everybody's out on the streets looking."

*"You better do more than look. Otherwise, I'm sending you down
to the Tower and you can tell the man himself why we can't keep our
borders clean."*

"Yeah yeah, okay okay..."

The connection broke and Carmody sat back, satisfaction coursing
through her like a strong shot of good whiskey. Finally, something they
could work with. The pressure was on, and the street-level muscle

never looked at the big picture. Cracks were starting to form and would get wider as the inevitable repercussions rained down from the top. The little guys would be looking to take care of their own asses first, and the best way to do that was to cut a deal. Someone would talk. She copied the file, noted date and time, triangulated the towers and the cell numbers associated with it, and called Frye.

❖

Dell got to the six a.m. meeting at Sloan's a couple minutes ahead of time, still drinking her second cup of coffee of the hour on the way up in the elevator. Sloan, Jason, and Watts were already in the conference room. She dropped into a chair next to them with a groan.

"Long night, huh, boyo?" Watts said.

Watts looked better than he had any right to look if he'd been up as many hours as she had, and she figured he probably had. After they'd wrapped up witness interviews at the Galaxy, Watts had volunteered to follow up on the tip from the ME about their Jane Doe with the homicide guys, and missing persons too. He'd seemed almost eager to roust a few fellow detectives in the middle of the night.

"Did you get anything?" Dell asked.

Watts gave a slow grin, looking like he was enjoying himself. Hell, he probably was. For all his reputation of being a laid-back cop, he was like a pit bull on the hunt. He never gave up.

"Homicide turfed a female OD a while back that sounded an awful lot like the trio tonight—and guess who ended up with the case?"

He looked around at the blank faces and his grin widened. He pointed a finger at Dell. "Your squeeze."

"Sandy?" Dell's eyes widened. "Fuck. She told me she was working a case that might have something to do with a bad package or two, but I didn't have any reason to put it together with what we heard on the wire." She shook her head. "Man, I think I dropped the ball on that one."

Frye said from the doorway, "No reason to connect her case to what little we had to go on from the wire." She shrugged out of her topcoat and draped it haphazardly over an empty chair back. "You know how these things run. A bunch of loose threads that don't point anywhere until one little bit starts to knit them all together." She smiled, an altogether feral smile. "Maybe we have that little piece or two now. Carmody's got something for us too."

Watts drummed his fingers on the table. "*I* might have another thing working, Loo."

"Good. Hold that until Carmody and the rest get here," Frye said.

Five minutes later Carmody walked in with Sandy and Nunez. Dell hadn't seen Sandy for almost twenty-four hours, and she looked so good in her off-duty skinny jeans and tight stretchy top, her body came wide awake.

"Hey," Dell said.

"Hi, Rookie," Sandy said softly, and the teasing tone shot right down to the pit of Dell's stomach and went off like a firecracker.

"Team's looking better all the time," Watts said, giving Sandy a wink.

She laughed and sat down across from him and Dell. "Sounds like you missed me."

"You know," Watts said, "if you ever get a hankering for a guy with a—"

"Uh-uh." Sandy shook her head, and slid Dell a slow smile. "Your *whatever* is probably awesome, but I'm just fine, thanks."

Watts chuckled and Sandy introduced Oz to those he didn't know.

"So here's what we've got," Frye said, and everyone straightened up and got serious. "Sandy and Oscar have been working an unidentified Jane Doe who overdosed from a synthetic opioid. Point of origin for the drug unknown." She paused, looked their way. "I take it you haven't tracked down the source or dealer?"

"We haven't hit on much of anything," Oscar said. "We've been waiting for a repeat, but nobody's talking about anything new or who might be handling the shit."

"No repeats until tonight," Dell muttered.

Sandy swiveled. "You got another one? At the Galaxy?"

"That's why I got you two out of bed," Frye said. "We've been looking for some kind of connection to Zamora and an unknown faction who might be looking to disrupt his business or put his people in the spotlight. The first hint we got of anything came over the wire, speculation of a body dump in his territory."

"Our girl?" Sandy looked like she was about to burst.

Frye nodded at her. "Yes, that's what we think. The ME made a connect with the drug envelopes on our scene tonight. Victim profiles match too."

Watts cleared his throat. "Positive ID is pending, but it looks like her name is Mary Ann Scofield. A senior at Schuyler."

Sandy pounced. "How did you get that?"

Watts gave her a waggle of his bushy eyebrows. "I went to the source and woke up the college president, who woke up the dean of students. Helpful guy named Davoud." Watts glanced at Dell. "Once you had that student ID, I figured, why not find out if they all knew each other. So I asked this guy if they could track students who dropped out, especially if they aren't official. You know, like just stopped showing up."

"They can," Sloan said, "but with all the colleges around here, you'd have to know where to look."

"Yep." Watts looked at his notes. "Anyhow, Schuyler has this process called Early Warning System. If a student is an unexplained no-show for longer than a week, the professor submits a report online and that sends out an alert to all sorts of people—including the dean."

"Did they call missing persons?" Dell asked.

"This guy says that's standard after they go through their protocols first—checking with family, friends, the usual. He's going to look into it first thing this morning, but probably just got lost in the system."

"But you have a name already," Sandy said.

Watts nodded. "Only two students on his list were girls, and I tracked down one of them with a phone call. No one has seen or heard of Mary Ann, including her parents, who were out of the country until just a few days ago."

"Photo?" Frye said.

"Davoud is emailing me one from admissions as soon as they open at eight."

"Send that to Sandy and Oscar." Frye looked at Sandy. "She's still yours. Follow up with the ME after you get the photo. They'll advise family if and when."

"Got it, Lieutenant." Sandy tipped her head to Watts. "Nice going. I should have thought of that."

"Don't feel bad, sweet thing. Would have been hard to chase down without knowing the school first."

Dell grinned to herself when Sandy smiled. If anyone else had called her that, she'd have castrated him. She said, "We're gonna have to track down the friends and associates and see if we can pin down a dealer."

Sloan said, "It will be simple enough to check if all four of them are students at Schuyler. We'll have that from class records and dorm assignments for you this morning."

"You know," Sandy said, "they're probably all coming into town to score. This kind of stuff isn't all that easy to get."

"If it's the Salvadorans," Frye said, "they're smart enough not to peddle the stuff on a college campus. Someone would turn them in. I think this is a street-corner deal, and it's probably going down in Zamora's territory."

"If they're selling here," Oscar said in his lazy drawl, "they are a lot dumber than we think. Or a lot smarter."

"I think you can go with smart," Watts said darkly, "smart like a wolf pack smart."

"What I don't get," Jason said, "is what they gain by messing around in Zamora's territory—besides a war."

"Could be the market is better in this part of town," Frye said. "The kids they're selling to might be uneasy going deep into Salvadoran territory for a night's fun. This is close to Center City, and that probably feels like a safe zone to them."

Dell said, "And if things go bad, like this, MS-13 doesn't have the problem on their turf. It's in Zamora's backyard. That's a win-win for them."

"Seems to me they're putting their hand in the wolf cage while holding a bloody steak," Watts said. "They're gonna get bit."

"The Salvadorans aren't afraid to fight." Frye scanned her team. "I don't think they have any idea who they're up against, and before things get very bad very fast, I want a positive ID on this girl of Sandy and Oscar's, along with any association with these college boys from last night. Sandy, ride the ME for tox and drug screens. Let's be sure we're dealing with the same street drug. Everyone work your snitches and your CIs, and let's get on top of this before we've got more deaths."

Frye turned to Carmody. "You want to play us what you've got?"

"Sure." She cued up the computer and played the file for everyone to hear.

Sloan whistled softly. "Now, that's what we've been waiting for. A drug connection or retribution against the Salvadorans from Zamora's people can give us the hammer to use on the RICO case."

"Another piece," Frye said, "but proving the act goes all the way to the top is the challenge. What we need is someone to turn. Start squeezing his lieutenants."

Watts rubbed his hands together. "This is going to be fun."

❖

A rail-thin doctor with salt-and-pepper hair and sharp blue eyes, wearing rumpled scrubs and a clean white lab coat, walked into the family lounge at a little before six a.m. and looked around. "Mrs. Greenly?"

Penelope Greenly, a short, round woman with auburn curls just going gray, stood up quickly. "That's me."

"I'm Dr. Villanueva. We spoke on the phone. Your husband did just fine. We placed several stents—small tubes—through areas of blockage in two of his coronary arteries to reestablish the blood flow to his heart muscle. Everything went very well and the follow-up studies so far look excellent."

Penelope let out a long sigh. "Thank you all so much for everything you've done."

"Not at all," the cardiologist said. "He'll be in the cardiac care unit for a day or two. If all goes well, he should be home soon after that."

"When can I see him?"

"If you wait here, the nurse will call you once he's settled."

She sank down onto the sofa as the cardiologist turned to go, and grasped Olivia's hand. "Thank you, Dr. Price, and you too, Dr. Reynolds, for staying. Our daughter's on a plane from LA. I don't know what I would have done here all alone."

"Please, call me Olivia," Olivia said. "I'm glad everything has gone so well. You should try to get some rest after you see him."

"Yes, yes, I will." Penelope's eyes clouded and she blinked away tears. "You know, we've been talking this past year about Howard retiring, traveling, now that our daughter is through college and settled. It seems to me this is a sign."

"I'm sure you'll have plenty of time to talk that over." Olivia squeezed her hand. "I'll be available if you need me. Just call the office."

"Of course, thank you again."

Olivia and Jay left her waiting to see her husband. Outside in the hall, Jay murmured, "I guess you're in charge now."

"Acting, I suppose, at least until the state health commissioner appoints an interim replacement." Olivia pushed the elevator button. Morning shift hadn't yet arrived, and night shift was just finishing up work in preparation for the changeover. The hall was empty.

"You want the job, don't you?" Jay leaned a shoulder against the wall while the numbers above the elevator counted down to their floor.

She looked remarkably untired for having been up all night. She also looked remarkably attractive.

Olivia suddenly felt very much awake, on every level. "I do. This isn't the way I would've wanted to get it, though."

"No, who would? But if he does plan on retirement, you're a perfect fit for the job."

Olivia regarded her curiously. "How do you know that?"

"You're smart, an excellent clinician, a good teacher, and you care about the office. You wouldn't just be an administrator, but you'd be good at that part. Sounds like an ideal chief to me."

Olivia laughed. "Well, you're certainly good for my ego."

The elevator came and Jay held the doors open. The elevator was as empty as the hall. When Olivia brushed by her, she caught a hint of spice. How could she smell good after a whole night awake? That didn't even seem fair.

Jay followed her in as the door slid closed. Her gaze traveled over Olivia's face, dark and intense. "You know, I'd sort of like to be good for quite a few other things."

In two minutes they'd reach the ground floor, the doors would open, and they'd no longer be alone. In two minutes she'd be safe from the ache in her depths turning quickly to hunger. She could risk two minutes, couldn't she?

"You already are." Olivia gripped Jay's shirt in both hands and backed her against the elevator wall. She kissed her, not even waiting for Jay's lips to part before sucking her lip between her teeth, nipping hard enough to satisfy the need rising through her like a summer storm. God, God, she tasted good.

Jay groaned, pulled her close.

A faint bell penetrated the haze clouding Olivia's brain and she broke away. Her lungs screamed for air. Her body screamed for more. She gasped in a breath, turned as the doors slid open, and stepped out. Staff waited to get on, and she held her mask in place.

Jay caught up to her after a few steps. "Olivia—Liv…"

Olivia stared straight ahead. "I need to call the office."

"Okay."

Olivia pushed outside, stopped, turned. "We need breakfast."

Jay nodded, the same dark look in her eyes. "Hasim?"

Olivia shook her head. "No. My place."

CHAPTER TWENTY-ONE

Jay ordered her legs to move but nothing happened. Her body had suddenly gone on strike. One second Olivia was kissing her brains out, the next she'd strode out of the elevator and disappeared. Jay blinked. Good, not totally paralyzed. Maybe she'd imagined the kiss. Or dreamed it. Maybe she was actually still asleep upstairs in the waiting area. Hell, maybe she was still in a coma, because nothing quite like this had ever happened to her before. She'd been hit on, sure, and had women not too subtly let her know they'd be available for some friendly frolicking, but she'd never been *handled* before. Never had a woman just take what she wanted, and boy howdy, could Olivia make what she wanted crystal clear. Jay had thought she was a pretty fine kisser, but Olivia made her feel like a neophyte. Olivia's kiss was like a forest fire, incinerating everything in its path. Jay ran her tongue over her lips, just to see if they were blistered. Intact, but damn, her lips still tingled. Every muscle that wasn't still paralyzed trembled.

Jay looked down. Her shirt was half out of her pants and still bunched up from where Olivia had grabbed it. When she raised her head, a ring of curious faces peered in at her as people waited for her to exit. Okay. Not dreaming, then—although it would have been one hell of a dream—and hopefully not hallucinating. She clutched her cane in a white-knuckled fist. Definitely awake. And alone.

Holy hell. One kiss or a hundred, she'd take whatever she could. But she wasn't letting Olivia get away.

The waiting hospital staff, intent on starting their day, finally decided she wasn't getting out and crowded into the elevator. Jolted to life, Jay muttered, "Excuse me, sorry, coming out, sorry," and once free of the bottleneck, hurried as fast as she was able down the long corridor past the ER and out through the double doors to the parking

She'd made the same trip hundreds of times, only now she felt as she were traversing a strange new land. Everything was familiar but just slightly out of focus. She passed people she knew, responded to several greetings, and barely noted who they were. She wasn't certain she knew who *she* was. The only thing registering in her blood and her brain was the sizzling aftermath of Olivia's kiss, a kiss that had thrown her so off balance she was struggling to catch up, to keep up, physically and mentally. Mostly, though, struggling to figure out what came next.

By some miracle, Olivia's SUV hadn't been towed and still stood outside the ER, a warning note on the windshield but no ticket. Olivia pulled the limp paper, damp from morning dew, out from underneath her windshield, folded it one-handed without looking at it, and pushed it into the pocket of her coat.

"Lucky," Jay muttered.

"Mmm. My lucky morning, I guess." Olivia looked across the hood at Jay and smiled when she took in the half-dazed expression. Jay was undoubtedly used to sex on her terms, or at least sex on her timetable. Olivia really liked seeing Jay, usually so sexily self-assured, upended by a kiss. *Her* kiss. A kiss she had enjoyed far more than she'd imagined, and she had a very good imagination where Jay Reynolds was concerned. Olivia opened her door, paused. "Coming?"

Olivia almost laughed when Jay bolted the short distance to the passenger side and jerked open the door. If she thought about what she'd done, what she was doing, she might reconsider, but she wasn't going to think about anything for the next few minutes. She was just going to ride the wild storm of desire and exhilaration she'd kept chained in some dark corner for a very long time.

By the time Jay settled into the passenger seat, Olivia had started the engine, switched her phone to voice control, and was already talking to Archie. As Olivia swung the SUV around the lot and out onto the street, Jay mentally tried out half a dozen openings, none of which seemed exactly what she wanted. *I've never been kissed like that before and I'd really like you to do it again. What exactly did that mean? What comes next? Is breakfast a euphemism for sex, because if it's a choice between food and kisses, I'll happily starve?*

She'd never been left in a place where she didn't know the next move before. She wondered if this was what Olivia's Go opponent experienced when they received an email with some unexpected move they had no idea how to counter, something not written in their playbook, a challenge that left them scrambling for a plan.

"I have no plan," she murmured.

Olivia glanced at her, a half smile that said she knew just what Jay was thinking. That smile played hell with Jay's hormones all over again, and she was back to thinking about the next kiss—*when, how, how soon?* Since Olivia was all business again, talking to Archie, Jay had no chance to ask and was left twitching with pent-up arousal.

Archie's voice came over the speaker. "How's Dr. Greenly? Is it true he arrested?"

"Dr. Greenly is in the CCU. He's stable," Olivia replied. "Until further notice, I'll cover for him. Anyone who needs me should call my cell. You and the rest of the team from last night should sign out to Markham and Osaka. They can handle finishing the posts. I'll be in later today."

Archie said, "Thanks, Dr. Price. Looks like they're all pretty straightforward. The answers are going to come from tox on these three."

"I agree," Olivia said. "Please let everyone know there will be a mandatory meeting of the entire staff this afternoon at four. In the meantime, you and Darrell should take a break."

Olivia signed off, turned down the narrow alley to the parking lot, and slid the SUV into her regular space. She switched off the engine and turned to Jay. "What about you? Do you need a break?"

Jay released her seat belt and swiveled to meet Olivia's gaze. "I'm used to being up all night."

"Yes, but you might be a little out of practice."

At a lot of things, looks like. "I'm good." *I'm practically destroyed, but hey, I'm good besides dying for you to please do that again.*

"You mentioned something about a plan," Olivia said softly, every word sliding under Jay's skin and teasing her like feathers skimming her most sensitive spots. "What kind of plan were you thinking about?"

"You." Jay's voice broke and she swallowed dryly. "Ah, I don't know what's happening."

"Don't you." Olivia relaxed in her seat, looking as if she had all day and nothing more pressing to do than chat. "You mentioned a plan. Do you usually have one where women are concerned?"

"I suppose not consciously," Jay said, still floundering through a strange sea of disorienting sensation. "I suppose I don't think about it all that much. Usually when things come up, it's just a matter of opportunity. But I—"

"Opportunity, I like that idea." Olivia pulled out her keys, pushed open her door, and stepped out. "I suggest you not worry about a plan. Let's go inside and see what opportunities arise."

"Right," Jay said, still wondering if she'd walked into an alternate reality. "Right."

Hurriedly, she got out and walked down the alley beside Olivia as if this were an ordinary morning and not one that had turned her inside out before coffee. By some miracle, the sun was up, the sky was clear, and the coming day promised to be warm. Olivia's street was one of the few in Center City still lined with mature trees, and their branches were covered with buds on the verge of bursting open. When had everything changed?

"It's spring."

Olivia smiled. "It is. My favorite season."

"Mine too," Jay murmured.

"Here we are." Olivia led Jay up the broad stone steps of the brownstone, unlocked the door, and held it for Jay to precede her.

The foyer was wide and deep, extending a third of the length of the first floor, ending in a wide staircase with a gently curving banister and delicately carved spindles. An oriental runner covered the gleaming hardwood. A set of open French doors with wavy glass panes on her left led to a sitting room with a fireplace, a high-backed dark blue velvet sofa, two matching wingback chairs, a low coffee table with a stone inlaid top, and a massive marble fireplace with mahogany mantel. Another ornate area rug covered most of the floor. The original woodwork, paneled doors, and wainscoting gleamed in rich mahogany and walnut.

If Jay's mind hadn't been overloaded with questions about just how Olivia defined *opportunity*, she would have taken more time to admire her surroundings. But this was no ordinary morning, and no way could she muster up her best guest manners. She stopped abruptly.

Olivia took one step past her before turning back, a question in her eyes.

"How hungry are you?" Jay asked.

"Very." The way Olivia looked at her, as if food was the farthest thought from her mind, burned the last shred of Jay's restraint.

Need as hot as a furnace flared deep within and scorched away caution. Jay said, "I'd rather another kiss than coffee, and that ought to tell you how much I want the kiss."

"You don't say." Olivia took a step toward her, and for some strange reason, Jay backed up.

Olivia laughed. "Scared?"

Discovering she liked being stalked, Jay took another step backward. "Maybe. Should I be?"

"You know what?" Olivia's eyes danced as she slowly advanced. "I think so."

Jay put a hand out, found the smooth banister, knew she was close to the bottom step. Holding Olivia's gaze, holding the dare, she backed up again. *Come and get me.*

Olivia took another step toward her.

The rounded top of the newel post rose beneath Jay's palm, and she swiveled around until she felt the bottom stair behind her foot. She lifted a foot, stepped up, a head taller than Olivia now. Olivia advanced, crowding her, Olivia's breath on her throat, then her mouth glancing so fleetingly over hers Jay might have imagined it. Except her body registered the touch, and she gasped. Another careful step up, and again, Olivia followed. She wasn't going to make it to the top before the blood rushing into the furnace in her depths left her too weak to walk.

"If you go upstairs," Olivia said softly, "the only place to go is the bedroom."

"No place to hide, then."

Jay took a step, Olivia followed. "None."

"Then consider me caught."

Olivia stepped up beside her, took her hand, and tugged Jay around to face upward. "Come with me."

Olivia led her up the rest of the stairs and through an open doorway halfway down a hallway covered with ivory flowered wallpaper above more dark hardwood floors. Olivia touched a light switch and a chandelier came to life in the center of the high ceiling. At one end of the large room, early morning sunlight cut a pale swath across the far end of a four-poster bed with a stack of pillows piled against the carved headboard. Another fireplace adorned the small sitting area at the opposite end of the room.

Olivia released her hand and moved a few feet away. "Last chance."

Jay shook her head, unbuttoned her shirt, and let it fall open over the tight black silk tank she wore beneath. Olivia made a low humming sound in her throat.

"Let me do that." Olivia slid her hands under the tails of Jay's shirt, clasped her waist, and rubbed her thumbs up and down Jay's stomach.

Jay's muscles tightened so quickly it almost hurt. She arched her neck and closed her eyes, giving herself over to the touch, to the heat streaking through her. Olivia's mouth was on her neck, her lips soft, her teeth sharp. She bit, tasted her. Jay swallowed, her breath so short she was light-headed. She liked being caught.

"You're trembling," Olivia whispered, kissing her way back down Jay's neck to the hollow of her throat. She yanked the tank free of the waistband of Jay's pants and slipped her fingers beneath, her nails lightly scraping Jay's stomach. "Want me to slow down?"

"I want you to devour me," Jay gasped.

"Oh," Olivia murmured, breath coming fast, vision blurring with the fierce need to take. "I'm going to."

Olivia knelt, pushed Jay's tank up with both hands, and kissed her stomach, trailing the tip of her tongue down the center of her abdomen until she reached the waistband of her trousers. She teased one fingertip underneath and swept back and forth, pushing lower with each stroke.

"Fuck!" Jay gripped Olivia's shoulders to steady herself. Olivia's mouth was so hot, her mouth so demanding, so perfect on her skin, she wanted to cry. She never wanted to move. Couldn't move. She'd never wanted a woman to take her so much. Waiting was driving her crazy, and the last thing she wanted was to rush. "Just don't stop."

"Why would I do that?" Olivia ran her hands up and down Jay's thighs, feeling the rigid muscles quiver beneath her touch. She rubbed her cheek against Jay's stomach, feeling like a cat claiming its mate. She stroked her, petted her, felt the heat pour from her body. Jay's skin was softly misted, taut and salty, demanding to be tasted, her body a mystery demanding to be explored. Stop? Impossible. She wanted to stop time, revel in this moment forever. The power was intoxicating, so potent the sound of her pounding heart was deafening.

Need formed a fist in her throat, driving her to feed her hunger. She must have her, would have her, all of her, and soon. Pushing to her feet, Olivia gripped Jay's shoulders and pressed her backward, step by step. When they reached the side of the bed, she yanked the covers down with one hand and then unbuckled Jay's belt, opened the tab trousers, slid down the zipper. "I want to see you naked."

Jay shed her shirt and tank and kicked off her shoes as Olivia pushed her pants down her thighs. Once freed of her clothes, she froze. She'd forgotten the scars until Olivia's mouth was on her chest, lips softly moving over the marred inner surface of her breast. "That's from—"

"I know," Olivia murmured. Another scar, another kiss, another absolution. "Your body is beautiful. Lie down now. I want to have all of you."

Jay stretched out on the pure white sheets, as soft as falling into driven snow. Olivia loomed above her, somehow naked now too, her breasts swaying gently just outside Jay's reach, her hair tangled around her face, her thigh pressed between Jay's legs. Olivia stroked her shoulders, her breasts, her belly, the length of her thighs. Olivia kissed the places she had just caressed, moving slowly down Jay's body, her mouth pausing on each scar until Jay quivered with need, lingering on the places that made Jay shiver and moan.

Jay closed her eyes when the pleasure stole her reason.

"I adore touching you," Olivia whispered.

Then Olivia was beside her, kissing her, stroking the inside of her thighs, fondling the fire between them.

Jay arched, her breath caught in her throat, willpower snapping like a high wire in the wind. One touch, one kiss, one perfect stroke. "I'm sorry, I'm sorry, I'm going to come."

Olivia laughed, a wild, fierce cry, and Jay flew into a billion blazing fragments, knowing to the very depths of her being what it was to be owned.

CHAPTER TWENTY-TWO

O h," Jay gasped. "That was—"
    Olivia pressed her fingers to Jay's mouth. "We're not done yet."

"Yeah, good, God, my brain is mush." Jay kissed her, just wanting more of…everything. The sight of her, the taste of her, the piercing pleasure of her touch. "I want—"

"So do I," Olivia whispered. She straddled Jay's thigh, braced her outstretched arms on Jay's shoulders, and leaned over, her hair curtaining Jay's face again, her eyes dark and wide.

Jay gripped her waist, fingers curled over her hip bones, and pressed her leg hard between Olivia's. "Ride me."

Olivia's head snapped back, the muscles in her neck taut, sunlight gleaming in her hair.

"I want to make you come," Jay murmured. "Don't hold back. Don't wait."

Olivia's fingers tightened on Jay's shoulders and she slid, slick and hot, along Jay's thigh in short hard thrusts, her body trembling, faint cries tearing from her throat. Jay urged her on, rocking her up and down, harder and faster, until Olivia's eyes slammed shut and she stiffened with a startled cry. A convulsion ripped through her, and she collapsed on Jay's chest, a string of soft whimpers buried against Jay's throat.

"Oh yeah," Jay breathed, wrapping an arm around Olivia's shoulders, caressing the satin skin, slick now with pleasure and need. Olivia roused with a murmur and rocked her leg into Jay's center.

Jay's clit swelled and her legs tensed.

"You want to come again," Olivia murmured in Jay's ear, "don't you."

"So bad right now." Jay shivered. "I can't help it, you seriously wind me up."

Laughing, Olivia shifted enough to slip her hand between Jay's thighs, gliding easily down and inside her. "I haven't even started."

Olivia squeezed and Jay's hips bucked. Her heart stuttered and skipped. She lifted her hips, pushed into Olivia's hand.

"Now you're going to come again." Olivia rose to her knees, one hand pressed between Jay's breasts, holding her down, and stroked long and deep inside her.

Jay's gaze blanked. The orgasm shot hard and fast out of nowhere, tearing through her, ripping her asunder. Again and again.

"You like that," Olivia's voice in her ear again, low and teasing. "Don't you."

"Fuck yes." Strength sapped, Jay's arms and legs flopped uselessly, her body utterly sated. She turned her head a fraction, found Olivia's mouth, and kissed her. "I've never come like that for anyone. Never even doubled up before."

Olivia smiled, an altogether self-satisfied smile. She nipped Jay's lower lip. "Then I'm honored."

"Take all the credit you want." Jay laughed weakly. "No one has ever made me feel the way I feel right now."

"And how is that?"

"Wasted. Totally satisfied. Like I've possibly seen God."

Laughing, Olivia leaned on an elbow, trailing her fingers over Jay's chest, circling the shallow scar on her breast. "You're amazingly beautiful. I love your body."

"Believe me, it's all yours."

"You should be careful, saying things like that," Olivia murmured.

"Why?"

"I have an appetite for you."

"Liv, you can have me. Anything you want. Hell, everything." Jay brushed a hand down her abdomen, her body still not her own, simmering and ready to boil again. "I've never said that to anyone before."

"It's the sex," Olivia said quietly. "Your brain isn't quite working yet."

"The hell it isn't. My brain is fine. I know what I feel, I know what I want, and I know what I want you to do."

"Jay, this isn't—"

"Wait. Let me say this." Jay gathered her strength, needing to be clear. Wanting, in this moment when needs had been filled she hadn't even known existed, for Olivia to hear her. To *know*. "It's not the sex. All right—sure, it is. The sex is fabulous, amazing, mind-blowing. *You're* amazing. You are all I've been thinking about day and night, since the first time I walked into your office. You fascinate me, excite me, drive me a little bit crazy."

Olivia's expression grew remote, her eyes cooled. "Jay—"

"What you do to me—what you make me want, make me feel. No woman has ever done to me what you do." Jay read the retreat in Olivia's gaze and hurried on. "I'm not asking for anything except another moment like this." She laughed shakily. "A million moments might not be enough."

"Mmm," Olivia said, trying to make light of the moment, trying to escape the wild hunger surging, aching, torturing her with unbearable desire. "Like I said, great sex—"

"It's more, Liv—it's more…I—"

"Take this for what it is," Olivia said abruptly, her tone still soft. "We're good together, like this." She slid on top of Jay, gripped both of Jay's wrists, pinned them gently to the bed, her body moving effortlessly over Jay's, igniting fires everywhere she touched. "You feel how good we are. I can see it in your eyes."

"I'm breathing, aren't I," Jay gasped. "When I'm anywhere near you, when I even think about you, I'm on fire. From the first minute I saw you. Don't stop. God, don't stop."

Olivia's mouth was on hers again, demanding, devouring, driving thought from her consciousness. Her flesh sang of need and desire, opening, yielding, surrendering. Olivia kissed her throat, her breasts, the hollow valley of her belly and the divide between her thighs. Olivia's mouth was fire, her lips the promise of release. Jay arched, twisting in the storm of sensation and need.

"Let me have you now," Olivia demanded, "all of you."

Jay climaxed at the commanding sweep of Olivia's tongue. She gave and gave until she was hollow, an empty husk and yet somehow completely full. Groaning, she cupped the back of Olivia's neck, fingers tangling in strands of hair. "You finished me. I'm way past done."

Olivia leaned her cheek against Jay's silky inner thigh. "Good. That's all that matters." Olivia rose above her, flushed and victorious, and kissed her. "Just be."

Jay closed her eyes. Olivia filled her senses, her body, her heart. Too late, way too late.

❖

While they'd slept the sun had moved beyond the windows, leaving behind a diffuse pale glow in the place of the brilliant shafts of early morning light. Olivia lay curled with her back in the cradle of Jay's body, her breath wafting across Jay's arm, her breasts rising and falling gently, her creamy skin shimmering in the soft haze. If Jay couldn't still feel the aftermath of sexual satisfaction lazing in her depths, she might have imagined she was dreaming. In a way she was. She'd never expected to wake this way, so intensely sated, so astounded by who she had been just hours before.

Oh, she'd awakened with women before, not all that often, maybe, but enough times to know she'd never experienced such contentment, or such unabated desire. She'd never shared herself so intensely with anyone, never given herself so completely, with such mindless magnificent abandon. Never wanted anyone the way she wanted Olivia. Again. Right now.

Jay kissed the back of Olivia's neck and lightly traced her fingertips along the curve of Olivia's hip and over her abdomen, inhaling the scent of her shampoo and the fragrance of her skin. Olivia shifted, pressed her hips into Jay's, and suddenly stiffened, as if startled to discover where she was. Her breathing abruptly changed, not rapid, not anxious, but careful. Cautious. If Jay had to put a word to it, she'd call it wary.

"It's me," Jay murmured.

"I know." Olivia turned onto her back, a subtle movement putting just a little distance between them.

Ordinarily, Jay doubted she would have even noticed, but now, even that slight withdrawal was a warning sign flashing at the crossroads of her mind. She waited, a tight kernel of trepidation knotting her insides. She braced herself for the words she expected to hear.

This was good, and now it's over.

"You don't need to look so worried." Olivia kissed her quickly. "Nothing has changed."

Jay probably should have been relieved, but somehow, the small kernel blossomed into something larger, something she couldn't define. Olivia wasn't the kind of woman to regret a night of passion, but she might not want to repeat it. Jay understood that, rationally at least. She'd been on the other side of this equation a dozen times—trying to explain why something pleasant, something mutual, wasn't something she wanted to continue. She had no reason to put Olivia in the position of explaining what they both understood. They'd made no promises or plans. "I'm not worrying. This morning was great. And boy, does that not do it justice."

"It was, and I'm glad you're good with it." Olivia kissed her again, threw the covers back, and rose. She picked up her watch from atop the spindle-legged walnut side table and glanced at it. "Almost noon. I need to get to the office."

"I should go home and shower and change," Jay said, quickly abandoning the bed.

"I'll drop you." Olivia smiled. "I still owe you breakfast, and unfortunately, I think that might mean a quick cup of coffee here and Hasim's after all."

Acutely aware she was naked, Jay searched for her pants, pulled them on, and spotted her tank top beside the bed. "That's fine. I'm always good with Hasim's. Just hope he has some fritters left."

"We'll find one somewhere." Laughing, Olivia picked up the discarded tank top and tilted her head, her gaze raking down Jay's torso. "You know, on second thought, I think I like that look on you—barefoot and shirtless with just the trousers."

The tank dangled from her outstretched hand like a dare. And there it was again, the swift flood of desire and need surging through her so fast and hard Jay shivered. "Come on, Liv. You only have to look at me to get me started. I'll be wound up all day if you keep looking at me like that for another minute."

"Will you?"

"I've been wound up since I opened my eyes and discovered I really was lying next to you."

Olivia's breath quickened and lust flared in her loins. She was walking a dangerous line. No, she'd already crossed it in the last few hours more times than she wanted to think about right now. The need and unbridled desire in Jay's eyes were a powerful aphrodisiac, so powerful Olivia trembled. The urge to touch her, taste her, take her to that fever pitch and push her to the pinnacle of pleasure again was a craving guaranteed to drive her mad. Being with her was intoxicating, addicting, and could so very easily be all consuming. She'd already let her own needs seduce her into bed once, and if she wasn't careful, she'd spend every second thinking about when she could have Jay again. When she could indulge in that mind-melting pleasure again. Just what she had no time for, no room for, in her life. Just what she'd schooled herself not to want again. She held out the shirt. "You should put this on. There's no time."

"I think I've already proved it would only take a minute."

"Believe me, I'll be thinking about that for quite a while." Abruptly, Olivia turned away and opened a door that led into a bathroom. "I'd invite you to share the shower, but I can't promise I won't want my hands on you again. I'm sorry."

Jay's thighs tightened. Another minute in the same room with Olivia and she was going to explode. "I can guarantee I'd have my hands on you, so you better go without me. I'll shower at home."

"The kitchen's in the back downstairs, and the coffeemaker's on the counter by the sink. Go ahead and make yourself a cup of coffee at least."

"Okay. It's just…hell…" Jay slipped her arms around Olivia's waist and kissed her. "I feel like I should say something about this morning."

Olivia shook her head. "Why? We both know what happened. Unless you want to tell me you have regrets."

Jay laughed shakily. "Hell, no."

"Then there's nothing to say. Because neither do I." Olivia gently disentangled herself. "I'll be down in just a few minutes."

"Okay. Sure. Thanks."

Olivia disappeared and Jay finished dressing. She found the coffee in a canister next to the coffeemaker and had just poured a cup when Olivia walked in, somehow completely put together, looking cool and professional and completely fabulous. Her tailored light brown trousers and milk-chocolate silk shirt made her blond hair gleam golden, and her makeup was just subtle enough to accentuate the elegant lines of her face. In her rumpled pants and unbuttoned shirt, Jay felt distinctly outclassed.

"I feel like kissing you right now, but I'm not worthy of touching you."

"Believe me, you are anything but that. And I like the casual look on you. Very sexy." Olivia accepted the cup of coffee Jay held out to her. "It's probably safest that we avoid touching at the moment, however."

At the moment. Jay took heart at the suggestion there'd be some other time. Grasping at straws maybe, but she had to. She wanted her that bad. "You look amazing."

"Thanks. I—" Olivia's phone buzzed. She slipped it from her pocket to check the number and sighed. "Dr. Price…yes, all right, thank you. I'll make the calls…I'll let you know when they're coming."

Jay took a final slug of coffee and dumped the rest in the sink. "Something happen?"

"That was Officer Sullivan. They've identified our Jane Doe."

"Who is she?"

"A college student." Olivia set her cup next to Jay's and headed down the hall. "I need to make arrangements with her parents to come and see her."

"Is there anything you need me to do?" Jay thought back to the times she'd had to tell friends and family their loved one had died. There was no easy way to do it, but even in the worst of circumstances, death had not come as a complete shock. An accident, an emergency surgery, a long difficult recovery always carried the possibility of tragedy, and as much as those waiting for word from her hoped for a different outcome, part of them had already started to prepare. This was different. This family would be coming to view the body of their daughter in the morgue, an experience most people could never even contemplate.

"No, I'll handle it." Olivia paused. "On second thought, yes. As soon as you get in, find Archie and compare notes with him on last night, make sure we have everything covered. And then check on the status of the posts. You can update me after I've made some calls and handled things with the family."

"Okay, sure. I can do that."

Olivia chose her next words carefully. She'd been trying to find the opening since she'd reclaimed some of her senses in the shower, and this was the perfect opportunity. "With Dr. Greenly in the hospital, I'm going to be tied up a great deal of the time. Just so you know it's nothing personal."

Jay flinched but managed to keep her expression neutral. There it was, the not-so-subtle notice she'd been expecting of how things were going to be—or not be, more likely.

Nothing she could protest about, or even had any right to. "Right. I understand."

"Good." Olivia gathered her purse and keys. "I'm glad we have that settled."

CHAPTER TWENTY-THREE

O livia leaned back in her desk chair and closed her eyes. Almost one in the morning and still one more family to meet with. The first notification of the night had been Jane Doe, who had become Mary Ann Scofield, age twenty years, six months, a junior at an elite private liberal arts college. Her parents had arrived at the ME's building just before seven, the first of three families scheduled to gather in the small, secluded lounge adjacent to a long, narrow, unadorned viewing room where a body, swathed in a white sheet, could be brought in on a gurney and exposed under too-harsh lights for the family to formally claim. Most of the time, the identification signaled the destruction of a family's hopes and dreams.

Mary Ann's parents had been part of a missionary group in Southeast Asia, out of contact for much of their six weeks abroad, and had not realized Mary Ann had dropped out of sight soon after they'd left the country. Even upon their arrival home a few days before, they hadn't thought it unusual not to hear from her right away. Her mother—pale, shell-shocked, and disbelieving—had explained in a monotone that Mary Ann had never been good about keeping track of time.

"Always missing the bus to school," she'd said in a choked voice, as if Mary Ann were still a child at home.

Neither she nor her husband could believe their daughter had been involved with drugs.

"She was raised to be smarter than that," her father said hoarsely, his red-rimmed eyes fixed on the pale frozen profile of his daughter's body. "She wouldn't have done something like that if she'd had any idea of the danger."

"Young people often don't realize that some of the things available to them can be deadly, even the first time," Olivia said, while knowing her words brought no comfort, at least not then. Perhaps at some later time, when something penetrated beyond the pain.

Victor Gutierrez's family had arrived shortly after that, his single mother and her mother, both inconsolable. No, they hadn't known Victor had any involvement with drugs. He was a good boy, a good student, a good son. He never would've done something like this unless his friends had urged him on. The next boy's father had boiled with rage, his timid wife cowering silently by his side. *How could the boy have been so stupid with his whole life ahead of him. A scholarship to a good college, the best, better than anybody in the family had ever been to, after all the family had sacrificed for him. He wasted it all.*

Olivia had no answers and no words of comfort that would temper his fury but slipped her hand behind his wife's elbow as she swayed unsteadily, staring at her son.

"Did he suffer?" the mother asked in a quiet, diffident whisper.

"No," Olivia said. "I don't believe he did."

Tasha and Armand Abraham, one of the other MEs, were just finishing the third boy from the club. She would wait until they were done and meet with the family. None of the other families so far had had any information that would've been helpful for the police. Similar stories—healthy, successful children, loved and held with high aspirations for bright, successful futures. Olivia suspected the last family would be much the same. She'd promised Sandy Sullivan a call when all the identifications were confirmed. Sandy would probably interview the families again at some time, but unless something definitive arose during Olivia's discussions with them, it probably wouldn't be a priority.

After almost forty-eight hours with little sleep, her mind was dull and sluggish. All the same, she was grateful to be so busy. The meeting with the staff had gone well, and after the shock of Greenly's sudden illness had worn off, everyone seemed comfortable with her taking the reins for as long as he was incapacitated. Greenly's wife had updated her late that afternoon, saying the cardiologist expected Greenly would be in the hospital for another four or five days and not ready to go back to work for at least six weeks.

After talking to his wife, Olivia wondered if Greenly would ever return.

At the very least she could count on six weeks of intense physical and mental work. She hadn't exaggerated when she'd told Jay she would be very busy, even if she was glad for other reasons. Every spare moment when she hadn't been wrestling with some administrative problem or consoling the bereaved, she'd thought about Jay. Her concentration was shot—glimpses of Jay in bed, errant snippets of past conversations, visceral imprints of the sound of her voice, the heat of her flesh—kept intruding when she least expected. Six weeks of intense obligation and round-the-clock work wouldn't be enough to dull the memories or the desire, but it would help.

Olivia swiveled to her computer, brought up the message from her Go opponent, and read it again.

I believe in five moves, you will have defeated me. Congratulations, you are a worthy opponent. Shall we meet again in another contest?

Olivia typed, *Yes. You are the perfect opponent, someone who challenges me to be better than I believed I could be.*

She read it over again, hit send, and then rose to return the Go board to its starting position. She carefully arranged the stones, obliterating her last battle plan, wiping out the strategy she'd spent hours contemplating, preparing for the next encounter. It wasn't lost on her that her closest confidant, the person who occupied more of her thoughts, who respected her in a way she appreciated, was a stranger she'd never met. Until Jay. Once that person had been her mother and then, she'd believed, mistakenly, Marcos. Jay had swept into that aching void in her life and swept away her determination never to allow her irrational needs to rule her reason again.

Olivia turned from the board, took in the shelves laden with journals and textbooks, the files stacked on her desk. This office was her safe haven, even if it served more as a hideout than a sanctuary. Jay was the only one who really spent any time in here, other than her. She hadn't noticed before how easily Jay had become part of her life.

Olivia sagged back into her chair to gather her wits and her waning energy before starting in on the next task on her list. Before she could decide what to tackle first, someone knocked on her door. Frowning, she double-checked the time. Slightly after one. Other than the night diener and Tasha and Armand in the autopsy suite, everyone should be long gone.

"Who is it?"

"It's Jay."

Olivia's heart galloped, a troubling reaction, but not as troubling as the throb of arousal that sprang up instantly. Her system, it seemed, had already established its new set of reflexes, and Jay was tuned to wake all her senses. She steadied herself, ignoring the fluttering in her chest and the quivering deep inside. "It's open. Come in."

Jay entered, a McDonald's bag in her right hand. "I went over to Children's Hospital for fuel. I'm willing to bet you haven't had dinner."

"Ah," Olivia said, searching for an excuse to decline. Her stomach rumbled, and even if she hadn't been famished, she wasn't good at pretending. She *was* glad to see her. Very glad. "No, I haven't."

"And as I recall, we missed breakfast, and lunch was a fritter."

Olivia laughed, a lightness she couldn't discount and had no desire to smother energizing her. "And so you decided McDonald's in the middle of the night was a good idea? Have you ever heard of heart disease?"

Jay grinned, that disarming, oh-so-sexy grin. "Surgeons are immune."

Olivia tilted her head. "Maybe, although I don't believe there's any evidence for that. But you—"

Jay set the bag on the desk. "I know, not a surgeon anymore. But I figure I've got a grace period."

"Does it still hurt when you say that?" Olivia asked, unable to treat Jay as if she didn't matter. Unable to pretend she didn't care.

Jay shook her head. "I'm pretty much used to the change in self-image now. Not as big a switch as I thought."

"Good. I'm very glad."

"Mind if I join you?"

Olivia glanced up, saw that Jay had closed the door. "No. Sit down."

Jay pulled the chair across the rug until she sat opposite Olivia at the desk and opened the bag. She passed Olivia a large order of fries and a double cheeseburger. "Besides, I could tell from our first meeting you weren't a vegetarian."

"Why is that?"

"You burn too hot."

Heat flooded her face at that. "I think most vegetarians would take issue with that, you know."

"I hope most vegetarians aren't in a position to know about you."

Olivia plucked a fry from the cardboard sleeve and munched on it. "None that I know of, come to think of it." She paused. "And none in a very long time."

"Mind if I ask you why? You're beautiful, you're passionate, you're so fucking sexy I've been walking around in knots all day long, just wanting you to make me—"

"Jay," Olivia warned. "Do you have an off button?"

"Not where you're concerned, apparently." Jay unwrapped her cheeseburger, took a bite. After a moment she said, "And you're not answering me again. Why not, Olivia? Why no lovers?"

Her tone was quiet, not challenging, but insistent all the same.

"It's not something I enjoy talking about."

"Because you think you failed or...no," Jay said thoughtfully, "because you think you made a mistake."

Olivia sat up, anger coursing through her. "I *know* I made a mistake. A colossal one. And no, I haven't forgiven myself."

"Absolution, I think you called it when you were talking about me and my guilt over the accident."

Olivia shook her head. "That's completely different. You stopped to help someone who needed aid. You were hurt, nearly killed, your life as you knew it destroyed, and here you are. Succeeding again. Excelling again. There's nothing to compare what you did, and my marrying Marcos Ramon."

"Why did you marry him?"

"Because I was young and stupid and he was very, very good at making me feel special and desirable."

"He wouldn't have had to work very hard at that," Jay said, fighting down a surge of jealousy that made her want to find the guy and remove a few body parts, "since you *are* special and sexy and a million other amazing things."

"What I was was a naïve young woman who fell for the charms of an older man who made me feel the way no one had before."

"I don't think I like this guy very much."

Olivia laughed, despite herself. "Actually, you probably would if you met him. He's sophisticated, accomplished, charming. He was a colleague—kind of a friendly competitor, as far as academics compete—of my mother's. That's how I met him. He came on a dig in the Andes when I was nineteen."

"And I take it he turned out to be a dick?"

Olivia sighed. "What he turned out to be was a very clever man who convinced me I was the most important thing in his world, while he was actually using me to gain access to some of the people working with my mother and, ultimately, to her. By the time I realized he was having an affair with one of my mother's assistants, he'd already compromised some of her work. I don't think she's forgiven me yet."

"You didn't put him up to it, I'm sure," Jay said.

"Of course not." Olivia took a bite of the hamburger and then set it aside. "But I also didn't see him for what he was. I was too caught up in my obsession with him, or at least my obsession with what he made me feel. I'm not even sure if I'd known, what I would've done. He was a drug."

"Nobody before him?"

"No," Olivia said, weariness making her less cautious than usual. "I traveled with my mother most of my childhood and teenage years, so I wasn't schooled conventionally. Actually, I tested out of the first two years of college, so I hadn't had much experience with…anything, really, when I met him. And Marcos was so enchanting, his attention bringing out a part of me I hadn't even known existed. The need to experience that…insanity…suddenly took over my life."

"Sounds like pretty normal puberty to me," Jay said. "Maybe you started a little later than most given your upbringing, but that kind of sexual and emotional insanity is pretty common. It sure was for me. Maybe you should give yourself a break."

"I wasn't an adolescent, and because of me, my mother's work and reputation were endangered." Olivia grimaced. "I would've done anything to keep feeling the way he made me feel. I was a fool."

"I understand what you're saying." Jay folded her empty cheeseburger wrapper into a precise square and dropped it into the empty red french fry sleeve. "I know what it's like when someone throws open doors inside you didn't know were there and you end up riding an incredible wave of excitement. You just want it again and again."

"I *don't* want it again," Olivia said. "Believe me, I'm done with mindless passion."

Jay let out a long breath. "What about pleasure, then, safe on your own terms?"

Olivia shook her head. "I appreciate it, but that's hardly fair to… someone, is it."

"Well, that would be for *someone* to say." Jay sat forward, done with word games. "What if I told you I was good with that? Your terms, your call when and where and how much."

"You might think now you'd be good with that, but you…" Olivia laughed softly. "You have too much inside you, too much power, too much passion, to hold anything back. You deserve to receive the same."

"Again, up to me to say," Jay said.

Olivia rose, gathered the trash into the white bag, crumpled it, and dropped it into her wastebasket. "Yes, you're absolutely right. It is for you to say what you want, and it's for me to say what I'm comfortable with, what I can do. What I *want* to do. And right now, the only thing I have room for, time for, is right here in this building. I have to go meet with the last family now."

"Of course." Jay grabbed her cane and stood as Olivia headed for the door. "Say, Olivia?"

Olivia looked back, one hand on the door.

"Are you sure it's Marcos you're trying to get away from? Because he's not here any longer."

Wordlessly, Olivia walked out and quietly closed the door.

CHAPTER TWENTY-FOUR

When Sandy walked into the bedroom, Dell was lying facedown on the bed, fully clothed and sound asleep. For half a second she contemplated dropping down beside her but decided she had to have a shower before anything else. She was pretty certain she could still smell the morgue in her hair. Even though the place didn't smell bad, with the ubiquitous hospital smell of cleanser and whatever else they used to sanitize places like that, in her imagination, she smelled death. The memory of cloying sweetness masking the bitter tang of decay was real enough, and not anything she wanted to take into bed with her and Dell.

Taking just a second to grab on to the scent of life, needing the warmth and excitement and steadiness Dell brought her, she leaned over and kissed Dell's cheek. When Dell's eyelashes fluttered, she whispered, "Hey, Rookie, you want to take a shower?"

Dell grunted and rolled onto her side, reaching out blindly with one arm, catching Sandy around the waist and dragging her down to the bed. Eyes still closed, she burrowed her face into Sandy's neck. "Depends. You're going to be there too?"

"What, you were thinking of someone else, maybe?"

Dell drew back, her lids lifting, her gorgeous mouth curved into a slow smile. "I never think of anyone else, baby."

Sandy kissed her. "Good answer. And yeah, I'm going to be there. It'll have to be a quickie, though."

"The shower or the sex?"

"Either or both. I gotta get some sleep, and then I gotta get back out there."

"Yeah, me too." Dell rolled onto her back and pulled Sandy on top of her. "You getting anywhere?"

"Uh-uh." Sandy braced herself on her elbows, her legs naturally fitting between Dell's, everything naturally fitting, just like always. The pall of pain and loss lifted, and then it was just the two of them, like always, in tune, together. "Didn't turn up anything more than what we already had. None of the dead kids had any serious drug history. We still have to talk to their friends, see if we can get a line on who hooked them up with whoever sold them the shit they took, but you know what that'll mean."

"Yeah, a lot of hours chasing after a bunch of kids who probably don't know anything or are afraid to mention anything they might suspect, but you never know, you might hit on something."

"Well, that's the job." Sandy shrugged. "But man, sometimes getting through to these privileged types is tough. They just don't believe bad things can happen to them. At least out on the street, people know the score."

"Funny, isn't it," Dell said, "how the so-called criminals are more help than the upstanding citizens."

"Well, the girls know we're trying to look out for them, at least." Sandy rested her cheek on Dell's chest. "What about you? Anything?"

Dell toyed with a strand of slightly curly blond hair. "The only thing everyone pretty much agreed on was seeing more in the way of street-corner turf battles. Small stuff that would have gone unnoticed if you weren't actually hunting for it."

"Huh. Retaliation, you think? Or testing to see if there's push-back?"

"If MS-13 is trying to play chicken with Zamora, they're in for a nasty surprise." Dell snorted. "Zamora's crew will come charging back."

Sandy sighed. "I hope we're wrong about what's brewing."

"All we can do is be ready." Dell rolled Sandy over, kissed her, and pulled her up from the bed. "Come on, let's take a shower and catch a couple hours' sleep."

"I've got a better idea." Sandy grinned. "Let's get reacquainted first."

"Okay, but I gotta tell you, baby…" Laughing, Dell pulled her shirt off over her head, tossed it aside, and headed for the bathroom. "I remember you."

❖

When Catherine heard the front door open and close, she poured a second cup of coffee. Rebecca walked into the kitchen a minute later, and Catherine held out the cup. "Long night."

"Ugly night." Rebecca kissed her, took the coffee, and sipped absently. Rebecca looked impeccable as always, but her eyes were tired and something else…worried, sad perhaps.

"What was it?" Catherine asked.

"Three kids dead from overdoses at a club."

Catherine's stomach twisted. She was a psychiatrist, but death was no stranger to her, not working with the police, not with a police detective as her lover. "That's a nightmare."

"Yeah, it is." Rebecca pulled off her blazer, dropped it over the back of a kitchen chair, and pulled Catherine into her arms. She closed her eyes and buried her face in Catherine's hair. Some of the despair seeped from her soul, driven out by the reminder of what was good and strong and beautiful in her life. She caressed Catherine's cheek, kissed her again.

"How did you get involved with that?" Catherine asked.

"We think there might be a connection between those kids and a previous girl who OD'd. All of them are on Zamora's turf."

"That seems too…convenient," Catherine mused.

"You're right," Rebecca said, "and that's why you are so good as a profiler."

"You think it's some kind of setup?"

"Maybe," Rebecca said. "Or just an opening volley in a war."

"Sooner or later, you'll stop it." Catherine sighed. "Are you going to be able to get some sleep? You've been out all night."

"A bit. Don't worry."

"How about I stay for a little while?"

Rebecca's brows rose. "You're all ready for work."

"Mmm." Catherine laced her arms around Rebecca's waist, leaned back in her arms. "Are you afraid to muss me up?"

"I've always thought you were incredibly beautiful and totally sexy no matter what you were wearing—pj's or one of your very elegant suits." Rebecca chuckled. "And I've never really worried about mussing you up. Do you have time to be mussed?"

"Actually, I do, if you have the energy."

Rebecca pretended to frown. "Are you questioning my prowess?"

Laughing, Catherine kissed her. "Not your prowess, darling. Stamina, maybe."

"You have no idea what you're in for, then."

"Oh, I think I do. But I wouldn't mind if you reminded me." Catherine grasped her hand and tugged, pausing when Rebecca didn't move. "What is it?"

"I love you—you know that, don't you?"

"I do," Catherine said gently. "I know that with every breath I take, and I count on it with every beat of my heart."

"I'm glad, because I don't know any other way to show you, except..." Rebecca shrugged. "Words don't work."

"Words are nice, wonderful," Catherine whispered, "but what really matters to me is that when you need a place to rest, a place to heal, a place to be happy, you come to me."

"Always."

"And that's how I know you love me, Rebecca." Catherine tugged her hand again. "Now, come on upstairs and muss me up a little bit."

❖

"What the fuck happened?" Kratos Zamora demanded of his stone-faced captain. "Why are the cops crawling all over my club? Benjamin has been on the phone since three in the morning. I'm going to have them in the lobby in another couple minutes."

"That's why Benjamin is your attorney. He'll throw up road-blocks." Spiro Pavlou dressed like a businessman at all times. His shirt was Irish linen, his tie silk, his charcoal suit custom tailored, and his imported Italian loafers gleaming. Kratos had no immediate successor. His children, a son and a daughter, were still too young to introduce to the business. Of the two, his daughter was more likely to follow in his footsteps. She was quick, tough, and incredibly loyal. At fourteen she had an inkling of where the family fortunes came from and didn't seem bothered by it. Kratos had already told her law school or business school first, preferably both, and then she could move into an office next to his. Until then, Spiro was the de facto heir, and he understood his position would be that of regent until Kratos's children came to power. For now, though, he was still accountable for the mistakes that happened, no matter whose they were.

Kratos chopped the air, a rare show of temper for him. "I'm not interested in how effective Benjamin might be in deflecting the police, I want to know why I even have to worry about it."

"Three kids OD'd—"

"I know that," Kratos said with exaggerated calm. "What I *want* to know is how it happened. Who the hell sold them the shit? According to what Benjamin could get out of the cops, they probably bought the stuff inside our club."

"We don't know that for certain." Spiro slid his hands into his perfectly creased trousers. Unlike Frankie and some of the old-time captains, Spiro didn't worry about telling Kratos what he wanted to hear.

"Where is it coming from?" Kratos asked.

"We don't know, but everything points to the Salvadorans dealing in our territory."

"In our clubs?"

Spiro didn't sugarcoat it. Bad was bad. "On the street for sure, and considering last night, probably in the clubs too."

Kratos rose, strode to the floor-to-ceiling windows, scanned the barges on the river a quarter mile away. He'd scaled back on the waterfront enterprises after the police broke up their lucrative trafficking ring, and he couldn't afford to have his clubs and the backroom enterprises they supported shut down while the police crawled all over them. "We can't have this—it makes us look weak and it puts us too much under the microscope with the police. I don't want that fucking Frye in my office."

Spiro grimaced. "I think that might happen. You do own the club, and considering these were college kids and not some ghetto rats…"

"I own a lot of things."

"Yeah." Spiro lifted a shoulder. "True."

"Send the little bastards a message," Kratos said. "It's time they stopped climbing up our asses. Let them know who the big dog is."

"How big a message?"

"One they can't misinterpret."

"All right," Spiro said carefully. "I'll see that it's done."

"And make it soon," Kratos said as Spiro turned to leave. "I want them to know if they piss in my yard, we're going to tear their throats out."

Spiro nodded.

When he hit the sidewalk, he pulled out his cell phone and made the first call.

CHAPTER TWENTY-FIVE

Jay waited for Archie to dictate the last post, coordinated all the field notes from the techs, and compiled summaries to forward to Olivia. By then it was almost five in the morning. Olivia had said she was going to meet with the last family, but they had come and gone, and a light still burned under her office door when Jay was ready to leave. She paused outside the door but didn't knock this time. She was tired, beyond tired, and Olivia must be too. As much as she wanted to see her, as much as she craved hearing her voice, yearned for a glimpse of the haunting, incandescent smile, she needed to regroup before she talked to Olivia again. She definitely needed to wrestle with her runaway emotions and totally out-of-control libido.

She wasn't too proud or too arrogant to court her, hell, to plead with her if necessary, but she also wanted to respect Olivia's needs and her wishes. Olivia had been burned by some bastard who made her believe that her feelings were somehow responsible for his unconscionable actions. And now Olivia wanted to disown the very passion that made her unique. If ever there was a crime, that was it, to incite guilt over what was so natural, so incredibly beautiful. Olivia hadn't forgiven herself yet for trusting Marcos and for the harm done to her mother, even though Olivia was guilty only of trusting the wrong person. Jay only hoped she could convince Olivia to dare to trust again.

Jay walked out of the building, fatigued from the long, arduous night of heartbreaking work and consumed with the unexpected revelation of how intensely she had connected with Olivia. She didn't register where she was until she stood in the hall outside the trauma admitting area, like a horse that came home to the barn out of habit, returning to the only safety it knew. She grimaced and spun around.

Ali stood an arm's length away. "Hey, what are you doing here?"

"Wish I could tell you that." Jay ran a hand through her hair. "Daydreaming, I guess."

Ali smiled, but her eyes were wary and worried. "At this hour of the morning, I'd have to say it was more like a nightmare. You okay?"

"Yeah," Jay said. "You're right, though, I'm beat. I was just walking. This is where I came."

"You're always welcome here." Ali checked her watch. "I've got a little time before rounds. Buy you breakfast?"

"Hey, I'm fine. You don't need to babysit me."

Ali didn't smile, just shook her head. "I guess you don't get that I miss you and, you know, I love you."

Jay sighed with equal parts shame and tenderness. "I'm sorry. I'm an ass. I miss the hell out of you too. Even more than I miss…" She lifted a hand. "All of this. I never thought that would happen."

"Come on, we've got time for the cafeteria." Ali squeezed her shoulder and didn't let go until Jay fell into step beside her. They went through the cafeteria line together as they'd done countless times before, choosing the too-yellow scrambled eggs, the underdone bacon, and the dry toast just like always. Extra-tall steaming mugs of coffee completed the ritual, and they grabbed a table by themselves over by the windows.

"I thought you were getting along okay there," Ali said, doctoring her coffee with three creamers and an honest-to-God sugar.

"I am." Jay dumped creamers into her coffee, thinking of all the times she'd brought Olivia coffee over the past few weeks. Everything she did somehow made her think of Olivia. "Just a long night, some senseless deaths—you know how that feels."

"I do. I'm sorry to hear it." Ali made a sandwich out of her eggs and bacon and took a big bite. A few seconds later, she said, "I've never really seen you thrown off stride by the tough ones before. Bothered, sure. Sad for the families. Pissed off at the waste and needless suffering, sometimes. But that's not what I'm seeing now. Somebody on your case? Giving you a hard time?"

Ali sounded like she was ready to go to battle. She probably would if Jay told her she needed backup. There'd been plenty of times when she was a kid that Vic and Ali had been ready to do the big sister protector routine. Jay smiled, glad to be home for a few minutes. "I don't think you can help me out of this one, but thanks."

Ali's brows lifted. "Ah. Woman trouble."

Jay laughed for the first time in what felt like a century. "You didn't just say that."

"I'm right, aren't I?" Ali's tone held a little bit of a challenge, a little bit of sympathy. "Tell me, is it the beautiful Dr. Price, assistant chief medical examiner?"

"Acting chief medical examiner now," Jay said. "Greenly's in the cardiac intensive care unit. Had an MI out in the field last night. Emergency cath. He's probably gonna be okay, but Olivia is in charge for now, possibly permanently."

"Wow. Sorry to hear about Greenly. Is Olivia happy about being interim chief?"

"Oh yeah. She's right for it, will be great at it."

Ali frowned. "Are you bothered by it?"

"No," Jay said, pushing her eggs around on her plate. "At least, I wouldn't be if she wasn't using it as an excuse not to get involved with me."

"Oh, the tangled web gets thornier." Ali leaned back in her seat, sipped her coffee, watched Jay for any sign of trying to skirt the issues. "So you made a move and she said *Sorry, not in my career path*?"

Jay laughed. "See, you just don't give me enough credit."

Ali smiled. "How so, hotshot?"

"*I* didn't make the move. Olivia took me to bed and thoroughly…" Jay's throat constricted. Images of Olivia stripping her down, straddling her, making love to her until she couldn't move a muscle crashed through her brain. Her mouth went dry, her words died, and her heart threatened to stop in her chest.

"Wow again." Ali looked intrigued now. "*She* took *you* down?"

"Thoroughly and completely."

"And then she dumped you."

Jay winced. "Not exactly. Not the *we should just be friends* line. Definitely not the *this was a mistake* line. More like *I'm going to be really busy and it's not a good time to get involved* line."

"Well," Ali said thoughtfully, "of the three, that's probably the best. It's not exactly *I don't want you, you were terrible in bed, and there's no future* kind of thing. It's more like…*I'm scared out of my mind*."

"Maybe," Jay said quietly. "Or maybe she really would just rather focus on work and her safe game of Go."

"Huh?"

"Go…she plays some high-level strategy game online. I don't think I could even learn the rules."

"Sounds like she's avoiding something."

"Maybe," Jay said again. "I don't want that to be me."

"There's more," Ali said carefully. "I can see it in your face. You don't need to tell me if it's Olivia's business. That's between you and her. But as a friend, you can tell me how you feel."

Jay pushed the tray away and cradled her coffee cup. "I'm pretty much helpless here. I—" She blew out a breath, shook her head. "I'm pretty much falling for her."

"More than sex."

"Way more."

"All right then."

Jay frowned. "All right then?"

"If you're in that deep, that way, you can't walk away until she tells you there's no chance. And you can't push too hard, because she might walk."

"Like I said—kind of screwed here."

"Oh, come on—since when did you get so cautious. You're observant, read her. Not what she says, what she does. Pay attention to that. Since you've never mentioned getting so hung up on anyone like this before, I have to believe it's different."

"It's definitely different." Jay let out a long breath. "Oh, man, is it different. I don't even recognize myself."

"She really took the legs out from under you."

"Actually, she did. Literally."

Ali laughed. "You know, I'm picturing her, and she's slender and elegant and, you know, you're not exactly delicate, and she…" Ali waggled her hand.

"Yeah, she did. Rolled me over and made me beg."

"I think I like her."

"That's good, because I love her."

Ali stared.

Jay had to remember to breathe. "Oh, fuck."

"Congratulations," Ali said softly.

❖

Just before seven, Olivia finally reached Greenly's secretary and got his calendar for the upcoming two months. By seven thirty she'd gotten through most of it, emailed colleagues and the state board members who needed to be informed about his status, and sent instructions to Pam to reschedule his meetings for her. She also had Pam reassign several seminars Greenly was to have given to the other MEs. When things looked like they were reasonably under control, she hurried outside for coffee before morning rounds. Jay was just paying Hasim when Olivia got to the food truck, and for one instant, she considered escaping before Jay saw her. And wasn't that ridiculous. Of course she could see her and not make an idiot of herself, sweaty palms or not.

"Hi," Olivia said.

"I got your coffee," Jay said.

"You didn't need to," Olivia said quietly.

"I was getting mine anyway. Bagel and cream cheese okay?"

"I'm not even sure I can eat anything," Olivia said wearily.

"You'd better. I know what you had for dinner."

Olivia thought back to the McDonald's in the middle of the night. Jay had been quietly taking care of her, thinking about her and what she needed, last night and now. The realization was foreign, the pleasure a little frightening. She couldn't think about it for very long or she'd give in to the urge to head back to her apartment with Jay, crawl under the covers, and sleep for the rest of the day.

"You should go home," Olivia said. "Technically, you're not even supposed to be here after twenty-four hours on call. It violates the residency—"

"Bullshit, Olivia." Jay's voice was low and dark, just a little bit angry. "I'm not going home."

"I could order you to go home," Olivia said, digging in her heels, and she wasn't even sure why. In Jay's place, she would stay too. Any responsible fellow who wanted to get the most out of their training never paid attention to the ridiculous residency rules about mandatory hours on call and off, as if medicine were a nine-to-five job and no one got sick at night. But she didn't think they were talking about the fellowship, and she needed to keep their relationship on the level of two colleagues, working together. "All right, stay until after morning rounds. Then you're going home."

"Thanks," Jay said tightly. She paid Hasim, handed Olivia her coffee, and juggled the food bag, her coffee, and her cane as they walked.

"How is your leg?" Olivia said quietly. "You're limping a little this morning."

"Just not used to all the exercise."

"Are you taking anything for it?"

"Motrin when I can remember, which is almost never."

"I've got some in my office. We can stop there first."

"I'm fi—" Jay nodded. "Yeah, that'd be good, thanks."

When they reached her office, Olivia set her coffee cup on the desk and rummaged around in her top drawer until she found the ibuprofen bottle. She shook out three and looked up to find Jay close beside her. Bruised gray circles smudged her lower lids, her dark hair was tousled, her face paler than usual. Olivia stopped just before she reached out to cup Jay's cheek, instead, offering the pills. "Are you sure you're all right? You're not in too much pain?"

Jay covered Olivia's hand, laced her fingers through hers. "Does it count if my heart aches?"

Olivia took a sharp breath. "Jay, I don't want to hurt you."

"Then don't write me off."

"I never said that."

"Then what's the *I'm too busy to see you* line mean?"

"It's true." Olivia paused, closed her eyes for second. "As far as it goes, it's true. And I suppose, yes, it's also a good excuse for me to put a little distance between us. I don't want what you make me want."

Jay's face blanked. "Right. Sorry. I'm pushing you and I didn't mean to."

"If we could just—"

"Hey, you already told me what you wanted." Jay took a step back. "I should've listened. I'm listening now. It's okay. We have to work together, and you've got a lot of work to do. I don't intend to make you uncomfortable."

"Thank you," Olivia said, pushing aside the irrational spear of disappointment. She'd gotten what she wanted, and sooner or later, she'd be glad about that. "We should get to rounds."

Jay picked up her coffee, tilted her head toward the bag. "Take the bagel with you. You can eat it when nobody's looking."

"What about you?"

"I had breakfast earlier with a friend."

"Oh, all right then. Then we should go."

Jay held the door silently as Olivia passed through. There was nothing left to say.

CHAPTER TWENTY-SIX

Olivia ate the bagel and didn't care who noticed her eating during rounds. She wasn't particular about formalities, and even if she had been, half the department had been up all night in the field and in the Graveyard. Everyone was drinking coffee and most were finishing a hasty breakfast. As much as her weary brain would let her, she focused on the residents, fellows, and students presenting cases. But even as she worked, she was aware of Jay, slouched in the front row, one leg stretched out in front of her, cradling her coffee cup on her thigh. Not noticing her took more effort than Olivia could manage—the spark of pleasure too addicting to ignore. And that was the problem, wasn't it? Already she was incapable of setting any kind of limits on her attraction, and the hunger she'd staved off for so long gnawed at her. Jay stirred all her appetites. Worse even than the physical craving, as dangerous as that was for her, was the ache of simply missing her.

When the session ended, concerned and curious colleagues waylaid Olivia, inquiring about Dr. Greenly's condition or attempting to schedule meetings they'd apparently been trying to set up with him without results. As she answered what she could, she caught sight of Jay walking out with Archie and Tasha. Jay didn't look her way.

When Olivia reached the hall, Jay was gone.

Chalking up the instant sense of deflation to fatigue, Olivia headed to her office to face a new onslaught of emails with directives from the Board of Medical Examiners about her transition, committee meetings she'd now need to attend, and reports on open cases. Pam called every few minutes for instructions on how to handle some of Greenly's appointments and correspondence. By the time Olivia had wrangled the backlog into a manageable state, it was midafternoon. Time to go home and sleep.

Out of habit, she made one final check of her mail and clicked on a new message from her Go opponent. An image appeared with the opening move in their new game. She shook her head, recognizing the classic first move that set up a familiar and difficult strategy. Having studied many previous games by the masters, she also knew the countermove, at least the conventional and probably anticipated one. The conventional would never be enough to defeat this opponent. She answered quickly with an unorthodox move of her own, documented the board with an image, and sent it off. The message she sent with it was brief: *What would be the point of playing a safe game when the risk is so much more interesting?*

She clicked send and didn't bother to ask herself why she suddenly felt like taking a risk.

She drove home in that half awake, half on the verge of sleep state she'd gotten used to after years of taking night call, and started shedding her clothes as soon as she got inside her front door. By the time she reached her bed, leaving a trail of discarded items behind her, she was nude and her mind was mercilessly empty. She pulled down the covers, dropped facedown, and slid her hand across the sheets to the space where Jay had lain beside her. Imagining the warm flesh beneath her fingers, she slept.

❖

Olivia's phone pulled her from a deep and dreamless sleep. Almost awake by the time she found it and answered, she said, "Dr. Price."

"Sorry to wake you, Doctor," Roxanne Markham, the tech on call, said briskly, "but we've got an all call."

An all call. Mass casualty alert. Olivia sat up abruptly, her mind completely clear. "What and where?"

"Initial report was a fire, but now we're getting first responder reports of a bomb. A bar at Second and Moore. Fire rescue, police on scene."

"Casualties?"

"Multiple, exact number unspecified."

Olivia stepped into the bathroom and turned on the shower. "I'm on my way. Are you notifying first and second on-calls?"

"I was thinking I'd call everyone."

"Put everyone on standby at least," Olivia said. "We can update them when we assess on scene."

"Got it."

"Thanks, Rox."

"We're rolling. See you there."

Not bothering to wait for the water to warm, Olivia allowed herself a minute under the lukewarm spray to rinse away the sleep, then dressed as quickly as she had showered. She was downstairs, out the door, and to her car in under five minutes.

Three a.m. The sky was cloudless with a bright, nearly full moon. She'd slept almost ten hours. Hopefully Jay had done the same.

The blaze was visible from five blocks away, a shifting tide of crimson churning in the sea of black. The traffic snarl started a block later, and she slapped her portable flasher onto her dash, adding her strobe to the dozens of others swirling atop the haphazard morass of fire trucks, ambulances, and police vehicles. Once she'd threaded her way through the progressively clogged streets until she couldn't drive any farther, she parked, pulled down her visor with the *ME on Call* sign clearly visible, and grabbed her gear.

This time the club itself appeared to be a victim, as well as its patrons. The face of the ground floor corner establishment was illuminated by emergency light bars and a large portable halogen light set up in the middle of the roped-off intersection. What had been plate-glass windows were now shattered into glistening shards and spikes and scattered over the street. The brick façade with its blown-out eyes was scorched. Black streaks climbed from the empty orifices toward the second floor like upraised arms searching for rescue, and sooty water dripped down from above, sluicing along windowsills and doorjambs to puddle in the street. The door itself, a plain black rectangle, hung askew on one bent hinge. Flames shot from the rooftop of the adjoining building, and two ladder trucks extended long mechanical arms into the air where firefighters doused the fire with high-pressure hoses.

Olivia approached a patrolman, identified herself, and asked, "Who's in charge?"

"Incident commander is Pete Gonzalez. He's around here somewhere—short guy, black hair, mustache, trench coat."

"I'll find him." She moved a few feet away, out of the stream of spent water falling from the hoses. "What's the status on the fire?"

"Last I heard it's contained. They expect to have it under control any minute."

"Clear to go inside?"

The patrolman shrugged. "Plenty of people been coming in and out, but officially I guess you have to ask Pete."

Olivia winced inwardly at the likelihood of the scene being compromised by all the activity, but nothing she could do to change that now. She just needed to ensure the bodies were undisturbed. "Thanks—will do. Is there somewhere we can park our vans to transport the fatalities?"

"I'll contact traffic control to see about that. We'll try to make some space, but"—he made a face—"it's pretty much a clusterfuck out here."

"Well, hopefully that will change shortly."

Olivia approached the site of the destruction, scanning the clumps of photographers, firefighters, police officers, and others milling around outside and coming and going through the entrance to the bar for someone who appeared to be in charge. Two sheet-covered bodies lay on the sidewalk, one with an arm extended toward the group of onlookers, the fingers curled plaintively. The other looked suspiciously small for a full cadaver.

Another uniformed police officer, a young female looking decidedly ill at ease, stood next to the two bodies.

"I'm Dr. Olivia Price, chief medical examiner," Olivia said, only half aware of how easily she'd said that. "Have these bodies been moved?"

The police officer actually snapped to attention. "No, ma'am, Doctor. This is where they landed."

"See that no one moves them."

"Yes, ma'am." The officer glanced down and then quickly up again. "Um, do you know how long that might be, ma'am?"

"Until CSU and our techs are done. It's going to be a while."

The officer tried to hide her disappointment. "Yes, ma'am. Thank you."

Olivia nodded. "Have you seen—"

"Dr. Price!"

Olivia turned. Darrell and Archie, and just behind them, Tasha and Jay, hurried toward her. She had only a second to reflect on Tasha and Jay arriving together before she had to put everything else from her mind.

"Where do you want us?" Darrell said. "Rox and Abe just pulled in too."

"Good. The four of you pair off," Olivia said briskly and pointed to the sheet-covered bodies. "Darrell and Archie, take one of these, Tasha—Jay's with you. Take the other one."

Jay looked surprised, as if she'd expected—hoped?—to be with Olivia, but she said nothing.

"Got it," Darrell said and Tasha echoed him.

"I'll be inside," Olivia said. "Tell Rox and Abe to find me."

"Sure thing," Darrell said.

Olivia spared a quick glance at Jay, who was still watching her. Jay looked slightly more rested than the last time she'd seen her, and Olivia wondered how she'd gotten there so quickly without a car. But then, she and Tasha had arrived together. The disquieting thought was a distraction she couldn't entertain. Abruptly, she turned away and strode toward the dark, gaping mouth of the club. A heavyset man with a broad jaw covered with a day's growth of beard was just emerging when she reached the doorway. "Detective Gonzalez?"

"Lieutenant," he said absently. "Who are you?"

"Dr. Olivia Price, chief medical examiner."

His face lit up, transforming him from intimidating to attractive. "Damn glad to see you, Doc. We've got a lot of work for your team. Two out here, half a dozen inside, and who knows what else in the building next door."

"I heard a rumor there was a bomb. Is that what you suspect?"

"Looks like a homemade firebomb from the level of destruction, and no evidence of any other incendiary. The fire marshal's looking into it now, so we're not official."

"We're clear to work the scene inside?"

"Yep. The bomb guys have come and gone."

"I'll have my team start as soon as CSU is done, then," Olivia said.

"You can climb right up their tail as far as I'm concerned. We need to get the bodies out of here."

"As quickly as we can." Olivia signaled to Archie. When he hurried over, she said, "We've got more casualties inside. Who's on camera?"

"Jay, right now."

"Good. Thanks. Tell her I need her."

"Right."

A minute later Jay approached. She was wearing the field jacket she'd borrowed from Olivia and carrying a camera. The jacket was still too tight, and she still looked great in it. Olivia cleared her throat. "We'll need photographs inside as soon as you're done out here."

"I'm pretty much set here."

"Good. I haven't gotten a good look inside yet, so you can photograph while we see what we're dealing with."

"Sounds good to me."

When Jay fell in beside her, Olivia said, "This isn't usual for us. Or who knows, maybe it's the new normal."

"You mean a constant stream of mass casualty alerts?" Jay said.

Olivia nodded. "The last one was a derailed Amtrak train, a year ago. Now we've had two in rapid succession."

"Similar too," Jay said.

"How do you mean?"

"Both bars, not-so-great part of town, seemingly indiscriminate victims. Death at a distance."

"You're right," Olivia said, making a mental note to examine the reports for possible connections. "Good call."

"Thanks." Jay glanced around. "I had a good teacher."

Olivia's face warmed, and she hurried to the entrance. Ridiculous to be so pleased by a throwaway comment. "If you've never done this kind of scene before, it could be a little overwhelming."

"I'll be okay," Jay said. "Sometimes there's not a lot of difference between what you see out here and in the trauma unit."

"Only a matter of minutes, sometimes," Olivia murmured.

"Or luck." Jay slowed. "Who are these guys?"

A man and a woman, both wearing black raincoats and dark suits, stepped in front of them, blocking the doorway.

Olivia paused, frowned. "I'm sorry, we need to get inside."

"Who might you be?" asked the tall, sharp-eyed brunette, her voice officious despite its bored monotone.

"I'm the chief medical examiner," Olivia said. "I need access to the scene."

"That won't be necessary, Doctor," the woman said. "DMORT is on their way and will handle the recovery of the bodies."

"DMORT?" Olivia suppressed a surge of annoyance. The regional Disaster Mortuary Operational Response Team was part of the national disaster network and often assisted in large-scale recovery and identification efforts. The word being *assisted*, and she hadn't asked for any help. "By whose authority?"

"By ours," the woman replied. She and the man took out badges and held them up. "Homeland Security."

"You're declaring this a federal crime scene?" Olivia asked.

"That's right."

"It's customary for the local authorities, particularly the medical examiners, to maintain control of the scene and liaise with DMORT."

"Not in this case." The male agent spoke for the first time.

Olivia blew out an exasperated breath. "Listen, this is no place for a turf battle. We are here, this is our scene, and I need you to let us pass."

The brunette looked almost apologetic, for a fleeting second. "The dead aren't going anywhere, Doctor. We'll see that you are copied—"

A barrage of loud cracks drowned out her words. The federal agents pulled their weapons.

Someone shouted, "Shots fired, shots fired, down, down, everyone down."

Jay grabbed her, and the next thing Olivia knew, she was falling. Pain stabbed through her forehead, a heavy weight forced the breath from her chest, and all around her, chaos raged.

CHAPTER TWENTY-SEVEN

"O livia!" Jay struggled to keep the panic from her voice. "Medic, I need a medic!"

Her call for aid was echoed everywhere. First responders tended the injured who lay in the street or struggled for cover. Jay never lost her composure in an emergency, but this wasn't a patient in trauma admitting, this was Olivia. The red flashing lights rendered Olivia's pale face otherworldly, as if she might slip away into another dimension any second. Jay grasped her hand and held it tightly. Olivia's eyelids flickered and opened a fraction. "Olivia, it's Jay. Lie still."

The fingers grasping Jay's twitched, then held more firmly. "What happened?" Olivia asked faintly.

"I'm not sure." Jay brushed blond hair away from the blood streaming down Olivia's temple. "Maybe shots, I don't know. There are wounded."

"You should go. Get to safety."

"Are you kidding? I'm not leaving you."

Olivia slowly propped herself up on one arm. "I'm fine. Lost my footing and struck my head."

"You're bleeding." Jay waved to a paramedic in a firefighter's turnout coat. "Over here."

The medic dropped down beside them. "What have we got?"

"Head injury," Jay said quickly. "Four-centimeter forehead laceration. She's oriented and moving all fours."

"Loss of consciousness?" The medic quickly strapped a blood-pressure cuff on Olivia's arm and pulled out an IV setup.

"I don't need that," Olivia said, waving away the IV. "I'm a doctor. I tripped and fell. I did not lose consciousness. You're needed elsewhere. I'm all right."

The EMT flashed a penlight in Olivia's eyes, seemed satisfied, and looked at Jay. "What about you, you hurt?"

"Bumps and bruises," Jay said.

"Okay—we can wait to transport." The medic tore open a clean four-by-four gauze and pressed it to Olivia's forehead.

Jay brushed his hand aside. "I can take that. She'll need sutures."

"Right now all the vans are full with level threes and fours," he said.

Olivia grasped Jay's arm. "I don't need to take up space in an ambulance. My car is right here."

Jay nodded. "Okay, I'll drive."

The medic said, "If you've got wheels, and she can walk, you might as well."

Olivia said, "I can't leave. I've got—"

"You're not staying, Olivia," Jay said. "Osaka and Markham are here. They can handle things for now. You're hurt and you need attention."

"I'm fine, it's just a bump."

"It's a bump that needs stitches, and you might need a head CT. We're going to the emergency room."

The medic quickly packed his gear. "If you're staying, get to cover in case the nutjob shooting at us starts again."

Olivia tried to get up. Her headache ratcheted up a notch and she winced.

Jay's arm came around her. "All right?"

"Yes, nothing too terrible. I need to speak with my people if I'm leaving."

"I'll get someone," Jay said, leading Olivia to the shelter of one of the big fire trucks. "Stay here."

A minute later Jay returned with Kim Osaka, one of the senior medical examiners, and Olivia handed the scene over to him. Officers directed them through a gauntlet of SWAT members to her car.

Jay backed out through the torturous labyrinth of stopped vehicles and crawled through the snarled traffic surrounding the crime scene until she reached a cross street that was open. Breathing fully for the first time since whatever the hell had happened, she glanced at Olivia. Just having Olivia beside her helped quell the anxious fear clawing at her ribs. "How do you feel?"

Olivia held the gauze against her forehead. A bloody patch the size of a quarter spotted the center. "I'm fine, really. A headache. I never lost consciousness. If you head to the ME building, we could put some Steri-Strips—"

Jay snorted. "Really, Olivia? That's down to muscle. It needs sutures. I know what I'm talking about."

"I know that," Olivia said quietly. "All the same, the ER will be busy with patients who need attention a lot more than I do. I'm not so vain that I'm worried about how this is going to look."

Jay gripped the wheel and stared ahead, using the demands of driving in the insane traffic to keep her nerves at bay. When Olivia'd cried out and crumpled to the ground, Jay thought her world had ended. The adrenaline rush still hadn't ebbed, and every muscle was jangling. Her fear was coming out as temper, and that wasn't Olivia's fault. "There's nothing in the world that could make you any less beautiful, but you're still getting sutures."

"Jay," Olivia said quietly, "I'm really all right."

Jay blew out a breath. "Okay, I know, but it's just—"

Olivia slid closer and rested her hand on Jay's thigh. "Are *you* all right?"

"Physically, yeah, fine. Maybe a couple of splinters here and there."

"What do you mean, splinters? Are you hurt?" Olivia unsnapped her seat belt and tugged at Jay's jacket. "Where? Let me see."

"Would you please get back over there and put your seat belt on," Jay said, calmer now that she could see Olivia was really all right. Nothing was going to take her away. "Some kind of debris hit me, I'm not sure what it was. Stings the back of my neck, that's all."

"Pull over. I want to look."

"Liv," Jay said, exasperated and relieved and wanting to laugh. "Have you looked around? I couldn't pull over if I wanted to. People are double-parked, trying to get closer to see what's going on, and the ones who aren't parked might as well be. We're crawling here."

"You know, I've got a med kit in the back of this car. You can take care of my forehead at my office."

Jay shot her a look. "You have suture and lidocaine back there? Because you know, Liv, you're not dead, so you might feel it."

Olivia smiled. "Do you know when you get aggravated with me, you call me Liv?"

"Do I." Jay shook her head, the desire a living thing inside her. "Actually, I think I call you that when I'm aggravated *and* when I'm trying to seduce you."

Olivia caught her breath. "I think it's the first at the moment."

Jay thought better than to tell her the desire was a constant. "We'll be at the ER in fifteen minutes. I know all the shortcuts. If I could just get through this last block, I'll have you taken care of and home in an hour."

"I'll need to go back to the scene."

"No, you won't. At least not for a little while." Jay maneuvered down an alley and came out on another block, cut back the way she'd come, hit another alley, and blessedly found a reasonably free through street that would take her north and west toward the hospital. "Not until we're sure you're feeling all right."

"I've got to handle this DMORT situation," Olivia said grimly. "I can't believe they're trying to take over our scene."

"I bet they'll try playing the terrorism card."

"Because of the bomb," Olivia said.

"That's what I figure."

Olivia grimaced. "That doesn't really make any sense, either. We won't even know what the incendiary was until the fire marshal signs off on the scene. It could have been a furnace that blew up."

"So there's something else going on we don't know about."

"That's more than likely. The feds rarely communicate exactly what they're doing and have very little respect for our jurisdiction."

"All the same," Jay said, jumping behind a police cruiser clearing a path for an ambulance toward the hospital, "not much is going to change down there for a few hours. Let's at least take care of that laceration and your headache before you head back into the fray."

"What headache?"

Jay laughed. "The one you're trying to hide."

Olivia sighed. "Are you always this stubborn?"

"Only where you're concerned." Jay covered Olivia's hand where it still rested on her knee. The pressure was so light she might not have noticed if it was anything else. If it was anyone else touching her. But it wasn't anyone else. It was Olivia, and the contact settled her more than anything else could have. Olivia was here, beside her, and Olivia had reached for her.

❖

Dell was having a great dream featuring Sandy in nothing at all, doing unspeakably outrageous and unspeakably exciting things to her while she lay helpless, her arms and legs tied to a bed. She was just getting to the part where she begged when her phone rang.

"Damn," Dell muttered.

Sandy flailed on the bedside table for Dell's phone, came up with her own, dropped it, and handed Dell's over. "Here."

Sandy put her head under her pillow as Dell answered. "Mitchell."

"Hey, sunshine," Watts said, sounding scarily cheery. "Time to climb out of the rack. Somebody blew up one of MS-13's clubs."

Dell sat up, wide-awake. "Whoa. Okay. I'm on my way. Where?"

Chuckling, Watts gave her the information. "You can take time to get dressed, you know. None of us want to see your skinny bare butt."

"Ha ha." Watts hung up and Dell kissed the back of Sandy's neck. "Gotta go, babe."

"What is it?" Sandy mumbled, her head still under the pillow.

"One of the Salvadorans' clubs got hit."

"What was it? Drive-by?" Sandy pulled the pillow off her head, turned on the light, and squinted in the glare.

"They're thinking a firebomb. Pete Gonzales called Frye when he asked around about the club and found out it was one of MS-13's main meeting places."

Sandy pulled the pillow off her head. "You think it's Zamora retaliating?"

"Good bet. Reports of shots fired too." Dell collected her clothes. "Looks like the war's started, babe. Might be a coincidence, but—you think?"

Sandy scoffed and jumped up. "Coincidence my ass. I'm coming."

"Okay, but get your vest on."

"Always do." Sandy kissed her quickly. "And you keep your head down, Rookie."

❖

Jay parked half a block from the hospital and flipped down the visor. Maybe Olivia's on-call placard would save them a ticket or tow. She really didn't care. "You sure you're okay to walk over?"

"Really, I'm fine. It doesn't even hurt all that much."

"Let me know if you feel dizzy."

Olivia linked her arm through Jay's. "I promise, if you promise to stop worrying."

"I can't."

"You have to trust me on this," Olivia said. "I wouldn't lie to you. I never have."

"I know."

Olivia leaned against Jay, not because she needed to, but because she felt Jay's anxiety and wanted to comfort her. And because the connection warmed her in a way she couldn't reject. "When we get there, I want to take a look at your neck."

"You first."

Olivia laughed. "All right, deal."

When they reached the ER, Jay had to admit Olivia had been right. The place was a zoo. The waiting room was full and the ER board had a name in every slot. Some of the rush was probably just the usual late-night ER traffic, but other patients had to be the least injured victims from the bar. The trauma unit was likely going to be full with the more serious casualties.

Jay flagged down a nurse who was hurrying by with an instrument pack. "Hey, Suli, can I grab a spot to take care of this?"

"As long as you don't need a cubicle. They're all full."

"Thanks!" Jay took Olivia's hand. "Come on, all we need is someplace for you to lie down so I can get a look at this."

"Are you planning to take care of this yourself?" Olivia said.

Jay raised a brow. "At least until we get to the stitches part." She squeezed her right hand. "I don't trust myself to do anything else."

"Jay," Olivia said gently, "I would trust you to do anything."

"Thanks," Jay whispered. She pointed to a lone stretcher tucked away in a hallway by the fire exit. "Over here."

Olivia obediently climbed up on the stretcher while Jay grabbed gloves, gauze, and a bottle of sterile saline from a treatment room. Her forehead stung as Jay cleansed it, but she could tell the wound was more of a nuisance than anything else.

"At least it's got a good orientation," Jay muttered, replacing the wet gauze with a dry one. "Here, hold that. I'll see if I can find someone to get this closed up."

"I don't mind waiting. Everyone's taking care of people who are a lot more seriously injured."

"I'll be right back."

Olivia sighed. "I'll be here."

Jay hurried around the corner to the trauma bay and found the controlled chaos she expected. All three acute treatment tables were occupied. X-ray and respiratory techs clustered around with their monitors and machines, residents and fellows and nurses worked over the prone bodies, and Ali directed all of the action with the absolute calm of a conductor of a symphony orchestra. Jay waited until she could catch her eye.

"Hey," Ali said as soon as she saw her, "have you seen Beau? We're getting reports there were shots fired out there."

"Yeah, I saw her," Jay said, "maybe forty minutes ago. That was after whatever the hell went down out there happened. She looked okay."

The tension around Ali's jaw relaxed. "Thanks. Thanks." Ali's gaze sharpened. "What are you doing here?"

"Olivia's hurt. She's in the ER."

"Why isn't she here?"

"She's okay. It's a forehead laceration, but it needs sutures. Can you spare anybody to close it?"

Ali glanced over at the three beds. "Unless we get another acute case, things are under control here. If you get things set up, I can run down and do it."

"Ali, no," Jay said. "Just give me one of the residents for fifteen minutes."

Ali laughed. "Jay. You think it will take me fifteen minutes to close a forehead laceration? You assist, and I'll get it done in five. They can spare me here for that long unless something else comes rolling in."

"I owe you."

"The hell you do. Go get ready."

"Okay. Give me five minutes."

Jay grabbed a suture set from the rack by the door on her way back to where Olivia waited on the gurney. "Ali's going to come down and close this up in a minute. Why don't you lie down."

"Ali Torveau, the trauma chief?"

"The very same."

Olivia frowned. "Jay, really. This is—"

"She's a friend. It's okay."

"All right. Thank you."

Jay opened the tray and got gloves for Ali and herself. Her hand was at least steady enough to cut suture. Once she was set up, she sprinted to the unit to let Ali know she was ready.

"You have any idea what's going on out there?" Ali asked as she followed Jay. "The victims are mostly burned, but a few are missing body parts. Looked like a bomb went off."

"Reports were pretty conflicted, although an explosion took out the bar. How many did you get?"

"Between the ER and the trauma unit, probably a dozen, most thankfully not too seriously injured. What about you?"

"Looks like whoever was close to the focus of the blast absorbed most of the damage. There are half a dozen dead on scene."

Ali shook her head. "It's crazy."

Olivia sat up straight as Ali approached. "Dr. Torveau, I really appreciate this. I told Jay—"

"Hi," Ali said, gently resting a hand on Olivia's shoulder. "I'm Ali. I'll get this taken care of in a couple of minutes. And I insisted." She glanced at Jay. "After all, Jay's family."

Olivia settled back, accepting she couldn't argue with both of them. *Jay's family.* And what did that make her? "All right, yes. Thank you very much."

Ali gloved up, injected the area with lidocaine, and loaded the suture Jay had pulled for her. She was quick, quicker even than Jay had ever been, and as Jay cut suture for her, she thought of all the times they'd done this together. She missed the camaraderie more than anything else, and that was a revelation. The work she did now challenged her as much, satisfied her in different ways, and she was learning to be part of a new team. And Ali would always be part of her life.

"That was less than five minutes," Olivia observed as Ali pulled off her gloves.

Ali laughed. "You needed the sutures, but fortunately, the laceration was straightforward. You won't have much of a scar."

"I'm not worried about that. Now if you would just tell Jay I'm fine and don't need to be babysat?"

Ali glanced from Jay to Olivia and shook her head. "I could, but you've probably noticed by now that she's on the stubborn side. I think you can expect a little hovering for a couple of hours. I'd recommend you not go back out into the field until you've had something to eat, some Motrin, and an hour or two for your system to settle down. You are going back out, aren't you?"

"Of course."

Ali glanced at Jay. "I think a meal and some pain pills are the best you're going to be able to do."

Jay lifted a shoulder and smiled at Olivia. "Okay, I'll take it."

"Good," Ali said. "I'd better get back in there. Take care of each other."

Ali disappeared, and Olivia sat up slowly. "She's very fond of you."

"Yeah. She knows how I feel about you."

Olivia caught her breath. "Does she."

"Come on," Jay said, thinking she was ahead so far and that was enough for now. "My place is around the corner. It's not much, but I actually have some food. It's closer than your place, and we won't have to fight the traffic so much."

"All right, for an hour."

"Ninety minutes," Jay countered.

Olivia laughed. "You win this one."

Jay held out her hand. When Olivia took it, Jay knew she'd never be happy until she won it all.

CHAPTER TWENTY-EIGHT

S orry to wake you up, Lieutenant," Carmody said.
"It's quite all right, Sergeant, I'm in the car." Rebecca slowed to let a black van with *Medical Examiner* stenciled on the side in tall yellow letters inch past. "What do you have?"

"I heard about the blast in South Philly, and the location tweaked something in my memory. There's been a real uptick in activity the last few days, so it's taken me a while to rerun the tapes."

"You hit something?" Rebecca slid her sedan to the curb behind an idling police cruiser. Yellow crime-scene tape blocked the street half a block ahead. She shut off the engine, checked her watch. Five a.m. Carmody must've been working all night.

"I think I might have caught a conversation we can use," Carmody said. "At least, I got a name for you."

Rebecca straightened. Names were like gold. Names meant individuals they could pressure for more names, more threads to pull. "Go ahead. Read me what you've got."

"Okay," Carmody said, excitement lacing her voice. "This is Spiro Pavlou outside Zamora's office yesterday. He's talking to one of Zamora's captains, the same one who reported on Mary Ann Scofield a while back. Carlos Faro."

"I've got a priority job for you. We need to send a message to our friends south of the border."

The Salvadorans, Rebecca presumed, who held the underworld territory south of Bainbridge.

"Here's Carlos," Carmody said and a rough, accented voice came on.

"Yeah, it's about time those little fuckers get what's coming to them. They been fucking with us too long already. After the Galaxy—"

"Spiro cut him off," Carmody interjected. "Zamora has never been able to train some of the old guard in the subtlety of surveillance."

Rebecca chuckled.

"Then Spiro spells it out," Carmody said, "and Carlos names his guy."

"We want the statement to be loud and definitive, if you understand what I'm saying. Someplace they'll know we sent it."

"Sure, I know just the place. I'll have Mickey the Match turn the lights on in that hole-in-the-wall down on Moore."

"Good. Make it soon."

Mickey the Match. Rebecca let out a breath. There it was, an order direct from Zamora, or as close as they'd ever come, with a name. "Did you run this Mickey guy?"

Carmody's smile came through the line. "Oh yeah, right away. Mickey the Match is one Mikolos Bakos, thirty-seven years old, did a stint at Attica for arson about ten years ago, has been a suspect in a couple of other firebombings, but no definitive evidence, and—get this—is married to the daughter of a low-level Zamora numbers runner."

"You might just have given us the break we've been looking for, Sergeant. Nice work."

"Thank you, Lieutenant."

"Hand this all over to Sloan and start working on all known associates. Let's broaden our net."

"Yes, Loo. Already called her."

Rebecca cut the call and wove her way past clots of SWAT and first responders to the crime scene. Uniformed and plainclothes cops huddled in front of the blown-out building, while firefighters hosed down steaming adjacent buildings. Pete Gonzalez appeared to be in a standoff with a couple of suits who might as well have been carrying big signs identifying them as federal agents. Rebecca paused and made a quick call to the assistant state's attorney, Jared Calhoun.

"You know what time it is, right?" Jared said, sounding perfectly awake.

"I do. Are you in the office?"

"Where else?"

Rebecca grinned. "I'll take that as a yes."

"What have you got for me?"

Rebecca filled him in on the firebombing and what Carmody had turned up.

Jared said, "You think if you squeeze this Bakos firebug, he'll give you Zamora?"

"He's likely to trade if we work him hard enough—maybe not Zamora right away, but someone else. You know it's always a game of dominoes," Rebecca said. "We've got a wedge, and eventually they all start to fall. Carmody has Spiro Pavlou on tape setting this up. That's a powerful persuader. He might not break, but someone else will."

"Well, that's how these cases get made," Jared said. "What do you need from me?"

"Right now? I need control of this crime scene. The feds are here."

"Of course they are. What else do they have to do. I'll make some calls."

"Thanks, Jared."

"Good hunting, Frye."

Rebecca pocketed her phone, energized by the sense of her quarry finally within her grasp. She could taste Zamora's blood. She headed over to let the feds know they were welcome to observe, but this was her crime scene now.

❖

"It's not much," Jay said, unlocking the door to her studio apartment, "but it's actually pretty clean, and I make a mean grilled cheese sandwich."

"I happen to be a big fan of grilled cheese." Olivia's stomach had seemed on the edge of revolt a short while ago, but now that the adrenaline had diminished, she was aware of being hungry. "You know you feed me a lot?"

"You mind?"

Jay held the door open, and Olivia stepped through into a tiny kitchen no wider than the foyer in her town house, with a table barely big enough for two against one wall and an efficiency-sized stove and fridge. The space opened directly into the living area beyond that. Enough light came through the single window to illuminate the narrow sleeper sofa. The whole apartment didn't seem much bigger than a dorm room.

"No, I like it when you take care of me," Olivia murmured. After all they'd been through, hiding what mattered to her was no longer an option. She could have died. Jay could have died. Her stomach clenched at the thought. Nothing came close to the fear that possibility stirred, not even the fear of being vulnerable to her own desires. She pulled out a chair. "Now it's my turn to return the favor. Take your shirt off and sit here."

"Sorry?" Jay's voice held surprise and uncertainty.

"I want to look at your back. The scrape, remember?"

"It's nothing, really."

"Mm-hmm," Olivia said. "Let's take a look and be sure."

"Okay. If that will make you happy." Jay shed her borrowed jacket, the one she *accidently* kept forgetting to return to Olivia, and pulled off her polo shirt. Her skin pebbled slightly even though the room was warm. While waiting for Olivia's touch, she sat in the chair, hands clasped in her lap, as tense as she'd been her first day as an intern.

When Olivia brushed the hair away from the back of her neck, she shuddered. Olivia's fingers were cool on her shoulders, the sensation like fire in her blood. Her nipples tightened and a swell of arousal cinched her insides into a painful knot. Her heart had already kicked up to double its usual tempo, and she figured there was no point in hiding what she was feeling.

"Looks like a shard of glass or possibly gravel hit the back of your neck." Olivia rubbed her thumb along Jay's hairline as she took in the long irregular abrasion in the skin below. Jay's body was hot, hot enough for Olivia to feel in her depths. She swallowed the desire suddenly blocking her throat. "You've got an abrasion that's through the dermis in a few places. It needs to be cleaned up."

"It'll be fine once I shower," Jay said.

"I'd rather get it taken care of now. Do you have any peroxide?"

"Uh…maybe in the medicine cabinet?"

Olivia laughed, running her hands up and down Jay's arms. "Which means you have no idea. Where's your bathroom?"

"Right around the corner." Jay tilted her head back and grinned. "It would be pretty hard to miss."

Olivia stared down into Jay's eyes. Tiny flecks of gold danced and teased in the deep gray irises. She'd never seen anything so enticing. "I'll be right back."

A minute later, Olivia returned, her tattered control hastily stitched together. If she didn't touch Jay any more than clinically necessary, she might preserve what little willpower was left to her. "Peroxide and antibiotic ointment."

"A true mother lode." Jay looked over her shoulder. "I told you I was well supplied."

Olivia cupped Jay's cheek, and the urge to kiss her rolled through her with the same primal urgency as the need to breathe. What she felt must have shown in her face. Jay's eyes darkened, grew heavy with desire. Olivia whispered, "Sit up straight so I can finish this."

Jay shivered again as Olivia used a washcloth she'd found in the bathroom to cleanse the wound and applied the antibiotic ointment.

"All done," Olivia said, setting the peroxide and ointment on the narrow counter behind her. "This is going to sting when you put your shirt on, but it's probably better to leave it open for a while."

There was very little room in the kitchen, and almost no distance between them. The back of Jay's head was at the level of Olivia's breasts, and when Olivia leaned forward, their bodies touched. Looking down, she watched Jay's breasts rise and fall, her quick shallow breaths matching Olivia's. A flush bloomed across Jay's chest, and Olivia trailed her fingers over Jay's collarbone and skimmed her palm between her breasts, lingering with her fingertips over Jay's heart. "You're very beautiful."

Jay pressed the back of her head against Olivia's chest and closed her eyes. "You did say you liked the shirtless, trousers-only look."

"Mmm. I do. Although I like you in pretty much anything." Olivia dropped her hand lower, and Jay's stomach tensed beneath her palm.

"If you take your hands off me," Jay said very carefully, "you're going to kill me."

"I can't."

"Neither can I." Jay pushed the chair to one side and pivoted to face Olivia as she rose. She grasped Olivia's shoulders and backed her up against the refrigerator, caging her there with both arms. If Olivia wanted her to stop, she'd have to say so, because she was done waiting.

A second passed and Olivia's arms slid around Jay's waist. Jay kissed her, melding their flesh with the weight of her body until no space remained between them. Olivia moaned and dug her fingers into the muscles on either side of Jay's spine. Olivia's touch was fire, her kiss the match that ignited Jay's desire.

"I need you, Liv," Jay gasped. "Please."

Olivia found Jay's hand, pulled it to her breast, and cupped Jay's fingers around her flesh. "Touch me, then. I need you to touch me."

Jay unbuttoned Olivia's shirt, slid her hand inside, and cradled her breast. Olivia was hot and pliant in her hand, hot and demanding in her mouth. "Come to bed. I want to make you come."

"Yes," Olivia whispered.

Jay pulled Olivia the short distance to the daybed beneath the window, shedding her clothes and helping Olivia out of hers, until they fell naked onto the sheets. Jay slid her leg between Olivia's and kissed her until Olivia tugged at her hair and murmured, "Hurry."

Jay made her way down Olivia's body, savoring the taste and scent of her until she reached her breasts. When she rubbed her cheek over Olivia's nipple, Olivia's legs came around the backs of her thighs, holding her tight between them. When Jay tugged the nipple lightly between her teeth, Olivia's hips bucked.

"Fast this time," Olivia urged. "I want you, I need you. Don't make me wait."

Jay knelt between her legs, light-headed with need and power, and filled her in a quick thrust as sure as any truth she'd ever known. Olivia cried out and tightened around her. Jay stroked her to the edge, breathlessly intent. Olivia raised up and braced herself on her elbows, watching Jay take her over. Jay had never seen anything so sexy in her life.

"I'm close, close—God, yes." Olivia threw her head back and came in sharp, short thrusts.

When Olivia sighed and dropped back to the bed, Jay stayed where she was, waiting for her heart to start again, for her breath to fill her lungs again, imprinting the image of Olivia in the deepest reaches of her soul.

"God, you're good," Olivia groaned.

"You make my head explode." Jay still knelt between Olivia's thighs, caressing the shallow valley just inside her hip bones, one of her favorite places—so sensuous and compelling, so female in its strength and elegance.

Olivia laughed softly, her face relaxed and supremely satisfied. So astonishingly beautiful Jay trembled.

"I love you," Jay whispered.

Slowly, Olivia opened her eyes, caught Jay's heart in their smoky depths. "Would you say that again?"

"I love you."

Jay was aware of her own breathing, as if her entire being was about to fly off in opposite directions, one way leaving her adrift and uncertain, the other finally finding a place from which to go forward—this time, not a recovery, but a renewal.

"You don't need to look so worried," Olivia whispered, covering Jay's hands with hers.

"I was just waiting," Jay murmured.

"Not a usual thing for you, is it, Flash," Olivia said, tenderly teasing.

"It's true, I have been known to rush in where angels fear to tread and all that—but with a plan. I've never been able to plan with you."

"Is that such a bad thing?"

"Uncharted territory. I've always known where I was going, from the time I can remember."

"And where was that?"

"Wherever Vic and Ali were going."

Olivia smiled, rubbing her thumbs over Jay's knuckles. "Sometimes I wish I'd had that kind of experience. The only thing I knew for sure was that I wasn't going where my mother was going."

"And where was that?"

"Into a self-inflicted pressure cooker, sacrificing everything for admiration and prestige and success."

"And yet you are successful and respected and have accomplished every bit as much as your mother in your own field."

Olivia shook her head. "Hardly. And obviously, I didn't fall far from the maternal tree. I still deal with the dead."

Jay leaned down, braced herself on her elbows, and kissed Olivia. "No, you don't. You deal with the living to help *them* deal with the dead. You're a scientist and a physician and a healer. That makes you very special."

Olivia threaded her hands into Jay's hair. "And that must be why I love you."

I love you. Jay closed her eyes. "You really just said that, didn't you? I didn't imagine it?"

"Is that so surprising?" Olivia stroked her cheek and kissed her. "I'm sorry if you didn't have any inkling of how I felt about you. I've learned to deny so many things, but I never wanted to deny you."

"You didn't." Jay opened her eyes. "And you don't have to apologize to me for protecting yourself. I get that."

"You were right to remind me that Marcos wasn't here any longer. He was, you know. He followed me around, the memory of him, or more accurately, the memory of who *I* was with him." Olivia let out a weary breath. "I couldn't sort out who I was from who he told me I was. That's so embarrassing to admit."

"You never hid who you are inside. And that's who I fell in love with."

"And that's another reason why I love you," Olivia said. "You love me for the parts of myself I tried to hide. You made me realize I have a right to be my whole self."

"If you mean the sensuous, passionate, unbelievably sexy self you are—you're damn right." Jay kissed her until she realized she wasn't breathing and pulled back, gasping and grinning. "And I want every bit of you. As often as possible for as long as possible."

"Is that right?" Laughing, her eyes shining with the joy of being free, Olivia grasped Jay's shoulders, lifted her hips sharply, and rolled Jay over on the narrow bed. Coming to rest on top of her, she kissed her back. "Well, I'm glad you feel that way, because I'm a planner too, and I've got a lot of plans for you."

Jay's pulse went from slow and cautious to fast and eager in a single stroke of her heart. "I sure as hell hope that too." She narrowed her eyes, looked over the side of the bed. "That was quite a move. How did you manage to do that without dumping us?"

Olivia laughed again. "Well, I do have a lot of practice moving inert forms from one place to another."

Jay groaned. "Okay, I'm sorry I asked that."

"You did ask." Olivia leaned down, nipped Jay's chin. "You know, I have constant thoughts of making love to you. Everywhere. All the time."

"You can have me any time, any place—for as long as you want."

"That will be a very, very long time," Olivia murmured.

Jay couldn't help but ask. "That's all I want. You. For a very, very long time."

"You have me." Olivia kissed her throat, her breasts, the sweep of her abdomen, and the butter soft skin on her inner thighs. When she reached the delta between her trembling legs, Jay grasped the back of her head and lifted her hips.

"Fast this time," she said, tight and desperate.

Olivia wrapped her arms around Jay's hips to hold her close, took her in, and pleasured her until she gasped and trembled against her mouth. She rested her cheek on Jay's thigh, wholly content, and finally whole.

"I love you," Olivia whispered.

CHAPTER TWENTY-NINE

Olivia lay cradled in Jay's arms, listening to her heart beat for a few indulgent and completely contented moments. With a sigh, she finally pressed a kiss to Jay's breast. As amazingly happy as she was, she couldn't ignore the rest of the world, and Jay wouldn't expect her to. "I should call Kim and get an update on the scene."

"I know," Jay murmured, lazily stroking Olivia's back. "My phone is right here. Let me grab it."

"Sorry," Olivia said.

Jay handed her the phone. "No need to be sorry. It's the job. I just wish to hell you didn't have to go back down there, at least until the place is more secure."

Olivia sat up, tucking the sheet around her waist. "If the scene hadn't been secured already, Kim would have notified me by now. I'll be careful. Don't worry."

"Don't worry? That laceration on your forehead could have been from a bullet instead of just a fall." Jay rubbed her eyes. "I don't know what I'd do—"

Olivia leaned over and kissed her. "You won't have to worry about that either. I'm not going anywhere." She paused, tapped Jay's chin. "And I guess I should break it to you now, I'm not letting you go anywhere either."

Jay grinned, the lightness in her chest such a foreign thing she almost laughed. "Oh, you won't hear me arguing about that. Just try to get rid of me."

"Not on your life." Olivia paused. So much to say. She'd give a lot to take Jay away somewhere for a few weeks and tell her—show her—how much she loved her. How much she wanted a life with her. "We need a honeymoon."

Jay stared. "Okay, sure. Whenever we get a break."

Olivia smiled. "Nothing ever throws you off stride."

"Not true." Jay pulled her down, kissed her. "You do every second. And whenever we can get away, I'm ready."

"Aren't you curious what I mean?"

"Hey, I know what a honeymoon is. Lots of sex, long moonlit strolls, more sex, candlelight dinners, more sex—"

"We're not waiting for moonlight and candles to have sex," Olivia said.

"Thank God for that."

Olivia laughed. "But we'll find time for just us. Then you've got to finish this fellowship and we'll have to talk about what comes next."

Jay sat up, reached for her T-shirt, and pulled it on. "Not much to talk about. You'll be the chief medical examiner officially soon, and I don't plan on going anywhere without you. I'll find something around here—we're lucky, plenty of hospitals and medical schools."

"For someone of your caliber," Olivia said, shaking her head, "only a top position is appropriate." She pursed her lips. "Although, as luck would have it, we're always looking for competent medical examiners. Should you have an interest, that is."

"Oh, I have an interest." Jay kissed her again and pointed to the phone. "I'm yours. Wherever you are, that's where I want to be. Including this morning. Go ahead and make your call."

Olivia finally reached Kim after the first call was cut off mid-ring. "Hi, Kim, it's Olivia."

"Sorry," Kim Osaka said, "the cell reception down here is terrible."

"How are things going?" Olivia asked.

"We've processed and transported four out of the six fatalities. We're working on the last two now."

"Has DMORT claimed jurisdiction?"

"No, that's the funny thing. They never showed up at all. We've just been working the scene like it's ours."

Olivia smiled in victory. "It is ours. I'll be down—"

"Are you still in the emergency room?" Kim's concern showed in his voice.

"No, I'm fine. I'm just ready to return."

"There's no need for that. We'll be done here in an hour. I can handle it."

"I should probably talk to the authorities, all the same."

"I don't think you have to worry about that," Kim said. "They've been looking over our shoulders all morning. They'll find you. If I were you, I'd hide as long as I could."

Olivia laughed. Kim Osaka would make an excellent assistant chief, and she intended to recommend that at the first opportunity. "All right then, I'll meet with you at the office, and we can get started on the posts."

"That sounds good to me," Kim said. "I'll text you when we leave with the last one."

"Thanks, Kim. I appreciate being able to count on you."

"That's okay," Kim said. "We all appreciate seeing the chief in the field."

"I'll see you all soon." Olivia handed Jay the phone. "It'll be at least an hour or two before we have to start the posts."

Jay tossed the phone onto the pile of clothes by the bed. "Then I say we put it to good use."

"A nap?" Olivia teased.

Jay pulled Olivia down on top of her. "After."

At ten that evening, Olivia and Jay finished the autopsy on the sixth victim. All the fatalities had resulted from the direct blast effect from an incendiary propelled through the front window of the bar. The resulting fire had been contained to the first floor and the adjoining walls between the bar and the adjacent building. Fortunately, the least injured patrons had been able to escape before being overcome by heat and smoke.

Olivia snapped off her gloves, pulled down her mask, and untied the back of her gown. "This is the first time I've seen anything quite like this. Feels a bit like a war zone."

"Definitely intentional," Jay said, carrying a tray of instruments to the sink for the diener to prepare for autoclaving. "Homicide."

"Yes." Olivia shook her head. "No pattern to the victims, other than all male."

"This seems so random."

"In terms of the victims, yes," Olivia said. "Unless one of them was a specific target, it appears that the attack was more on the establishment rather than the individuals."

"Several of them had the same tattoo," Jay said.

"Gang tats."

Jay removed her gown and gloves, disposed of them, and opened the door to the antechamber. "Looks that way."

"We have a database of those." Olivia handed Jay her jacket. "We'll run them for our report, but that's what it seems."

"I'll get started on those."

"Tomorrow is soon enough." The hall was empty, and Olivia reached for Jay's hand. "I think we can—" Olivia's phone rang and, with a sigh, she answered. "Dr. Price."

"It's Kim. I was just leaving and I ran into a couple of police officers who want to talk to you." He lowered his voice. "I can tell them you're still in the Graveyard."

Olivia closed her eyes for a second. "Thank you, but I'll see them now. Can you send them to my office."

"I'll give them directions. 'Night."

"Good night, Kim. Good work tonight."

"Thanks, Chief."

Olivia glanced at Jay. "Feel like talking to the police?"

Jay laughed. "Absolutely. Makes my day."

"All right. Then, barring another callout, we're getting out of here."

"We are?"

"Unless you have other plans?"

"I seem to have a lot of plans where you're concerned now."

"I'm very glad to hear that. I have a few myself." Olivia unlocked her office, tugged Jay inside, and kissed her quickly. "The first of which is for you to come home with me."

"That could be habit-forming." Jay sat in the chair she'd occupied the first time she'd met Olivia, when she'd been lost in so many ways. She still couldn't see all the path ahead, but she was certain of what mattered most. "I love you."

"I love you too. I have mentioned that, haven't I?" Olivia laughed softly. The need she'd once feared, the passion she'd denied, had become part of a future she wanted more than anything in her life.

"You have, and I can tell you right now, I'm never going to get tired of hearing you say it."

"And I can promise you, I never will." A knock sounded on the door, and Olivia sighed. "Come in."

Sandy Sullivan entered with a tall blond woman Olivia recognized from the Galaxy. The blonde, strikingly handsome with ice-blue eyes that held intelligence and authority, held out her hand. "Dr. Price, I'm Detective Lieutenant Rebecca Frye. Thank you for meeting with us. I know it's been a long day."

"That's all right," Olivia said, shaking Frye's hand and nodding to Sandy. "This is Dr. Reynolds, one of our forensic fellows. Please, have a seat."

Jay started to rise and Frye waved her down. "We'll make this quick. I realize you won't have an official report yet, but preliminaries will be helpful."

"I can give you a general overview of what we have," Olivia said. "That would be appreciated."

Olivia recapped what she and Jay had found. "I don't think we have anything you didn't anticipate at this point."

"I'm sure you're always thorough with your reports," Frye said with careful deliberation.

Olivia cocked her head, listening for whatever message was underlying the entire visit. "I assure you, you can rely on our reports. Are you expecting something unusual regarding our testimony?"

Frye's eyes glinted with appreciation. "As a matter of fact, I expect you will be preparing for a grand jury hearing, and probably more than one."

"You've made an arrest?"

Sandy said, "We picked up a shooter tonight, a gangbanger from MS-13 who probably hoped murdering first responders would win the favor of his gang bosses."

"But he's not your arsonist."

"No," Frye said, "but we have a strong lead on him too. Hopefully, we'll have him in custody soon."

Jay leaned forward. "So you're expecting other arrests in the future."

Frye nodded. "We believe we will be targeting some high-profile individuals, yes."

"Then I wish you speed and success," Olivia said. "You can be sure this office will be prepared to present whatever evidence is relevant."

"I'm sure of it," Frye said.

"You'll have our reports by midday tomorrow." Olivia sent her own message. "And I assume you will keep us in the loop."

Frye nodded. "Officer Sullivan will be our liaison with your office."

Olivia smiled. "Excellent."

The officers left, and Olivia glanced at Jay. "Were you able to translate all of that?"

"They want to be sure we dot all the i's and cross all the t's because they're going after some heavy operators, probably organized crime."

"Yes, that would be my impression too." Olivia came around her desk and held out her hand. "Just another day at the office."

Jay stood. "Well, this job is turning out to be a lot more exciting than I ever expected."

Olivia laughed and threaded her arm around Jay's waist. "Just the job?"

Jay kissed her. "Excitement doesn't even come close to how the rest of this turned out."

Laughing, Olivia rested her cheek against Jay's shoulder. "Let's go home."

About the Author

Radclyffe has written over fifty romance and romantic intrigue novels, dozens of short stories, and, writing as L.L. Raand, has authored a paranormal romance series, The Midnight Hunters.

She is an eight-time Lambda Literary Award finalist in romance, mystery, and erotica—winning in both romance (*Distant Shores, Silent Thunder*) and erotica (*Erotic Interludes 2: Stolen Moments* edited with Stacia Seaman and *In Deep Waters 2: Cruising the Strip* written with Karin Kallmaker). A member of the Saints and Sinners Literary Hall of Fame, she is also an RWA/FF&P Prism Award winner for *Secrets in the Stone*, an RWA FTHRW Lories and RWA HODRW winner for *Firestorm*, an RWA Bean Pot winner for *Crossroads*, an RWA Laurel Wreath winner for *Blood Hunt*, and the 2016 Book Buyers Best award winner for *Price of Honor*. In 2014 she was awarded the Dr. James Duggins Outstanding Mid-Career Novelist Award by the Lambda Literary Foundation. She is a featured author in the 2015 documentary film *Love Between the Covers*, from Blueberry Hill Productions.

She is also the president of Bold Strokes Books, one of the world's largest independent LGBTQ publishing companies.

Find her at facebook.com/Radclyffe.BSB, follow her on Twitter @RadclyffeBSB, and visit her website at Radfic.com.

Books Available From Bold Strokes Books

Canvas for Love by Charlotte Greene. When ghosts from Amelia's past threaten to undermine their relationship, Chloé must navigate the greatest romance of her life without losing sight of who she is. (978-1-62639-944-0)

Heart Stop by Radclyffe. Two women, one with a damaged body, the other a damaged spirit, challenge each other to dare to live again. (978-1-62639-899-3)

Repercussions by Jessica L. Webb. Someone planted information in Edie Black's brain and now they want it back, but with the protection of shy former soldier Skye Kenny, Edie has a chance at life and love. (978-1-62639-925-9)

Spark by Catherine Friend. Jamie's life is turned upside down when her consciousness travels back to 1560 and lands in the body of one of Queen Elizabeth I's ladies-in-waiting...or has she totally lost her grip on reality? (978-1-62639-930-3)

Taking Sides by Kathleen Knowles. When passion and politics collide, can love survive? (978-1-62639-876-4)

Thorns of the Past by Gun Brooke. Former cop Darcy Flynn's heart broke when her career on the force ended in disgrace, but perhaps saving Sabrina Hawk's life will mend it in more ways than one. (978-1-62639-857-3)

You Make Me Tremble by Karis Walsh. Seismologist Casey Radnor comes to the San Juan Islands to study an earthquake but finds her heart shaken by passion when she meets animal rescuer Iris Mallery. (978-1-62639-901-3)

Complications by MJ Williamz. Two women battle for the heart of one. (978-1-62639-769-9)

Crossing the Wide Forever by Missouri Vaun. As Cody Walsh and Lillie Ellis face the perils of the untamed West, they discover that love's uncharted frontier isn't for the weak in spirit or the faint of heart. (978-1-62639-851-1)

Fake It till You Make It by M. Ullrich. Lies will lead to trouble, but can they lead to love? (978-1-62639-923-5)

Girls Next Door, edited by Sandy Lowe and Stacia Seaman. Best-selling romance authors tell it from the heart—sexy, romantic stories of falling for the girls next door. (978-1-62639-916-7)

Pursuit by Jackie D. The pursuit of the most dangerous terrorist in America will crack the lines of friendship and love, and not everyone will make it out from under the weight of duty and service. (978-1-62639-903-7)

The Practitioner by Ronica Black. Sometimes love comes calling whether you're ready for it or not. (978-1-62639-948-8)

Unlikely Match by Fiona Riley. When an ambitious PR exec and her super-rich coding geek-girl client fall in love, they learn that giving something up may be the only way to have everything. (978-1-62639-891-7)

Where Love Leads by Erin McKenzie. A high school counselor and the mom of her new student bond in support of the troubled girl, never expecting deeper feelings to emerge, testing the boundaries of their relationship. (978-1-62639-991-4)

Forsaken Trust by Meredith Doench. When four women are murdered, Agent Luce Hansen must regain trust in her most valuable investigative tool—herself—to catch the killer. (978-1-62639-737-8)

Letter of the Law by Carsen Taite. Will federal prosecutor Bianca Cruz take a chance at love with horse breeder Jade Vargas, whose dark family ties threaten everything Bianca has worked to protect—including her child? (978-1-62639-750-7)

New Life by Jan Gayle. Trigena and Karrie are having a baby, but the stress of becoming a mother and the impact on their relationship might be too much for Trigena. (978-1-62639-878-8)

Royal Rebel by Jenny Frame. Charity director Lennox King sees through the party-girl image Princess Roza has cultivated, but will Lennox's past indiscretions and Roza's responsibilities make their love impossible? (978-1-62639-893-1)

Unbroken by Donna K. Ford. When Kayla and Jackie, two women with every reason to reject Happily Ever After, fall in love, will they have the courage to overcome their pasts and rewrite their stories? (978-1-62639-921-1)

Where the Light Glows by Dena Blake. Mel Thomas doesn't realize just how unhappy she is in her marriage until she meets Izzy Calabrese. Will she have the courage to overcome her insecurities and follow her heart? (978-1-62639-958-7)

Her Best Friend's Sister by Meghan O'Brien. For fifteen years, Claire Barker has nursed a massive crush on her best friend's older sister. What happens when all her wildest fantasies come true? (978-1-62639-861-0)

Escape in Time by Robyn Nyx. Working in the past is hell on your future. (978-1-62639-855-9)

Forget-Me-Not by Kris Bryant. Is love worth walking away from the only life you've ever dreamed of? (978-1-62639-865-8)

Highland Fling by Anna Larner. On vacation in the Scottish Highlands, Eve Eddison falls for the enigmatic forestry officer Moira Burns despite Eve's best friend's campaign to convince her that Moira will break her heart. (978-1-62639-853-5)

Phoenix Rising by Rebecca Harwell. As Storm's Quarry faces invasion from a powerful neighbor, a mysterious newcomer with powers equal to Nadya's challenges everything she believes about herself and her future. (978-1-62639-913-6)

Soul Survivor by I. Beacham. Sam and Joey have given up on hope, but when fate brings them together it gives them a chance to change each other's life and make dreams come true. (978-1-62639-882-5)

Strawberry Summer by Melissa Brayden. When Margaret Beringer's first love Courtney Carrington returns to their small town, she must grapple with their troubled past and fight the temptation for a very delicious future. (978-1-62639-867-2)

The Girl on the Edge of Summer by J.M. Redmann. Micky Knight accepts two cases, but neither is the easy investigation it appears. The past is never past—and young girls lead complicated, even dangerous lives. (978-1-62639-687-6)

Unknown Horizons by CJ Birch. The moment Lieutenant Alison Ash steps aboard the *Persephone*, she knows her life will never be the same. (978-1-62639-938-9)

The Sniper's Kiss by Justine Saracen. The power of a kiss: it can swell your heart with splendor, declare abject submission, and sometimes blow your brains out. (978-1-62639-839-9)

Divided Nation, United Hearts by Yolanda Wallace. In a nation torn in two by a most uncivil war, can love conquer the divide? (978-1-62639-847-4)

Fury's Bridge by Brey Willows. What if your life depended on someone who didn't believe in your existence? (978-1-62639-841-2)

Lightning Strikes by Cass Sellars. When Parker Duncan and Sydney Hyatt's one-night stand turns to more, both women must fight demons past and present to cling to the relationship neither of them thought she wanted. (978-1-62639-956-3)

Love in Disaster by Charlotte Greene. A professor and a celebrity chef are drawn together by chance, but can their attraction survive a natural disaster? (978-1-62639-885-6)

Secret Hearts by Radclyffe. Can two women from different worlds find common ground while fighting their secret desires? (978-1-62639-932-7)

Sins of Our Fathers by A. Rose Mathieu. Solving gruesome murder cases is only one of Elizabeth Campbell's challenges; another is her growing attraction to the female detective who is hell-bent on keeping her client in prison. (978-1-62639-873-3)

Troop 18 by Jessica L. Webb. Charged with uncovering the destructive secret that a troop of RCMP cadets has been hiding, Andy must put aside her worries about Kate and uncover the conspiracy before it's too late. (978-1-62639-934-1)